Over fourteen million people tuned in to see Nadiya Hussain win *The Great British Bake Off* in 2015. Since then she has captured the heart of the nation. Born in Luton, she lives in Milton Keynes with her husband, Abdal, and is mum to three gorgeous children. *The Secret Lives of the Amir Sisters* is her first novel.

THE SECRET LIVES OF
THE AMIR SISTERS

Fatima, Farah, Bubblee and Mae, the four Amir sisters, are the only young Muslims in the quaint English village of Wyvernage. On the outside, despite not quite fitting in with their neighbours, the Amirs are happy. But on the inside, each sister is secretly struggling. Fatima is trying to find out who she really is — and finally pass her driving test. Farah is happy being a wife but longs to be a mother. Bubblee is determined to be an artist in London, away from family tradition. And Mae is coping with burgeoning YouTube stardom. Yet when family tragedy strikes, it brings them closer together and forces them to learn more about life, love, and each other than they ever thought possible.

NADIYA HUSSAIN
with AYISHA MALIK

◆

THE SECRET LIVES OF THE AMIR SISTERS

Complete and Unabridged

CHARNWOOD
Leicester

First published in Great Britain in 2017 by
HQ
an imprint of HarperCollins*Publishers* Ltd
London

First Charnwood Edition
published 2017
by arrangement with
HarperCollins*Publishers* Ltd
London

The moral right of the author has been asserted

This novel is entirely a work of fiction. The names, characters and incidents portrayed in it are the work of the author's imagination. Any resemblance to actual persons, living or dead, events or localities is entirely coincidental.

A catalogue record for this book is available from the British Library.

ISBN 978–1–4448–3426–0

Published by
F. A. Thorpe (Publishing)
Anstey, Leicestershire

Set by Words & Graphics Ltd.
Anstey, Leicestershire
Printed and bound in Great Britain by
T. J. International Ltd., Padstow, Cornwall

This book is printed on acid-free paper

I would like to dedicate this book to my Baba. For putting up with my teenage angst and telling me 'One day you will actually like me young lady'. As much as it pains me to admit it, you were right, and I do actually quite like you now.

1

Fatima

It's going to be fine. I wiped the palms of my hands on my trousers that crinkled from the sweat. Before I realised it my hand lunged towards my bedside drawer, shuffling around to try and find my stash. *How could I have run out?* Going downstairs wasn't an option given that I heard Mum on the phone with Jay. That's the first time he's called in two months. Every time after a conversation with him there's always this odd kind of quiet that's filled with trivial stuff like, *Did you get the toilet paper?* And *Let's re-arrange the family album.* Mum can never quite look any of us in the eye, while Dad goes into the garden to inspect the flowers. I took a deep breath and went to open the window in my room. Just as I'd predicted, there he was, standing with his hands on his hips, staring at his begonias.

I glanced at the next-door neighbours and quickly looked away. Marnie was out, sunbathing, stark naked. My eyes hovered towards her again. Amazing, isn't it? She hasn't a care in the world about who's looking at her and what others might think. What about all the insects in the grass? What if they decided to make a detour right up her . . . *ugh*. Still, that is what you call *being sure of yourself*. Her whole

1

family's like that. Naked, but sure of themselves. Dad scratched his head and bowed it so low it looked like he might've dropped off to sleep. I wanted to go down and talk to him about his flowerbed, but I hate leaving my room — the comfort of its four walls and dim light. I turned around and reached into my drawer again, just to double-check its contents, and right there at the bottom I felt the steely tube; crumpled, but there was hope. Lifting it out, I saw that my tube of Primula cheese had been squeezed to within an inch of its life. I unscrewed the lid and pushed into the top — a meagre bit of cheese poked out of the nose and back in again. Just then I heard Mum rapping at the kitchen window.

'*Jay's Abba*. Come inside,' she said to Dad.

I watched Dad peer in at her, confused. Not because she referred to him as Jay's dad — we're Bangladeshi, after all, and there are some traditions you can't let go of; like calling your partner by your eldest child's name. Except in this case — even though *I'm* the eldest — it's Jay's name because he's their only son. It doesn't bother me though — not really.

'*Come inside*,' Mum repeated to Dad.

I guess she saw that Marnie was out too. There was nothing for it; I had to go down eventually, anyway, considering what day it was. So, I made my way down the stairs and into the kitchen.

'Don't be nervous,' said Mum as I sat down at the table.

'I'm not,' I said, trying to smile without wanting to be sick everywhere.

She blew over me after having muttered a prayer.

'Have you said your prayers?' she asked.

'Yes,' I lied.

She patted my head and put a plate of biscuits in front of me, before going to make tea for Dad. He looked towards Mum, standing at the kitchen hob, and then over his shoulder. Reaching into his pocket, he handed me some money, putting his finger to his lips. I forgot about my nerves for a minute as I mouthed 'Thank you' and tucked the money into my jeans pocket. I don't know why he hides the fact that he gives me money for all my driving lessons from Mum — but it's become our little secret.

'Remember,' he said, clearing his throat. 'You look into the rear-view mirror every few seconds, they will pass you.'

'That's what you said last time, Abba,' said Mae, who'd wandered in, holding her phone's camera towards us. 'It's time for some new advice. For my video, thanks.'

'Switch that off and help me make the dinner,' said Mum to her. 'Farah is coming later.'

Mae rolled her eyes. 'Or maybe you should get a new driving instructor,' she said. 'Because he's obvs not doing something right.'

Dad scratched his jet-black hair. I wish he'd let it go grey like normal dads do. No-one actually believes his hair is that black.

'No,' he said. 'You know how long it took to find a Bengali instructor? Lucky he is just in the next town.'

But Mae had already stopped listening and

was tapping something on her phone.

'Don't worry, Abba — I'll remember to check all the mirrors,' I replied before turning to Mum. 'Is Farah coming alone?'

'Yes, she's not staying long,' said Mum.

Of course she wasn't. She'd be going home to her husband. I imagined her greeting him as he walked through the door. Or maybe she'd be in the bathroom and he'd call out to her? I do like it when the two of them come over sometimes, though. It's like watching TV but in real life. Only, every time they leave I'm left with this hollow feeling inside, because it *is* real life — just someone else's. I picked up a biscuit to go with the squeezy cheese Mum had just put on the table for me, but it was snatched from my hands. Mae, of course. She handed me a carrot stick instead while eyeing a bottle of olive oil.

'Mum, that isn't organic,' she said.

'Mae,' said Dad. 'We didn't have organic in our day and we are fine and healthy.'

'Yeah, right,' she retorted.

A car horn beeped outside. I gulped as my mum and dad both looked at me. *Everyone takes their driving test,* I tried to reason with myself. *What is there to be nervous about? So what if, at the age of thirty, I've failed before? And the time before that? And so many times before that?* My heart felt too big for my chest. I took the tube of cheese as I got up and made my way to the front door.

'Say bismillah before you begin,' Mum shouted out.

Bismillah. In the name of God. What was the

4

point in telling Mum that I'd tried that before each driving test and it's not exactly worked so far?

'I will,' I called out.

I steeled myself as I put my hand on the front door handle. *You can do this*. Because whatever happens you don't just give up on a thing, do you? Opening the door, I saw my instructor's red Nissan Micra parked outside our home. Ashraf lowered his head, dark hair flopping over his eyes, and waved at me. I took another deep breath before setting foot outside the door.

★ ★ ★

'You shouldn't get so nervous,' he said as I steered the car into a parking spot outside the test centre after I'd had my lesson.

I tried to swallow the lump in my throat as I looked up at the brown building. *I can't fail again.*

'Okay,' I said.

'Don't just say okay. Mean it,' he replied, softening his tone. 'You drove well.'

'Okay.'

'Fatima, the problem isn't whether you can do this or not — the problem is you *believing* you can do it.'

I stared at the steering wheel because he was right, of course. But it was all such an embarrassment. Which thirty-year-old woman struggles this much with a driving test? It's just that I *know* if I can do this, I'll be able to get my life in order. I'd be free. *Independent* — not have

5

to rely on someone to drop me off or pick me up for my next hand-modelling shoot. I looked at my hands — my source of income.

'And don't feel sorry for yourself,' he added.

I looked at him. 'I'm not feeling sorry for myself.'

'Okay, okay,' he replied, putting his hands up, the cuff of his electric-blue shirt riding up. 'Just checking.'

I took a deep breath and got a whiff of Ash's aftershave. Maybe I was feeling sorry for myself.

'How's Sam?' I asked, glancing at the clock and wanting to forget that my test was in under fifteen minutes.

'Teenage girls will be teenage girls,' he replied. 'But she's a good girl, really. Just hiding it well. Really well. Either that or she'll take after her mum,' he added.

I tried to give him a reassuring smile. 'No. She's half you too,' I replied.

'I'm not sure that counts for much. But at least my son's tamer. He might be two years her junior but he's also about ten years wiser.'

'He does sound it,' I replied, remembering all the stories I'd heard about him.

It's so weird to think that Ashraf has two teenage children when he's not more than five, maybe six or seven, years older than me. It'd be rude to ask.

'She probably regrets things,' I said.

He smiled and brushed something off his black jeans. Mae would have something to say about a man who wears black jeans. '*So uncool.*' I wish I had been as sure of myself at that age; to

6

be able to say what you think out loud. I wish I was that sure of myself *now*. My little Mae, who's able to say what she wants and still manage not to offend anyone.

'If my ex-wife regrets leaving, then her getting married to another man is a huge mistake,' he said.

'Oh. I didn't know. Sorry.'

'Don't be. He's giving her a detached house and an expensive car — all the things I couldn't. Or didn't. Either way, it doesn't matter.'

How did we even get talking about his wife? If you have a driving instructor for long enough you'll probably end up knowing more about their life than you do your own brother or sister's. At least, that's how I feel. I remember when I started my lessons he'd only just left her. She did sound like a bit of a shrew; not that Ash would say as much, but why would you come all the way from Bangladesh to England to marry a man, only to get permanent stay here, then make his life so miserable that he's forced to leave you?

'What matters is your test,' he added. 'Did your mum tell you to say your prayers?'

I nodded.

'And your dad told you to check your mirrors?'

'Yes.'

'And Mae . . . ?'

'Gave me carrots.'

'Good — so everything as usual then.'

I laughed. He must think my family is crazy. They do sound it when I talk about them. Funny that I always feel fonder of them when I tell him about the latest drama in the Amir household. My hands had stopped sweating and when he said it was time to go I didn't want to reach into my bag for some Primula cheese.

Because we should always remember: *what doesn't kill us, only makes us stronger.*

2

Mae

'What doesn't kill you makes you stronger. That's my sister, Fatti's, motto every time she fails her driving test, which would be — not even exaggerating — for the *fifteenth* time now. That's right. *Fifteen*. It's kind of a rich thing to say when she walked into the house, with cheese all over her chin. Remember, guys: saturated fat does not make you stronger. Just looking at the gooey substance smeared on her face made me want to take a shot of wheatgrass. Anyway, ciao for now. More on the trials and tribulations of a millennial living in a Wyvernage later.'

I came out of Snapchat and stopped jogging on the spot for my warm-down after my run. Checking my Fitbit as I walked into the house, I called up to Dad from the passage.

'Bet that run would've taken care of your headache, Dad.'

Headache — *yeah, right*. I walked back into the kitchen because where else would Fatti be? 'Look what I made,' I said, carefully placing the phone upright so the video captured me opening the fridge.

Fatti looked at the celery salad in disgust, scrunching up the pudgy nose she hates so much, even though I think it's cute in its own way. But, hey, I'm the youngest in the family

9

— what do I know?

'Is that camera on again?' asked Fatti. 'Where'd Mum put the prawns?'

Of course the camera was on again. What would it take for my family to realise that this wasn't some hobby now — it was *work*. I'd have the best GCSE media project in the year. No other student had eleven thousand subscribers on their YouTube channel. I stepped in front of our huge silver fridge. 'It's a scientific fact that celery can speed up your metabolism,' I said, putting the bowl down in front of her.

'Don't worry, Fatti,' said the mothership who'd walked in. She adjusted the drape of her sari and glared at me, which meant I should move out of the way or I might have a slipper thrown at my face. 'You will pass the test next time.'

And she handed her the prawns, which I guess brought a bit of balance to the synthetic cheese in a tube.

'Mae, can't you eat like a normal girl?' said Mum, looking at my salad. 'Don't you want your amma's delicious curries?'

No, thanks. I'd rather not have a heart attack, but of course I didn't say that because it would've been rude. I stepped back and zoomed the camera in on Mum who put her hand on Fatti's cheek. I had to shirk off this weird feeling I got — as if I'm missing out on something. I tried to remember the last time Mum put her hand on my cheek. I couldn't. Just then the front door opened and slammed shut again. Farah tumbled in with about seven shopping bags as

10

Fatti went to help her. There was a look on Farah's face, which I wanted to capture, but I couldn't zoom in close enough — what was it? Like sadness, but it disappeared too quickly, because as soon as Mum came into view Farah put on a smile.

'I see Mae's busy with her high-school assignment,' said Farah, raising an eyebrow. 'Perhaps put the camera down for a moment and help with the bags?'

I rolled my eyes. The thing is, I don't mean to, but it kind of just happens. Apparently it's called having an attitude problem. Whatever.

'Is . . . ' Farah cleared her throat. 'Is Bubblee here?'

Farah's movements slowed down as Mum told her: 'She's so busy in London. She said she can't make it this weekend either.' Mum's sigh was audible.

'All she'd do is smear mud all over the carpet and call it art. Ugh,' I said, repulsed at the chocolate digestives that Farah put on the breakfast table. 'Do you know obesity is one of the top killers in the UK?'

'Tst,' said Mum to me as she continued: 'If Bubblee comes I might be able to show her some boys. She is so beautiful — maybe someone will marry her before she opens her mouth. And then at least *she* will give me grandchildren.'

Mum glanced at Farah not so discreetly, waiting to catch her eye, just so she could give her an aggrieved look. Because that's how Mum rolls.

'You haven't heard that for five minutes, have

11

you?' I said to Farah.

She pursed her lips as she turned to Fatti. 'Well. How'd the test go?' she said, a hopeful look on her face.

Fatti shook her head. 'But it's okay. What doesn't kill you — '

' —Yeah, yeah,' I said, catching Fatti staring at Farah's wedding ring. 'We know.'

Mum slapped me across the back of the head. I swear I have a bald patch because of her. I got my phone and tapped on the Twitter icon:

Some people have alopecia, others suffer from male-pattern baldness — I have a mother who likes to hit me across the head #Abrasiveparents #Hairloss #Aintfair #Meh #Whatever

Fatti walked out of the kitchen as I saw Farah's eyes settle on our sister's widening arse. I mean, *hello*, why doesn't anyone say anything to her? I'm the only one who cares enough about her arteries to make a celery salad, and then I'm the one everyone shouts at for being 'insensitive'. Yeah, well, when she's in hospital because she needs a bypass at the age of thirty-five, then we'll talk about who's been insensitive.

'Mum, you really need to stop buying all that cheese in a tube,' said Farah.

Mum, as usual, opted for selective hearing and asked Farah whether she got more prawns. Fatti likes to mash them up and mix it with the cheese. If that doesn't make you vom, I don't know what will.

'Here,' said Farah, handing an envelope to

Mum. 'Five hundred.'

Mum quietly took it and slid it into her drawer. More money. From Jay, the prodigal son. Why our brother doesn't give it to Mum and Dad directly, I don't know. I decided that no-one cares about what I have to say and took the bowl of salad upstairs to Dad.

'Come in,' he said as I entered Mum and Dad's room.

He was lying on the bottom bunk, scratching at the wood panel above him, but sat up, craning his head forward so he didn't hit it against the bunk's panel.

'How's the headache?' I asked.

'Hmm? *Oh*, yes,' he replied, putting his hand on his head. 'Better.'

Of course it was.

'Mum was on top last night then?' I said, settling down next to him, holding on to the bowl of salad.

He looked at me, momentarily taken aback. 'Oh. Yes. On top,' he replied. His eyes settled on the salad.

'I guess you don't want it either,' I asked.

They say youth is energy. Like, you should be grateful for it and stuff. But youth to me feels like wading through a mass of crap, wishing someone would give you direction because you can't see (because there's crap in your eyes, obvs). Dad's top lip twitched — his eyes still on the salad.

'Yes, yes. I'll have it,' he said, picking up a celery stick and crunching into it. It took him about five minutes to swallow the thing.

We sat in silence for a few minutes. Then Dad said: 'How is school?'

'Yeah, cool,' I replied.

He scratched his chin. 'And, er . . . this video,' he said, looking at my phone with concentration. 'You are filming things?'

'*Correcto-mundo*.'

He looked at me, confused.

'It just means, yes, Abba.'

'Ah, good, good,' he replied.

'My teacher said I've got talent,' I told him.

'That's very good.'

I waited for him to ask me some more questions: like, what kind of talent, and what will you do with it when you leave high school? That kind of thing.

After a bit more silence, he asked: 'You like those smoothies, don't you?'

'Only the homemade ones, because you can't trust what supermarkets put in stuff.'

'But we buy everything from supermarkets.'

'Yeah, but they've got all those e-numbers and stuff.'

'E-numbers?'

I nodded. 'It's unhealthy. It's *killing* us.'

'But there is nothing wrong with us,' he replied, looking at his body up and down as if it was an example of supreme health.

It was like trying to explain fashion to Fatti. I gave up.

'You know what is healthy?' he asked.

'What?'

'YouTube,' he answered. 'Very good. For the brain.'

14

What the hell was my dad going on about?

'Er, okay.'

He hesitated then said: 'You said you had scribers.'

'Subscribers, Abba.'

'Oh, yes. That's what I meant.'

'And?'

He cleared his throat. 'Just . . . carry on.'

'Sure, Abba. Thanks.'

We both sat in silence for a few minutes.

'Oh, I know,' I exclaimed. 'I'll make tofu curry tonight. For dinner.'

Dad nodded, as if there was someone forcing the movements of his head, and patted me on my back. It's not on the cheek. Not like it is for Fatti, or a hand on the head like it is for Farah; the pinching of the nose like it is for Bubblee. But who really cares?

3

Bubblee

'You need to get the contours right,' said Sasha, clearing her throat and observing my latest piece. 'It's . . . it's coming along.'

I looked at my sculpture, Sasha's hand resting on the hip of my centaurian woman. The idea is to subvert expectation by showing the interchangeability of sexuality.

'But that's the point,' I replied. 'What *is* right?'

'Still,' she said, walking towards the window of my poky studio flat and lighting up a cigarette. She regarded the sculpture again. 'I'm not sure your aim is quite, you know, coming across.'

Sasha really has nothing good to say about anything. My mobile rang and 'Mum' flashed on the screen.

'You gonna get that?' asked Sasha.

'Later,' I replied, looking at the sculpture.

Something was amiss, but why should that be wrong? Isn't it like in life, where the imperfections are hard to pinpoint and yet are just *there*?

'You've go to stop over-thinking things,' she said. 'Your problem is you always want to create something with multiple layers of meaning, but that should be the end result, not the starting point. Art is about feeling.'

'A glimpse of the world as you see it,' I muttered, reminding myself.

Well, I definitely see it as being amiss, so I must've been on the right track. My phone rang again. This time Dad's name flashed on the screen.

'How many times do they call you in a day?' said Sasha. 'No point in exhaling. They can't hear you. Just pick it up.'

'I'm busy.'

Before I knew it, Mae was FaceTiming me.

'Is someone dying?' I said, picking the phone up, staring down at Mae's pixie-like face. 'I'll call you back.'

'She failed again,' she said.

'Who failed?' I asked.

'Fatti.'

'What?'

'Tst, her *driving* test, of course. Don't you remember?'

'Oh, yeah. I forgot. I hope you hid the cheese from her,' I said.

I glanced over at Sasha who was still leaning out of the window, puffing away.

'One sec,' I said to Mae, muting the phone and putting it face-down on the sofa while I asked Sasha to put her cigarette out.

'It's not like your family can see me,' she responded.

'What if they do? Then they'll think I smoke and it'll be something else for them to rail against. It's bad enough I've left my family home and that I'm living alone in London; thinking that I smoke will give someone a heart attack,' I whispered, even though I'd muted Mae.

Sasha sighed and shook her head, throwing the cigarette butt out of the window.

'You wouldn't know you're a twenty-eight-year-old woman,' she said as I got back to Mae's call.

'What was that?' Mae asked.

I saw her scan something behind me and it was Sasha, waving at her. Mae waved back unsurely.

'I'll see you tonight, Bubs,' said Sasha before leaving the flat.

'Don't you, like, have any other friends?' asked Mae.

'What do you want, Mae?'

Mae seemed to be sitting on the steps on the staircase. I recognised the green carpeting against the cream walls. I could just imagine her peeking over the railing, spying on everyone with them unaware of exactly what she's catching on camera. On the one hand it's an ethically dubious thing to do, but on the other, I'm glad she has some kind of passion that isn't related to a bureaucratic, unimaginative career-choice. Thank God there must be some kind of an artistic gene in our family. She made her way down the steps and everyone's face flashed in front of me.

'Look who's here,' she said, as Mum squinted and recognised me.

'I tried calling you — where were you? Why didn't you pick up? I was worried.'

Before I had a chance to answer, Farah's face was in front of me.

'Say hello to your fave,' said Mae.

Farah straightened up from stuffing the kitchen cupboards with God knows what.

'Salamalaikum,' she said.

'Hi,' I managed to mumble.

The sun shone from the kitchen window, right into her eyes.

She shielded them as she asked: 'How's the big smoke?'

I shrugged. 'Better than home,' I said, lowering my voice.

She gave a faint smile. We might be identical twins, but our smiles are different — hers is soft and sweet. Mine? Well, not so much. She looked away but I couldn't see what she was doing with her hands. I always did hate it when Farah looked like that; so helpless and at a loss.

'How's your *husband*?' I asked. Only it didn't come out in the well-meaning way I intended.

Before I knew it Farah was out of screen-shot, and swiftly replaced with Mae's face.

'Where's Fatti?' I asked Mae, pretending it was normal to have Farah walk away like that. Actually, it had become quite standard.

'Well done,' Mae said, ignoring my question. 'Farah's only gone and left now, and I needed to ask her about my tofu curry recipe. You need to let it go, it's been five years. I mean, come on — so what Farah's married?' she added, looking at the leftover shopping. 'Now I'm going to have to put it all away.'

I wanted to tell her she's lucky she has Farah who manages to do that for her, as well as everything else.

'So, she was helping out at home as usual. Not much change then,' I said.

'And handing over money from our dear brother, as per,' added Mae. 'Who, by the way, decided to call Mum and Dad today. Ugh.' Mae leaned into the screen as I realised that she'd caught sight of my sculpture. 'What's *that*?'

'A work in progress,' I replied, turning the phone the other way.

'What? Like you?' She found this a lot funnier than I did and laughed as she made her way up the stairs again.

'*Wait*. I wanted to speak to her,' I heard Mum call out after Mae as she passed the living room.

Not that Mae listened. 'I'll pretend I didn't hear. You can thank me later. Ssh.'

I saw she'd stopped outside Fatti's room and leaned into the door. Mae put her finger to her mouth, waited for a few moments before shrugging and going into her own room.

'How's school?' I asked, turning around to look at my sculpture, wondering what it was that made it seem so incomplete. What did Mae know? My sisters were so uncultured when it came to anything to do with the art world.

'Better than your relationship with Farah,' she replied.

'Not now, Mae.'

Would I ever be able to say anything to Farah without her taking offence?

Mae shrugged. 'Whatevs. I've got more interesting things to do than think about everyone's crises anyway.'

Just then there was a loud knock on her door.

20

'It's Abbauuu,' she said, smiling at our dad. 'What's up, Abs?'

'Your amma needs to talk to Bubblee.'

'Our amma always needs to talk to someone,' she replied.

If I'd said half the things at her age that she did I'd have been locked in the cupboard under the stairs.

'Soz, sis. I did my best but we are all veterans of our familial battles.'

'Just pass the phone, Mae.'

Before I knew it there was Dad's face as he spoke. 'Fatti failed her driving test again so your amma is a little more stressed than usual. Just speak to her for five minutes and make her feel easy.'

'She's not going to feel easy until I move back home. And let me tell you, Abba, that's not happening.'

'I know, I know.' He paused as I saw him stop at the top of the stairs. 'Erm, what is that?'

I'd turned around again without realising that Dad could see the sculpture.

'Something I'm working on,' I replied.

'Hmm.' He furrowed his eyebrows. 'And this is what you're doing in London? Making sculptures of women ... ' He leaned in closer. 'Animals? What is it?'

'Never mind, Abba. Just give the phone to Amma so I can get the conversation over with.'

I don't mean for my words to sound short or irritable but that's just how they come out.

'I'll speak to you properly later, okay, Abba?'

He was still looking at the sculpture, worry

lines spreading over his features.

'Hmm? Okay, Babba.'

By the time he'd walked downstairs I heard Mum complaining about Naked Marnie who was apparently out again, basking in the glory of unexpected sunshine.

'It is a free country,' I heard Dad say to her.

'What do you want then?' said Mum, taking the phone from him and giving me a view of the kitchen walls again. 'For us all to go out naked?'

'No-one wants *you* to go out naked,' he replied.

'*Hello?*' I said. I had a sculpture to work on, after all.

'Yes,' said Mum, putting the phone up to her sour-looking face. 'I called you two, three times and you didn't answer.'

'I was going to call back.'

'When? Next week? Next month? Next year?'

I didn't see why, between Fatti failing and Jay calling, I had to be the one who faced her aggression. This is why I make a point of calling home as little as possible. What's the point when you're only going to get told off? I'm an adult, for God's sake. I bet Jay doesn't get this antagonism. No, the golden child is probably showered with all manners of kindness.

'Poor Fatti failed again,' said Mum without any prompt from me.

'Hmm.'

'You know how hard it is for her. She doesn't have your confidence — you should help her but you don't even answer your family's calls.'

'It's not as if I'm loafing around, Amma. I'm working.'

She looked up at my dad, presumably, and decided to mirror his worried face.

'But, Bubblee, what kind of work? Look how beautiful you are — such a small nose and light-brown eyes. You shouldn't take these things for granted. Maybe you should think of getting a proper job where you are making some money. Maybe banking, hmm? Whenever I have a nice boy's amma on the phone who asks me what you do, I tell her and I never hear from them again. If you had a normal job they would see you and then your beauty would do the rest.'

'These aren't exactly the type of people I want to know anyway, and you need to stop trying to find me a husband. I don't want to get married yet.'

'Your youth won't last for ever. Already you're so old for marriage.'

'I'm twenty-eight, Amma. And Fatti's older than me. Why don't you bug her about marriage? I'm pretty sure she cares a lot more about it than I do.'

Mum shook her head and looked up at the ceiling. 'Allah, what have I done to deserve a girl who answers back so much? A girl who doesn't even speak to her own twin sister?'

Which was, of course, a complete exaggeration. I speak to Farah. When we're in the same room. Which, granted, might not be very often, because I avoid it as much as humanly possible, but that's for her sake as well as mine.

'And why?' Mum continued. 'Because she married a man?'

'A man who's not her equal,' I replied, feeling the heat rise in my cheeks.

Why does everyone find it so hard to understand? Why couldn't they see that my twin sister deserved better than this prosaic, uninspired individual? Why does a husband have to be horrible, or abrasive, or neglectful to not be right for you? Of all the things Farah could've done with her life, achieved or aspired to, she decided to settle down and marry the first man that asked her. Forget the first man — her first *cousin*. And I bet it was all because he wanted to stay in England; coming here to study and then conveniently 'falling in love' with my sister, who then — naïve woman that she was — decided to fall in love right back. I mean, don't even get me started on the notion of falling in love, let alone marrying your mum's sister's son.

Mum sighed and muttered something under her breath. 'And when will you visit your family? Or do we have to wait for someone to die?'

'Jay's Amma,' said Dad. 'Don't say things like this.'

I looked as Dad seemed to be putting grass in the blender.

'What are you doing?' I asked.

He turned around as he put the lid on the blender after adding a banana to the mix. 'Making Mae a smoothie,' he explained.

'With *what*?'

'She likes fresh things, you know. Says that supermarkets are no good, so I took some leaves

24

from the hedges for an extra . . . *boost.*'

'I only say what is true, Jay's Abba,' replied Mum, ignoring what was happening in her kitchen.

I mean, how can I take seriously the words of two people who refer to each other as the parent of their only son? Their only son who comes and goes as he pleases, hardly ever showing his face and exists more as an idea than an actual being. Not that he gets any flack for it because, of course, he's a boy and the same standards don't apply.

'Maybe at Jay's wedding,' I said, straight-faced.

'Bubblee,' said Dad, abandoning the blender and taking the phone from Mum as he glanced at her. 'Remember she is your mother.' He looked from side to side as if he wasn't quite sure of this fact. Or perhaps he was just looking out for a slipper that might come flying his way if he did anything but agree with her.

'Yes, Abba. Thanks.'

He gave a short nod and winked at me before he 'accidentally' hung up on me. Dad will probably end up paying for that in rationed dessert servings tonight.

I exhaled as I sat on the edge of my chair and looked at my sculpture. It was difficult to concentrate, what with Mum mentioning Farah. I turned to look at a photograph of us on my wall; it was taken on our thirteenth birthday. We were so excited about being teenagers. We thought there'd be this shift where things would change and life would somehow be more exciting. And it was in some ways; I discovered art and how a painting could make you feel things that life somehow couldn't; how there was beauty in the stroke of a brush or the curve of a shape; the way a drawing might speak a truth that reality only hinted at because it never stayed long enough for you to capture it. But art — it kept that feeling static in time, and you could re-visit it and be moved by it all over again, in a different way. I wanted to make people feel that way with *my* art. And I wasn't about to give up until I succeeded. Farah never took to art. Or literature. I waited for her to talk passionately about something. I urged her to read the same books as me, but she'd be tidying up after Jay, or straightening out her room, sewing a button on someone's jacket. Always busy but never with the important things. Never outraged at a news story, or delirious with joy when a dictator had been overthrown, or even about something stupid, like winning fifty quid on the lottery.

'Oh, Farah,' I whispered, picking up the photo, rubbing my finger over the frown on my face as if that'd wipe it away.

Why does no-one understand that I wanted more for her? After all, isn't that what sisters are meant to do? Want great things for each other? I turned my attention to my sculpture again, pleased with what I was in the middle of creating. This was going to wow people. I just had to get it right. It would be spectacular. I shook my head at my family and their ways. No-one understands: there's nothing great about mediocrity.

4

Farah

House cleaned? Check. Shopping done? Check. Shopping delivered to Mum and Dad's, along with money from Jay, that's not actually from Jay but me? Check. I needed a minute and ended up collapsing on the sofa. Bubblee's face swam in front of me even though I tried to blink it out of existence. It shouldn't bother me — it's been five years since I've been listening to the same passive-aggressive tone. I suppose you just don't get used to your twin's disappointment. The doorbell rang. It was Pooja who came to give back the electric screwdriver she'd borrowed.

'Have you seen the monstrous boutique they've opened up on Henway Road? The *designs* of the Indian suits are awful. And you know our neighbours will be queuing up to buy some if there's a South Asian wedding within a ten-mile radius.'

I smiled and gestured for her to come in but she said she had to go and make sure her husband didn't feed her children Tuc biscuits for dinner.

'Oh, an email's gone around to confirm our meeting. You're okay with next week?' she asked.

There was a burglary a few months ago and we'd set up a neighbourhood watch as a result.

'Yes, that's fine and let's have it at mine. I'll respond to everyone.'

'As long as we don't ask Marge to bring snacks, because honestly, I don't think I could stomach it,' said Pooja.

I laughed and told her I'd delegate with that in mind as she said goodbye. Since I was up I checked whether Mustafa had paid the bills I'd found a few weeks ago. They all still needed to be paid. I picked up my mobile.

'Hey,' I said to Mustafa.

'Hon, listen, I'm on my way to an important meeting. I just *know* this idea's going to be the one,' he said.

Which is what he said last time, and the time before that, and the time before that. I'd told him before that I knew this company was his dream — a place where he and his associates would get together and think about new inventions and apps — and then try to create them. But all the money he made in the stock market, coming out of university, was being used up in this company to no avail. Still, it was his money, and he still traded, which gave us a comfortable life, so I couldn't complain. There was just no nice way of saying that his ideas were . . . *not good.* I didn't want to be the cynical wife, though, because maybe, just maybe, he'd surprise me. And it would make me happy to see him happy.

'I'll call you in a bit, okay?' he said, sounding distracted.

'I just needed to know when you were transferring that money into our joint account.

28

You still haven't paid those bills, so I thought I'd do it.'

He paused.

'Today,' he replied.

'Babe, that's what you said last week. And the week before that.'

I included the 'Babe' to stop myself from sounding like a nagging wife. I waited for him to speak but it took a few moments.

'I know. I'll sort it out today. I promise,' he added. 'Are you okay?'

'Yeah, fine.'

'What's wrong?' he pressed.

'Nothing,' I said, then lost the will to pretend. 'Bubblee.'

'Oh.'

Why didn't she see that despite the fact that this man's been shunned by her, he still manages to bite his tongue when her name's mentioned. But I suppose rage isn't his thing. It's neither of our thing. That's what I love about him.

'How is she?' he asked.

'Still Bubblee.' I sighed and took out the groceries from the bag, putting them on the kitchen counter. 'I thought going to London might soften her a bit.'

He laughed. 'For a born-and-bred Britisher, you don't have a very good idea of what London's like.'

It still amuses me when he says 'Britisher'.

'You'll transfer the money then?' I said, suddenly feeling tired from having to talk about Bubblee.

I don't need her to understand my marriage to

Mustafa — *I* understand and so does he and that's all that matters. I waited for him to respond. Five years with a person can help you to read their silences and hesitations as well as the intonation of their speech.

'Is everything okay, Mustafa?' I asked.

I just had to check — his silences weren't normal. I don't see how things couldn't be okay. We had everything, after all. I looked around the house and the lack of toys cluttered everywhere; no playpen, no children's books, no pieces of Lego or dolls left lying around. I hear people complain about what their children have or haven't done and it stirs something inside of me — making me want to shout — not sure what I'd shout, but that doesn't matter.

'Everything's fine, Far,' he added. 'I'll always look after you. You know that, don't you?'

Of course he will. He always has.

'Have you heard from Jay lately?' he asked.

'He emailed last week. Why?'

'Just wondering,' he said. 'I er . . .' He paused. 'I promised your parents I'd get him to help out with work. Just to give him a hand.'

'Oh.'

It was the first I'd heard of it. Why hadn't anybody told me? When I asked Mustafa he simply said that it was only bits and pieces Jay was doing — nothing major.

'I'll see how he gets on — it's nothing permanent.'

'Thanks,' I said. 'For helping him out.'

'You're happy with it?'

'I know it'll mean a lot to Mum and Dad. But

take it one step at a time with Jay. I love him but it's not exactly an ideal plan.'

'Yeah, yeah, of course.'

'And come home early tonight if you can,' I added.

He replied that he would as he put the phone down, when the doorbell rang again.

'Hi, Abba,' I said as Dad walked into the living room and switched the television on.

'Your amma thinks I've gone out to buy some things for the garden,' he said.

He settled down on my large white sofa, giving a satisfied sigh and smiled as *The Arti-Fact Show* flashed on our fifty-inch screen.

'I'll make the tea,' I replied, glancing at the television screen. 'The presenter's put on weight, hasn't he?'

'Look at that,' said Dad, observing what can only be described as a painting of a swan, studded with crystals. 'Beautiful. Even your amma would like that,' he added, turning to me, and possibly seeing the disgusted look on my face.

I gave him his tea with a slice of cake and sat down next to him.

'You're okay?' he asked, not taking his eyes off the television screen.

'Yeah.'

'Bubblee's ideas are different,' he said, sipping his tea.

I picked a bit of walnut off my cake and put it to the side.

'London,' Dad said, shaking his head. 'Everyone talks about London, but we are happy here, aren't we?' he added, putting his arm around me, squeezing my shoulders.

'Yes, Abba.'

'She's a good girl, but if she could just get married so your amma would stop worrying, it would help me very much. Now your brother, on the other hand; we might not always see him but he still thinks of us, sending us money. Plus, you know boys will be boys.'

It was useful to have the TV as a distraction, because the look on my face might've given my secret away. I couldn't quite bear the idea of Mum and Dad thinking that their only son's one redeeming feature of sending them money was actually me.

'Before I forget,' said Dad, taking out a letter. 'What is this?'

I read through it.

'It's just about parking meters. You can read, Abba.'

'Yes, yes, but the English sometimes is confusing.'

'It's nothing,' I added. 'Won't affect our road.'

'Very good.' Dad smacked his legs with his hands and got up to leave.

'Don't forget to get the soil that's on offer, Abba,' I said. 'Not the full-price one. Mum won't stop telling me about it otherwise.'

He nodded, gratefully, kissed me on the head and left.

★ ★ ★

When he'd gone I wandered around the house. I do this often; when all the chores are done and the kitchen and bathroom can't get any cleaner. I look at the high ceilings and arched doorways, the mowed lawn, with flower beds dotted all around. Mum used to tell us that a woman makes a house a home. But sometimes these spaces seem so empty I'm not sure what else I can do to fill the void that seems to stretch. There are potted plants in the home, picture frames and even some organised clutter I've arranged, but nothing fills the emptiness apart from when my husband comes home.

I remembered the day we moved into this house. I couldn't believe we'd be living in a place so big and beautiful, but thanks to Mustafa's job and some help from Mum and Dad we were able to afford it. There's nothing quite like making your own home; filling up the spaces with things you've been given or have bought; deciding where to put the television; disagreeing over the paint, only to settle on a colour that looks dangerously close to Magnolia. Mustafa had come up behind me and put his arms around me.

'Do you like it?' he asked.

'I love it,' I replied.

'The small room upstairs would make a perfect nursery, wouldn't it?' he added.

I shook myself from the memory and sat at my laptop, looking at baby items on the Internet. If I had a baby girl I'd dress her up in pink — I don't care what people say about the colour; it'd look beautiful on her. And my boy would be in blue. I'd want the girl first so she could play me to our baby boy, who'd obviously have some of his Uncle Jay's looks. She'd hug him when he fell over, cover for him whenever he got in trouble with me or Mustafa — she'd call him when we asked where he was before he'd come stumbling home, careful not to wake us. Before going to sleep he'd creep into her room and plant a kiss on her forehead, which she'd accept before hitting him on the arm for making her lie again. I laughed at the memory it conjured and missed Jay so much, I wished he'd visit us. Five years ago it would've been Bubblee I'd have gone to, but now he's the only one I could tell: *No, Jay. I can't have babies.*

I looked through my inbox and clicked on his latest email to me.

From: Amir, Jahangir
To: Lateef, Farah
Subject: Hi

Hi Sis,

Thanks for sending through that money again. You know how much I appreciate it. I promise I'm trying to get my life together. Sometimes it's hard, but this time I really think I'm going to get my big break. I've a friend who's got a business plan and he wants me to be a part of it.

Don't tell anyone about it yet, not until it all goes through. I know it's been a while since I've called Mum and Dad but I promise I'll do that too. I'm just concentrating on this business plan.

34

Take care,
Jay

P.S. I do know how I'm lucky to have a sister like you.

God, please let this work. At least he did call Mum and Dad, even if it was five days later. I'd asked him what this plan was but he didn't want to go into detail because he said he'd jinx it. I don't know why it is that for some people things just don't seem to go smoothly. It's always been something with him — whether it was school or work. I prayed that next time he emailed, it would be good news.

★   ★   ★

I ended up falling asleep on the sofa. When I awoke it was already six o'clock and Mustafa wasn't home yet so I called him. No answer. Whenever I get up from a nap I feel anxious — as if I've missed something while I was asleep. I need to stop looking at Internet sites for baby clothes.

'Right — dinner,' I said to myself.

Adding the tomato puree to the fried onions, I glanced over at the clock. Six thirty-five. As the chicken simmered in the pan I reached for my mobile and called him again, but it went straight to voicemail. When it got to seven-thirty the demeanour of easy-going wife began to slip. I checked our joint-account balance online and saw no money had been transferred.

Why doesn't he just tell me when he can't do something? Why does he have to lie? But the anger dissolved as I looked at the dinner that was getting cold. That's when the doorbell rang.

'You're late *and* you forgot your keys,' I called out as I opened the door.

I looked up at two young men in police officers' outfits.

'Mrs Lateef?' one of them said.

What had happened? Had there been another burglary on the street?

'Yes?' I replied.

'Is there anyone home with you?'

I shook my head. Just then Alice from next door was coming home and stopped to look at what was going on.

'Everything okay, officers?' she asked, walking over.

'Is this lady a friend of yours, Mrs Lateef?' asked one of the officers.

'Yes, I am,' replied Alice.

The police officer gave a constrained smile as he looked at me for confirmation. I nodded.

'What's going on?' I asked.

I didn't know why but a knot formed in my stomach as I gripped the door handle.

'It's your husband,' one of them said.

I couldn't quite focus on their faces as my heart began to thud so loudly it muffled my hearing. Their image became a blur.

'I'm afraid he's been in an accident.'

5

Mae

'Mae, *put* the camera away,' Fatti whispered into my ear.

Was she mad? This was prime videoing time; all these faces, the hospital, the tension.

'Put it away or I'll throw it in the bin,' exclaimed Mum.

Everyone in the waiting room looked at Mum. Didn't look like she cared. I tucked the phone under my leg as Dad gave an exhausted sigh. Fatti got up and made her way towards the door, outside, where Farah was sitting on her own. Looked like Dad was lost in a world of his own, so I got up and walked towards the door too with my phone. I'd just got a message from the girls from school.

Omg. Jus saw on your snapchat that your bro inlaws been in an accident. Are you alright?? Hashtagged on Twitter #Pray4family. Lemme know if you need anything. Xxx

I knew it wasn't ideal to video all of this but it was my GCSE assignment. Plus, it's weird how people find my family so interesting. Whenever I put something on Snapchat about them it always gets loads of hits, because some people appreciate creativity — and not the Bubblee

37

kind, but the real, gritty, *my*-generation kind. What my fam fail to understand is that they don't actually have peripheral vision. Yeah, in the literal sense they have it, but not in the metaphorical sense (I'm going to ace my GCSE English too). For example, as I walked up to the door, Mum and Dad in the waiting room couldn't see how Fatti looked, sitting next to Farah. I sneakily got my phone out again. Of course Farah's going to be crying and all sorts but when I zoomed in on Fatti, just a little, there was something more than upset there. A look no-one would've noticed if it weren't for me and my trusted camera.

The doctor came and paused in front of Farah and Fatti as they both looked up. She started saying something about Mustafa being in a medically induced coma.

'A coma?' said Farah, looking confused.

'It's just a precaution to avoid nerve and brain-stem cell damage that can be caused by the swelling of the brain,' she said.

'But he's going to be okay, isn't he?' said Fatti. 'I mean, he's going to come out of it.'

The doctor removed her glasses. 'It's too early to tell. The injuries to the head have been severe. We'll have to wait to see the extent once the swelling has reduced and we take him out of the coma.'

'Oh, God,' said Farah, clutching her stomach.

'So, the coma's not permanent?' said Fatti.

'No, no. Just temporary and reversible.'

Farah shook her head. 'I told him,' she said to Fatti. 'Always use your head-set. You'll get caught by the police. You'll have an accident.'

I felt a lump in my throat but pushed it back. Fatti rubbed Farah's back, not saying much. She did look a little slimmer at this angle.

Every1s asking what's goin on with ur bro-in-law. U should tweet sumthin.

I tweeted:

Bro-in-law in coma. In hospital with amazin staff. #Pray4Family

'Who was he speaking to?' asked Fatti.

Farah shook her head. 'Don't know. His phone's dead — '

She stopped and did this weird staccato intake of breath as if she'd forgotten how to breathe. I realised only then that I didn't think I'd ever seen Farah cry. Fatti cries all the time. I know because I sometimes hear her in her room. All it takes is me offering her a salad before her eyes fill with tears. Bubblee cried the day she said she was moving to London. Those were more tears of rage, though. What a drama that was. I should watch that video back one day — 'You're stifling me! We're human beings, not just girls who are made to get married and churn out babies . . . ' On and on it went.

Fatti took Farah into a hug and I zoomed in on Fatti's face again, looking so sad and sorry that I decided to switch the camera off. Though I did wonder: what's she got to be sorry about?

When Bubblee came running down the corridor, Farah looked up as if she couldn't believe her eyes. Bubblee slowed down to a walk as she approached us and took the seat next to Farah. When I was a child I used to pretend that Farah and Bubblee were the two ugly step-sisters (except they weren't ugly, obvs) and Fatti was my fairy godmother.

'You came,' said Farah. Not like she sounded grateful or anything — just surprised.

Bubblee gave a tight kind of smile. Smiling never did come naturally to her.

'What do the doctors say?' Bubblee asked.

'Severe head trauma,' replied Farah, pressing her hand to her forehead.

I couldn't help it. I had to get my phone out again. I put it on video and then tucked it into my shirt pocket so it recorded everything without anyone going, *Mae, turn it off. Mae, stop it. Maeeeeeee.*

'But what does that mean?' asked Bubblee.

Farah looked at her. 'It means they don't know if he'll make it.'

'Oh,' replied Bubblee.

'He'll be okay,' added Fatti. 'You'll see. He'll be just fine.'

Unlike Fatti's eating habits, her voice is kind of even. Some might say it's monotone — they're people who have a problem with consistency — but right then her voice had a note of panic.

'Why are you being so weird?' I asked her later when she got up to use the bathroom.

'Am I? No, I'm not.'

She looked at herself in the bathroom mirror.

'It's not that bad,' I said.

'What?'

'Your face,' I replied, laughing.

She sighed. 'You should go and sit with Farah.'

'And say what? Sorry your husband's in a coma?'

'*Mae.*'

Fatti closed her eyes and splashed her face with some water. The problem with Fatti is that she's a worrier. Every little thing will have her crease her eyebrows, look from side to side and probably throw up.

'Poor Farah,' she said, under her breath. 'She doesn't deserve this,' she added, looking at me.

'You're telling me.'

'And *Mustafa*. Lying there with all those wires going through him, not having a clue that his wife's crying her eyes out.'

I squirted some disinfectant soap and rubbed it into my hands.

'He's too nice to be in a coma,' she added.

'Yeah, well, it'd be great if only murderers and rapists got put in comas, but I don't think that's how it works.'

She paused, leaning against the sink. 'Did you finish your history homework?'

'Not exactly top of my list of priorities right now,' I said.

'You've had all week. You've got subjects other than media and English, Mae.'

'Have I?' I said, leaning forward in shock as if I'd just found this out. I leaned back and rolled

41

my eyes. 'Don't know how I'd keep up if it wasn't for you.'

Fatti dragged me by the arm as we came out of the bathroom and sat me down in the waiting room.

'My poor daughter,' said Mum. 'My poor sister.'

I glanced at Fatti as Bubblee walked into the room. 'Has anyone called Mustafa's mum to let her know?'

We all looked at each other. No-one had enough of their head about them to actually call Mustafa's mum in Bangladesh.

'She won't forgive me,' said Mum.

Bubblee sighed and got her phone out. 'You didn't drive into him, Amma. What's her number?'

'No, no. I'll call her myself.'

With which Mum got her special calling card out and left the room. Dad got up a few moments later and followed her out of the room.

'Amazing, isn't it?' said Bubblee. 'Her sister's son is married to her daughter and they still only speak to each other once every few months.'

'Weird, for sure,' I mumbled, scrolling through Twitter, reading all the messages I was getting about Mustafa.

Bubblee nudged me and looked over at Fatti who was wringing her hands. She's mostly like a human but also a bit like a puppy — especially when she looks up at you like she did just then.

'I don't want Farah to be unhappy,' she said.

Er, obviously.

'Then you'd better stop looking like some-one's about to die,' said Bubblee. 'Because that's the last thing Farah needs.'

★ ★ ★

We all came home that night — Bubblee volunteered to go home with Farah so she wouldn't be sleeping alone. Mum, Dad, Fatti and I went to bed but when I got to my room and put my hand in my jeans pocket I realised I'd forgotten my phone, recording and propped up against the bread-bin in the kitchen. Walking past Mum and Dad's bedroom, I heard them muttering. I'd have just walked past but something made me lean in and listen.

'Did you see how short she'd cut her beautiful, long hair?' I heard Mum say to Dad from outside their bedroom.

Amazing, isn't it? Their son-in-law's done in and in a coma, and Mum wanted to chat about Bubblee's hair.

'I spoke to Mrs Bhatchariya about boys for her. She said she'd send me some details, but you know what I think. We shouldn't have let her go to London,' added Mum.

'Why couldn't she be like our Faru?' said Dad.

I was surprised they didn't say Fatti. Nothing Fatti does is ever wrong. Speaking of the expanding devil, she came up the stairs and saw me crouching outside Mum and Dad's door.

'What are you doing there?' she whispered, crouching with me.

'Shh. I thought you'd gone to bed.'

'Is that Mum crying?' she asked.

I nodded.

'Do you think Dad's comforting her?' she asked.

I let out a stifled laugh. 'Yeah, right.'

Fatti began shifting on each leg until she couldn't take it any more and sat back, leaning against the wall.

'Why do you think that's weird?' she asked. 'They're always chatting in that room.'

'Are they?' I asked.

'You might notice if you weren't on your phone all the time.'

'I only know what I need to know, thanks,' I replied.

Fatti shook her head at me.

'You think he's going to be okay?' she said.

'Who?'

'Mustafa.'

I shrugged. 'Dunno. Hope so.'

'What if he's not, though?' Fatti looked at me, fear in her eyes. 'What if he . . . *dies?*' Tears welled and were in danger of rolling down her cheeks.

'You always think the worst's going to happen.'

Fatti looked like she was about to say something when we heard Dad speak.

'Malik is getting on a flight and coming as soon as possible.'

Our aunt and uncle are too old to travel and so their third eldest is coming instead.

'Maybe this is why it's all happened,' said Mum. 'Malik will come and then . . . '

Fatti struggled off the ground, interrupting my eavesdropping with her deep breaths and suppressed sighing.

'Do you think Bubblee and Farah are okay on their own in Farah's house? Maybe I should've stayed with her instead?' she said as she hovered over me.

'They'll be fine. It's not like they'll kill each other — not while Farah's husband's in hospital,' I replied.

'You shouldn't be eavesdropping,' said Fatti, putting both hands on her hips.

I shooed her away. She was killing my buzz as I continued to listen in to my parents' room, so she plodded away.

'But is it the right time?' said Mum.

Right time for what? I leaned in closer as they both went quiet. Then Dad spoke.

'It doesn't matter that he's coming. Mustafa is here and you never worry about it.'

'Mustafa is different. He's the same as us now,' said Mum. 'Maybe Malik will also be like us one day. It will be the answer to our prayers and then we could tell her.'

'We've waited very long,' said Dad.

What were they talking about? Annoying Fatti who made me miss half the conversation with her anti-eavesdropping morals. Before I knew it, Mum and Dad began talking about shopping that was needed and how Farah should stay with us while Mustafa's in hospital. Then I heard the creaking of the bunk as they both seemed to get ready to sleep.

I went downstairs to get my phone and switched off the recording. Before I deleted it I thought I might as well check what it had caught and, sure as anything, there was Fatti, stuffing her gob with mashed prawns and cream cheese.

★　★　★

'Has someone tried to call Jay?' asked Bubblee. 'Farah'll want him to know.'

I looked at Fatti. Fatti looked at me. It hadn't occurred to any of us that he should be told, given that he never knows what's going on in the family anyway. Mum and Dad were walking down the hospital corridor where we'd congregated.

Farah was in Mustafa's room. When we asked them, Dad said: 'No, no. Better to keep him out of it for now.'

'He'll just worry,' said Mum. 'Such a busy boy, trying to make something of himself.'

Bubblee scoffed as she folded her arms. Mum looked at her and raised her finger, while Dad mumbled something about needing some tea. It's not as if Bubblee actually said anything, but God forbid anyone even suggest that Jay's a waste. Which, as the youngest, I can appreciate without feeling too bothered about it. Bubblee's bothered about everything, though. It's just who she is.

'Your amma is already worried enough. Don't worry her more,' said Dad to Bubblee. 'And she isn't wrong.' He looked towards Mum who was staring at him. 'You're getting old and must think about getting married. Look at Mustafa and think how things can turn out.'

It's not like he raised his voice or anything, but it was a bit off-topic.

46

Even in the middle of a hospital Asian parents have to speak about marriage. *#Obsessed #Marriage #Coma.*

★ ★ ★

Bubblee went to protest but Fatti nudged her as Mum looked at her.

'Our son is trying to be a man,' she said. 'You should try to be a woman.'

Dad looked at the ground and followed Mum as they both walked away, leaving Bubblee, basically bubbling with anger. Who can blame her? I mean, bit harsh telling her that the only way she's a woman is if she gets married. Plus, what did that make Fatti, who'd turned a shade of red too when Mum said that. Our amma needs to get with the programme. Can't fight these oldies though, they're stuck in their ways. Shame, really. Mum's all right when she's chilled out and not worrying about the fact that Farah's not had a baby, the rice has run out or that Bubblee's not married. She's even interesting when you listen to the stories she tells about her childhood.

'Unbelievable,' Bubblee exclaimed as soon as they were out of earshot. The nurse behind the desk shot us a look. 'Our brother-in-law's in a coma and all Mum can think about is me getting married.'

I think it was a good idea to have a hidden camera running — you have to love media equipment. This would've been the time I'd have had to switch it off otherwise. Fatti fidgeted with

47

her hands. I put my arm around Bubblee.

'You're twenty-eight, Bangladeshi and single. What else are they going to think about?'

Bubblee looked at me as if she was about to tell me to go to my room, before glancing at Fatti.

'I don't understand why they're not on your back,' she said to Fatti, shrugging my arm off her shoulder. 'You're two years older then me.'

'Mae, go check if Mum's okay,' said Fatti to me.

'You check,' I replied.

She gave me her fairy godmother look so of course I had to listen. I swear, being the youngest in the family sucks.

'All right, Ma?' I said, slouching in the seat next to Mum and resting my arm on her shoulder.

'Mae — sit like a girl.'

'Oops, sorry,' I said, putting my hands in the air before crossing my ankles. I pointed at them to show Mum how careful I was with her instruction. She ignored me. I tell you, it takes some kind of resilience to put up with this stuff.

'So, er, Jay,' I said.

'Tst, *Jahangeer*,' pronounced Mum. 'We give him this beautiful name and you spoil it.'

Talk about touchy.

'He's the one who prefers it,' I replied. 'He hates his name. Jahangeer. *Jahangeeeeeer*,' I said, spreading my arms out in dramatic Bollywood fashion. I sat back after Mum slapped my leg. 'I mean, who can blame him?'

She chose to ignore this before she said: 'Go

and see where your abba is.'

'But I want to talk to *you*, Amma.' I gripped her shoulders and shook them. 'See how you're feeling, talk about what's going on in *here*,' I added, patting her bony chest.

She didn't brush my arm off, so that was something. Mum stared at the wall in front of us that had disaster warnings of AIDS and Meningitis and all the diseases under the Wyvernage sky.

'You girls don't understand the struggles we've gone through.'

'Okay,' I said.

'You know how easy your life is?'

I wanted to say *easy*'s not the word I'd use, but best not to rattle cages in hospitals and all that. Mum turned to me, her eyes softening. If I could've angled my video camera right then I'd have focused on those eyes.

'You were such a good baby.'

This had me straighten up in my chair with pride.

'And then you started speaking,' she added. 'Every time I would tell you to be quiet, Fatti would take you and talk to you.' She smiled at the memory. 'Oh, I forgot to tell her I brought some of her cheese for her.'

She rummaged in her handbag to look for it, found it and put it carefully in one of the bag's pockets.

'Now check if your abba is fine,' she said finally.

'All right then. Good talk, Mum.'

I lifted myself off the chair and went in search

of Dad who was standing in front of the vending machine, looking a little hard done by.

'Every time,' he said. 'You put in money and nothing comes out.'

I nudged him out of the way and grabbed both sides of the vending machine, shaking it. That didn't work so I bent down and shoved my arm up to get hold of his packet of Maltesers that had got stuck between the Bounty and M&Ms. It was too far up for me to reach. I saw him shaking his head at me. With one last try I flung myself at the machine, hitting it with my arm, and out fell the Maltesers.

'You're welcome, Pops,' I said, handing him his packet of e-numbers.

He looked at the packet, turning it around in his hands.

'You know, sometimes your amma is a little harsh.'

'No kidding,' I said.

'But it's only because she wants the best for you girls,' he added, shaking his Maltesers at me.

He handed them to me and said: 'Now go and give these to Faru.'

I sighed and walked down the quiet, grey corridor, cleaning my hands at one of the hand sanitisers attached to the walls. Farah was sitting on the green leather chair, next to Mustafa's bed, staring at him.

'Hey,' I said, looking around for Bubblee and Fatti.

I opened the packet of Maltesers and handed them to her. She put them on her lap.

'How're you doing?' I asked.

She nodded. What did that mean?

'You've got to hope for the best,' I said, looking at Mustafa.

I wanted to prod him, just to see what reaction, if any, I'd get from him: would he twitch? Give a deeper intake of breath? Just stay motionless? But I don't think Farah would've been too happy about that. I'd have been accused of not taking anything seriously. It's just that, granted he wasn't dead, but he wasn't exactly alive either, was he? It was kind of fascinating — all of us watching a man in limbo.

'Jay's the one who calls himself Jay, isn't it?' I said.

She looked at me. 'What?'

'Mum goes on at us as if we're the ones who've spoilt his name.'

She looked at me like: *What the hell are you talking about?* 'Has he called?'

'No, I mean he doesn't like being called Jahangeer, does he?'

She looked at me, confused, but I was just trying to make conversation that didn't have to do with Mustafa.

'Mae — go and see if Mum and Dad are okay.'

★ ★ ★

You've got to wonder, don't you? Who's making sure I'm okay? So I took out my phone and decided to check my Twitter account — and what do you know? I got thirty-two new followers.

6

Fatima

Oh God, oh God, oh God. *Was it my fault?* I looked up at the sky, in case I got a sign whether it was or not. Did I give my sister the evil eye? It's not as if I wanted to marry her husband — just that, what would it be like to come home to someone who loves you? What's worse is that I can never stop my tears from falling and everyone looks at me like I'm this pathetic person. How do you make yourself disappear? So you can feel what you feel without worrying about what other people see?

When we got home after the second day at the hospital Mum and Dad insisted that Farah come and stay with us — we'd all be together under one house, just like old times.

'Apart from Jay,' said Mae without looking up from her phone.

'Look at this,' said Bubblee, picking up the local newspaper. 'Front page news.'

She skimmed through it and dropped it on the table. Mae went to read the article.

'Car accident leaves old lady's prize-winning poodle in need of veterinary care.' Mae laughed. 'The victim . . . ' She looked up. '. . . That'd be our bro-in-law — is in a coma. He is thought to be in a critical but stable condition.'

'This place,' said Bubblee, shaking her head.

'A poodle's disturbed and it's front-page news.'

'Marnie was complaining about the traffic on Bingham Road because of the branch that fell from the tree,' added Dad.

'That's Mrs Lemington,' I said. 'She loves her dog. We should probably send her something.'

Farah stared at the page and didn't say anything.

'Animals matter more than humans here.' Mum shook her head as she went straight into the kitchen and I followed her to help prepare dinner for everyone. Bubblee loomed in the doorway.

'*This* is just typical.'

How does she manage to fill a room like that without being fat? I always seem to fill it in the wrong way — not knowing where to put myself — where to shift or pause. But not Bubblee. She enters a room and people have to look. You can't not look at beauty: her brown hair, chopped and cut messily; her big eyes darting between Mum and Dad; rose-bud mouth pursed in her usual annoyed way. All this and living her independent life in London, not being tied to what people tell her; knowing what she wants and then just going out to get it. It's almost as if she knows she has a right to it. Or at least a right to try. I suppose everyone has that right, but how do some people just *feel* it? I'm told she and I have the same eyes, but I don't see it. I see nothing of myself in any of my sisters.

'When was the last time Dad entered the kitchen?' Bubblee added, putting down her patchwork bag that bulged at the seams.

She walked in and I had a sudden feeling of the room being too full, a need to be in my own space, within my four walls.

'Is this how you'll speak to your husband when you're married?' said Mum, looking at her. 'You should go and borrow some clothes from Faru. I'm not letting a boy see you like that in such tight jeans and T-shirt.'

'What boy?' said Bubblee as I got the ghee out of the cupboard.

'You'll see him tomorrow,' replied Mum.

Tomorrow! I remembered. I had a hand-modelling shoot tomorrow. When I told Mum that I'd cancel it she said: 'No, no, no. You must still go. I want to add it to my pile.'

She opened her drawer to show the plastic wallet she has of all my hand-modelling pictures.

'Bubblee will drive you.' She looked over at her. 'And you'll wear something nice when you both come after to the hospital.'

'No, I won't,' answered Bubblee.

'Bubblee — for so long your dad and me have let you do what you want. Do you know the talk we have to hear when people know you live in London?'

Why don't my parents ask me about marriage? Do they think I'm too fat and unattractive to be married? They wouldn't be wrong, but aren't your parents at least meant to see the best in you? Isn't that the point? Dad was standing behind Bubblee. She didn't see him until he said: 'Malik.'

Bubblee turned to look at him.

'Your amma and I have talked about it and we

54

think it would be very good if you married him.' He glanced over at Mum who was staring at Bubblee, a frown etched in her brows.

I opened the can of ghee, trying to concentrate on the sizzling onions, trying to forget that Malik — last I remembered — was thirty-two. Only two years older than me — wasn't that the perfect age for me? I reached into the cupboard and got the cheese tube out, squirting it in my mouth while they weren't looking.

'But I don't even know him,' Bubblee exclaimed. 'Anyway, I have to go back to London tomorrow. Sasha has an exhibition and I promised I'd be there.'

Mum adjusted her purple sari and lit the hob. 'Sasha is not more important than your family.'

'You shouldn't spend so much time with just one girl,' said Dad, clearing his throat. 'Please, Bubblee,' he said, taking her hand. 'Open your mind that you might like something that your parents think is good for you. Why would we want to see you unhappy?'

'But I'm happy *now*,' she replied.

Mum and Dad were both turned towards Bubblee — me hovering in the background, frying onions. I wondered: what does happiness really feel like?

★ ★ ★

The following day everyone else went to the hospital as Bubblee drove me to my shoot. She'd given in and worn a pair of jeans with a kaftan, which made me think that sometimes she could

55

do things, against her principles, just to keep the peace. She'd called Sasha and let her know she wouldn't make her exhibition.

'And no-one appreciates it,' she said to me, one hand gripping the steering wheel and the other resting on the gear-stick. 'That I'm putting my life on hold. It's all expected.'

Weird how she didn't expect it of herself.

'Farah needs us all here,' I said.

She took a deep sigh. 'I know, I know. God, there's no need to make me feel worse than they do. It's just Mum is impossible and Dad nods at everything she says. It's infuriating.'

'At least it's not the other way around,' I replied.

Let's face it, Bubblee would've been up in feminist arms.

'Doesn't make much difference, given that Mum's intent on ruling my life and telling me what to do. All because it's *expected* that I'll get married. It's *expected* that I'll be a good little wife.' She beeped at someone, who I'm pretty sure had the right of way. 'Like good old Farah.'

We all know that Bubblee's ideals — however weird they seem to me — stop her from liking the fact that Mustafa married our sister, but I never understood the strength of her opposition to it. It's not as if we get to like everything in life, but we accept it and get on with it. There are a thousand and one things I'd change about mine: not having a driver's licence being one of them; losing weight; being able to walk into a room with the same confidence that all my sisters seem to have. I might cry about it in my own room but

I don't make a song and dance about it to everyone — how uncomfortable would that be? There are some things that you just keep to yourself.

'Did something happen?' I asked her.

'What do you mean?'

'For you to hate Mustafa so much.'

She paused at a traffic light. 'I don't hate him. He's *fine*.'

'Then what is it?'

She looked at me like I was an idiot who'd missed the point completely. 'Why did Farah settle for *fine*? All this playing house is so . . . *conformative*.'

I didn't really understand what she meant by *playing house*. I thought that was just life — you meet someone, you fall in love, then you marry them. Wasn't that just being happy?

'God, I hope Mae doesn't do the same,' she added, picking up her phone, checking for messages then throwing it back down. 'What another waste it'd be.'

'Is that what I am?' I mumbled.

It wasn't meant to come out loud at all, but somehow the words tumbled out. I hoped she hadn't heard them.

'What? Don't be silly. You're just *you*.'

What did that mean? Maybe Bubblee just had higher hopes for a sister who's her twin and the other sister who's so much younger than us, she's practically a different generation.

'What I meant was . . . ' continued Bubblee, but not quite finding the words, it seemed.

I scratched at the skin around my fingernails,

peeling it as I felt Bubblee's eyes on me.

'You just *seem* content with everything,' she said. 'I mean, you like staying in your room and getting on with your own stuff. Oh, you know what I'm saying.'

Actually I didn't. 'Yeah, yeah. I know.'

'It's just, with Farah, it's like she could've wanted more.'

I looked up.

'That came out wrong,' she said. 'It's like Mustafa came along, made her fall in love with him, and she never got the chance to see what she could've been, because she was too busy being in love with him.'

I nodded at her, even though with every word she said I felt something pinch at my insides.

'You've had more time to figure out what you want. And this seems to be, just, you know . . . *you*.'

What was me? A thirty-year-old who'd failed her driving test a hundred times and had nothing but a portfolio of nice pictures of her hand because her face isn't worth photographing?

'And it's great. You're a hand model,' she added, glancing at me with encouragement.

It didn't exactly sound like she actually thought that was impressive.

'Listen, if you'd got married at twenty-three to someone who was just *fine* I'd probably be furious with you too.'

Except no-one wanted to marry me or be with me at the age of twenty-three. Or any other age, come to think of it. Bubblee began to look like she was trying to pass some really uncomfortable wind so I just smiled and said, 'Of course' before pretending to be really interested in the sky.

'Are you okay, Fatti?' she asked.

'Oh, yeah. You know. Bit grey out,' I replied, as we got to my destination.

Bubblee said she'd wait for me in the car as I went in and sat to have my hands made up.

'Beautiful,' said the woman, admiring my hand as she gave it back to me.

I wondered what it'd feel like for someone to look at all of me and say that?

★ ★ ★

When we got to the hospital the nurse was checking Mustafa's vital signs.

'Well?' I asked as the nurse left the room.

Farah shook her head, rubbing her tired eyes.

'No change,' said Dad.

Mum asked me how the shoot was as Bubblee went and sat on a chair. Mae was obviously on her phone. I stood around for a bit before noticing that it'd started pelting down with rain. As I sat, facing the door, dying for some prawns and cheese on crackers, this figure appeared, drenched. I couldn't quite see his face under his dark-grey trilby until he removed it, holding it against his chest. Then our eyes met. I noticed his dark lashes and slightly hooked nose, his chest rising and falling as if he were out of breath. When he smiled at me it was the weirdest thing — it's like there was something familiar about him, but I couldn't decide what.

'Kala. Mama,' he said, looking away from me

59

and at Mum and Dad.

They both turned around and got up.

'Malik,' said Mum as she burst out crying.

He put his arm cautiously around her, pursing his lips.

'Shh, shh. He'll hear you. You know my brother doesn't know what to do when someone cries,' he said in Bengali.

This made Farah smile for the first time in days. It didn't seem to have quite the same effect on Bubblee, who sat as if glued to her chair.

'What a surprise — everyone gathering around the man who enters a room,' said Bubblee, quietly, glaring at him.

For a moment I wished I could be like Bubblee — unafraid to say what she thinks, not caring how people might react. I was ready to give up my seat for him, go and get him a drink, ask him what his favourite food is, and there was Bubblee, looking as if ready to murder him. Malik's gaze fell on Mustafa, lying there with tubes attached to machines.

'He will be okay,' he said, so assuredly it made me wonder what I'd been worrying about. If I'd accidentally given my sister the evil eye, then he was here to do the opposite — to make things better. What was that feeling of familiarity? Maybe it's because he looks a lot like Mustafa. Of course I knew *of* Malik — he's family, after all, but it'd been so long since any of us had met him. He wasn't able to come to England for Mustafa and Farah's wedding and we hadn't been back home in over twenty years. Last time we saw him we were all just children. I hadn't realised that my nails were digging into my palms as I stared at him. I stood up.

'Have my seat,' I said.

He looked at me and smiled. 'Fatima.'

Was it me or did he hold my gaze a little longer than normal? Then he looked around at all of us and said: 'How you've all grown.'

His eyes settled back on me. I pulled my skirt down, trying to cover my thighs. Why hadn't I put on a bit of make-up before leaving the house? It was only when he'd taken my seat that I realised I'd put him next to Bubblee, who'd turned around and pretended to look out of the window, even though it looked like it might give her a crick in her neck.

'I remember, when we were children, you were the one who pushed me when I called you a girl,' he said to her.

Mum laughed and said in Bengali, 'She was always spirited.'

'I didn't push you,' she said. 'I punched you. And you went crying to your amma.'

He observed her for a moment before looking back at his brother.

'Bhabi,' he said to Farah. 'We are all praying for him.'

She looked at him, grateful. What was she thinking when she looked at Mustafa like that? What exactly was going through her mind? Mum and Dad went through the story with Malik about the police coming to Farah's and telling her about the accident, us all rushing to the hospital, Bubblee coming up from London, how difficult these past few days have been, but how glad we were that he was here. Malik rubbed his eyes and continued to stare at Mustafa.

'Amma and Abba wouldn't be able to look at this,' he said.

Then he took Mustafa's hand, leaned forward and kissed his forehead. 'That's from Amma.'

'You should've told us what time your flight was getting in,' said Dad. 'Someone would've come to collect you.'

'We would've sent Bubblee,' said Mum. 'This isn't right — you've flown all this way, come straight here and didn't tell us. You know Jahangeer is away, so you are now the man to come and look after us.'

I stole a glance at Bubblee who looked like she might throw something at someone.

'He's just so busy,' continued Mum. 'Working, working — sending us money.'

Mae snorted and looked up from her phone as everyone stared at her. 'Sorry.'

'If he were here you'd be able to speak with him, but you'll have to settle for all these women,' said Mum as Dad cleared his throat. 'And your mama,' she added, looking at Dad.

Malik stared at them both before he waved his hands around as if it were all too silly to talk about. Mum and Dad looked at each other, approvingly. I guess they were thinking he was perfect for Bubblee, and when Farah's husband wakes up, there'll be another family wedding and everyone will live happily ever after. I probably still won't have passed my driving test. *Oh, God!* I remembered I'd forgotten to cancel my lesson the following day. I texted Ash and told him what had happened, if he hadn't already read it in the paper.

From, Ashraf: I'm so sorry to hear that. Hope he recovers soon. Just let me know when you're ready for your next lesson. Are you okay?

To, Ashraf: Yeah, fine. Just weird when something like this happens. Makes you realise how short life is. The sooner I pass my test the sooner I can start living mine.

I thought about it for a second before sending it, but Ash is always saying stuff like this to me — telling me what's going on with him, so why not? I didn't think he'd respond, but he did, saying something like I don't need to pass my test to do that, but he doesn't understand. Passing my test means being in control. Just once, I'd like to feel like I have some of that.

★   ★   ★

'Ewww!' exclaimed Mae. 'Bubblee? Marry Malik? Gross.'

'What do you mean?' I replied. 'He's nice-looking.'

'Er, yeah,' replied Mae, 'but he's like, from Bangladesh. That accent is *vom.*'

I'd laid out a blanket for her on the floor of my bedroom because Malik was staying with us and Bubblee and Farah were sharing.

'Mae, you shouldn't say stuff like that about people,' I said, thinking about his trilby and how

63

English he looked when he walked into the hospital room.

'What? Be honest?'

I looked up at the ceiling as I lay down on my bed. 'You need to learn that some things should be kept to yourself.'

The light from her phone shone on her face. 'Yeah, well, I don't expect people to read my mind.'

Wouldn't that be great. If people could do that. My mouth never quite manages to say the words my brain thinks. It could save me a lot of trouble. While I was thinking this, someone knocked on the door before opening it.

'Is she still on her damn phone?' said Bubblee, walking into my room and plopping herself on my bed.

'How's Farah?' I asked.

Mae put her phone down as Bubblee switched on my bedside lamp and looked around my room.

'Every time I ask she just replies 'Fine.' I think you need more colour in this room, Fatti. Maybe a painting or two? Something to add a little character.'

What did she mean? Doesn't she think I have character?

'Are you gonna marry that Malik guy?' asked Mae.

My heart seemed to beat a little faster.

'Over my dead body,' replied Bubblee, observing my book-shelf. 'There's something very reflective in the orderly way you've piled your books, Fatti.'

Mae shot a look at me, suppressing a laugh. I had to hold mine back too.

'I mean, we can really draw parallels from our surroundings about our personalities.'

'Oh yeah,' said Mae. 'What's your flat like then?'

'You can come visit and see for yourself one day.' Bubblee looked at her. 'If you do well in your GCSEs, you can even come and stay with me for a while.'

Mae sat up. 'Shut your face.'

I had a sudden bout of panic. If Mae leaves here, then I'll be alone — with my parents.

'We can go to exhibitions and sit in cafes. You can get a part-time job.'

'A job?' said Mae.

'Yes. A job. That thing that funds the life we want to lead.'

Mae lay back down. 'London would be something.'

'Fatti, you can come too,' said Bubblee, hitting me on the leg.

I said: 'That'd be great.' But a hundred questions came to me: *What would I wear? How would I act with Bubblee's artist friends? I need to lose at least twenty pounds before going to London.* The whole idea made me want to reach into my drawer for cheese, except I couldn't with Mae around. But she was right, London would be something.

'You'd better not marry that Malik before I get a chance,' said Mae.

Bubblee threw a pillow at her. 'I'm not marrying him. He's so uninspired.'

'But you don't even know him,' I replied.

Why do people make such quick judgements about others? Why does no-one give anyone a chance? I think Bubblee said something, but I was too lost in these thoughts to hear. So lost that I ended up saying aloud: 'I feel like *I* know him.'

Mae let out a snort of laughter. I felt my face flush, unable to look at Bubblee, who I could tell was staring at me.

'Haha. Fatti fancies Mal-meister,' said Mae, getting her phone out again.

'Don't even think about hitting the record button,' I said, the heat in my face rising. 'And I don't fancy him. I'm just saying. He is family, anyway.'

'Exactly,' said Bubblee. 'It's unwholesome to even think about marrying him. I mean, Farah married her cousin and that's bad enough.' Bubblee looked at the ground. 'Look what she's got to show for it,' she added.

It seemed so obvious to me. Was I being stupid? Did no-one else see what I saw?

'Let it go, man,' added Mae. 'How much longer are you gonna hold that against her?'

'I'm here, aren't I?' replied Bubblee. 'Can you believe how Mum was going on and on about Jay? I was embarrassed for her.'

'He does send money,' I said.

'Not nearly enough to make up for the fact that we never know where he is, or what he's doing. He couldn't give a crap about any of us.'

I wondered if Bubblee realised that a lot of the time we don't know where she is or what she's

66

doing either. My bedroom door opened again and it was Farah. 'This is where you're all hiding.'

I folded my legs to make room for Farah on my bed.

'Bubblee's the one hiding,' said Mae, still tapping on her phone. 'From her husband.' After which she made kissing noises.

'She could do a lot worse than him. They're a good family. Good brothers,' replied Farah, still standing at the doorway.

'Good enough for someone else, maybe,' mumbled Bubblee.

'What?' said Farah.

'Nothing,' she replied.

Farah's hand rested on the door handle — she was still as a statue. 'If you have something to say, you might as well say it. It's not like I have other things to deal with.'

'*Nothing*,' repeated Bubblee.

I don't understand how someone can be so stubborn about something. I've seen the way Mustafa is around Farah — the way he's looked after her. He might not be funny and clever — all those things that Bubblee goes on about — but he was kind, at least. *Is* kind. Which is more than can be said for a lot of men. God, I hope he lives.

'Mae — get off your phone and sleep in the room with me tonight,' said Farah.

Mae sighed deeply, picked up her pillow and left the room with Farah closing the door behind her.

I watched Bubblee who was staring at the closed door.

'You can sleep on the bed,' I said to her. 'I'll take the floor.'

'Thanks,' she replied, sounding as if she were somewhere far away.

★ ★ ★

I woke up early, absolutely starving. Creeping out of the room, I walked passed my parents' room and heard weird noises coming from inside. Sounded like Mum's arthritis was pretty bad, as she seemed to be moaning. When I went downstairs Malik was at the breakfast table, eating a bowl of cornflakes.

'Oh,' I said.

'You're up early,' he replied.

I couldn't think of anything to say and wished I'd at least put my bathrobe on. My green polka-dot pyjamas weren't exactly the most flattering in the world.

'My jet lag's bad,' he added as I went over to the kitchen cupboard, forgetting what I was looking for. A plate — that's it.

'Yeah,' I replied. 'Must be.'

What I wanted was squeezy cheese and mashed prawns on my four slices of toast but I couldn't let him see me do that. I grabbed an apple and sliced it into pieces, along with some tangerines and a banana.

'Fruit?' I offered.

'Yes. Please. Thanks.'

I handed him the plate of chopped fruit and made myself another one, thinking of the cheese I couldn't eat. As I took the plate and made my way out of the kitchen, he said: 'Sit with me, Fatima.'

No-one ever calls me Fatima like that. It's always *Fatti, Fatti, Fatti.* As if even my name lives up to the expectation of who I am. I took a seat opposite him and looked at my plate, feeling my face flush again. *He's meant to marry Bubblee. Even if she won't marry him. It doesn't matter. He'll never look at you after having looked at her, anyway.*

'You're very shy for the eldest,' he said.

I shrugged. 'I don't have much to say.'

'That can't be true,' he said, putting a slice of apple in his mouth, munching so loudly it filled the room.

'Did you sleep okay?' I asked.

'Yes. Thank you.'

When I looked up he was staring at me. Our eyes met and he didn't look away, just smiled. I peeled off the white veins of the tangerine.

He seemed to laugh at something.

'What?' I asked.

'Nothing, it's just that . . . well, you have your kala's hands. My amma's hands.'

He observed my hands carefully.

'They're beautiful,' he said.

That much I knew was true, or I wouldn't be modelling them — long, slender fingers, petite and soft, finely shaped nails that never really need to be filed. It's the only attractive thing about me.

'Oh. Thanks.'

'Tell me about yourself, Fatima.'

The house felt so quiet we could've been the

only two people there. Is this what being with someone would be like? You'd wake up in the morning and just talk casually about anything; this little space made of you and them, like a secret society of privileged members. For a moment I pretended that we were married and that it was just another day in our lives — the happiness seemed to swell inside me, until I realised that it wasn't real and that I was even more pathetic than I thought.

'Nothing to tell,' I said.

'What do you do? What do you like?' He paused. 'Have you had many marriage proposals?'

Many? The banana pieces were already getting black, the juice from the tangerine touching the sliced apples.

'I er . . . no. I'm learning how to drive.'

He leaned forward, putting his plate to one side. 'And?'

'Well, once I pass, you see, I'll be able to get around and maybe get a proper job. Right now, I just help around the house.' I put out my hand. 'I make money modelling my hands in a magazine.'

'Good. I'm not surprised,' he said, looking at my hands again. 'Why haven't Kala and Mama found you a husband yet? You're the eldest — you should be married now.'

Imagine if he'd said that to Bubblee — she'd have thrown her plate at him. But it was nice being asked, because it was as if it was possible that someone like me *could* be married.

In his eyes, it wasn't only possible, but actually

70

weird that I *wasn't* married.

'Maybe. One day,' I replied.

'Someday *soon*, inshallah,' he replied. 'There should be no maybe. Of course you'll get married.'

It was nice to have someone believe that would happen for me, even if it was just to make me feel better.

'And how's your brother,' he said, clearing his throat. 'Jahangeer? He hasn't come home for Mustafa?'

We heard something drop and looked outside into the passage.

'Oops,' said Mae, bending down to get her phone.

'Mae, if you were recording without us knowing . . . ' I began.

'I wasn't, I wasn't,' she exclaimed.

Her eyes rested on my plate of fruit.

'Amazing, Fatti. Well done. Better than those hundred slices of toast you eat when you think none of us are looking. All right, Mal-meister?' she added, opening the fridge and getting some kind of smoothie concoction out.

'Mal-meister Baia to you,' he replied, his back turned to her as he winked at me.

'Ooh, yeah, of course,' she said, making stupid hugging gestures while he couldn't see. 'Doesn't Fatti have to call you Baia out of respect too? I mean, if you're my brother then you must be hers too, right?'

I could've killed her, laughing like that, without him seeing, while I could do nothing but look and listen. She took a sip of her smoothie.

71

'Ugh!' she exclaimed, spitting out its contents and looking at the bottle and wiping her mouth. '*Gross.* Dad's at it again, isn't he? He made me this weird smoothie days ago and it tasted like he'd put a spoonful of sewage in it.'

She tipped it out into the sink and threw the bottle in the recycling bin.

'You're almost half her age. She deserves your respect,' said Malik.

'And she gets it, don't you, Fats?' she said, messing up my hair while she walked past.

I tried to hit her on the leg but she just about escaped out of the kitchen. He must think everyone walks all over me. I just shook my head and pretended to laugh. 'Kids,' I said.

He leaned forward and put his hand on mine. I was so taken aback, I couldn't move. What was he doing? Why was he touching me? No-one's ever held my hand before. All that fruit was churning in my stomach, and it wasn't sitting very well.

'She's right, though, Fatima. You must know . . . '

We heard footsteps come down the stairs just then. Mae must've woken everyone up, as Mum walked in and Malik took his hand away from mine.

'Oh, Malik, you must let me make you a proper breakfast. This is no good.'

He gave her this weird look. 'No. Thank you.'

She insisted but he kept saying no and I did think, just let her make you some chapatti and lentil stew. Mum hesitated a little and then smiled at me.

'Fatti,' she said, getting out my prawns and tube of cheese. 'Shall I make you toast?'

What must he have thought of me?

'No, thanks, Amma. I'm just having this.'

She looked at my plate of fruit and frowned.

'You can't just eat that,' she exclaimed and was already making me a cheese-and-prawn sandwich when Bubblee came down.

'Morning,' Malik said to her.

I took the sandwich Mum handed to me as I watched them and munched on the huge bite I'd taken. Bubblee simply gave him a nod as she made a cup of coffee for herself.

'Amma, I really think you should call Jay,' she said to Mum.

Malik glanced at her as she said this. 'Bubblee is right, Kala,' he added. 'Wouldn't he want to know?'

Mum looked annoyed but turned around and got the flour out for the chapattis.

'I know Farah'd want to talk to him,' added Bubblee. 'And she's in no state to call him herself, or tell him what's happened.'

Mum shot her a look before turning to Malik. 'There's no need to worry him,' she said.

I saw Bubblee shaking her head in disbelief. I probably wouldn't have noticed if it wasn't for the fact that Malik was staring at her. I took another bite of my sandwich and wished I hadn't as Malik looked at me — my mouth full — while Bubblee's delicate mouth sipped at her coffee. He smiled at me though, so kindly that I didn't know whether to swallow what was in my mouth, or cry.

7

Bubblee

This place kills me. I'm, quite frankly, dying on the inside. I always knew Wyvernage was pedestrian, but it's never seemed so closed-minded as it does to me now that I've actually lived away from it. And everything, absolutely *everything*, ends up revolving around Jay. The male XY chromosomes — a blight to all our lives — only our parents are too visually impaired to see it. The golden child, simply because he's a boy.

I walked down the steep curve towards the town's green, passing the small shops — the store I'd always go to because it was the only one that sold *Arts Illustrated*; a crafts shop where I'd buy paint and utensils; the off-licence and grocery store and charity shop. Even though none of them were new, I had to get out of the house — away from that Malik. Not to mention Farah. I made it to the park and sat on the bench, watching white families with their white kids, living their middle-class lives in their white little bubble. I'm told you can find art anywhere, but not here. Art should be messy and full of grit — this is all so clean. You can't feel things here. You can't create something. I noticed that someone had left a glass bottle by the bin because it was full. I stared at it as an empty packet of crisps fell out of the bin. Walking up to it, I knelt down and saw there were still a few crumbs left in the crisp packet. I emptied it out next to the bottle, tipping the bottle onto its side as I observed the effect. Taking a photo with my phone, I sent the image to Sasha. It was the most art I'd get out of this place. I mean, of all the things my twin sister could've done with her life, she chose to stay *here*; to get married to a man who's exactly like this place — uninspiring. I had to laugh as I shook my head; I mean, if you live your life trying to fit in here, there's got to be something wrong with you.

* * *

When I walked back home I saw Farah opening her car door. She paused as she saw me. I noticed the way the sunlight hit her heart-shaped face, her black hair shining as it hung loose over her shoulders. It reminded me of how she looked when, as kids, we'd play out in the garden in the sun — Mae crawling around on her scrawny hands and knees, Fatti in her bedroom, looking out at us. Jay destroying something or other. Only Farah used to laugh a lot back then. She doesn't laugh like that now.

'Last one in's a rotten bean,' shouted Mae as she seemed to come out of nowhere and sprang into the car. She popped her head out of the window from the passenger's side.

'You might as well get in — do you know the carbon footprint we leave behind because we're too lazy to plan journeys or get a bike?'

75

I walked up to the car. 'Go sit in the back like the family dog you are,' I said to Mae.

'Get lost. You're sitting there with your husband — oh, look. There he is.'

And out he walked in his ridiculous trilby, trying to be something he's not. As if a hat can make you English.

'Wish Mum and Dad hadn't forced Fatti to go in their car,' said Mae as I got into the back. 'Him in the middle and both of you either side.' She burst out into laughter.

'*Mae,*' said Farah as she got in and Malik followed suit.

'Bubblee,' he said.

Even his voice was annoying. I bet he was looking at me, thinking how nice I'd look on his arm when we went out, and how much nicer standing in the kitchen, making his dinner for him. I looked out of the window. Does it look like I was born yesterday? My parents might not have said anything to him about marriage, but I know these men from Bangladesh — especially one who's in his thirties and ready to get married. When he looked at me, I could imagine just what he was thinking.

A few minutes into the journey he said: 'This is a very nice green place, isn't it? Mustafa would talk about it and I never could picture it. He was very happy here,' he said, looking at Farah through her rear-view mirror. 'What are your neighbours like?' he asked.

'Starkers,' said Mae, turning around.

He looked at Mae, confused. She stuck a carrot-stick in her mouth. 'Naked, Mal-meister.

76

Sorry, Mal-meister *Baia*.' She chomped on the carrot. 'They don't wear clothes. Nudists, through and through.'

He frowned. *Yes, here we get to live as we please*. Although, the sight of them in the garden is always a little disturbing.

He shook his head. 'What is the world coming to?'

'I suppose you'd have everyone covered, head to toe, not being able to leave the house?' I replied.

He smiled. 'Ah, you think all men from *back home* are like that.'

I thought he might say something else, but he simply looked out of the window.

'Don't worry, Malik,' said Farah, turning the car into the hospital car park. 'Our Bubblee doesn't really think well of anyone.'

★　★　★

'No change?' asked Farah to the doctor who was looking at her clipboard, scribbling notes.

'We're monitoring him closely, Mrs Lateef.' She looked up. 'Situations like these are impossible to predict. You have to remember that the lacerations were large from the closed head injury. Take heart that he's stable for now.'

The doctor looked over at all the family faces: *What are all these people doing here?* she was probably thinking. She gave a small smile and walked away, her black plimsolls padding against the floor. Mum got her rosary beads out, letting her tears run freely. Isn't she the one who always

77

says that whatever God does is for the best?

'What will happen?' she asked, looking at Malik, as if he had the answer. 'This is why you don't wait so long to have children, Faru. Anything can happen.'

Farah's face drained of colour.

'*Mum*,' I said. 'For God's sake. Not now.'

'They said he is stable, Kala,' he replied, though he didn't look particularly convinced.

'All she heard was 'injury',' I replied. I put my hand on Farah's arm before walking away to make a phone call.

★　★　★

'How's it going in the sticks?' said Sasha.

'Dire,' I replied.

She asked how Mustafa was, so I gave her an update.

'Your sister must be a wreck.'

I turned around and looked at my family huddled together, Fatti looking perturbed, Mae's eyes fixed on her phone, Mum and Dad solemn. Malik was saying something to Farah as she smiled at him.

'Listen, I'm so sorry I missed the exhibition. How'd it go?' I asked.

'I kept looking out for you, wondering if you'd make a surprise appearance.'

'Bubblee?'

I turned around and it was Malik, completely ignoring the fact that I was on the phone.

'Sash, sorry, I have to go. I'll call you later tonight, okay?'

'Yeah. Sure.' She paused. 'I hope he gets better, Bubs.'

I wanted to hope that too. Except I couldn't. People might say that I should've felt ashamed thinking like that. Wishing for someone not to recover is horrid, I know. But he's not important to me. My sister *is*.

'What?' I said, putting my phone in my jeans pocket.

'We need to get in touch with Jahangeer,' he said.

'No kidding,' I said, folding my arms.

Who is this guy? He might be family but he doesn't know us or what we're about — coming over here and sticking his nose into our business about Jay. He furrowed his eyebrows and folded his arms as well.

'Your sister, Bubblee,' he said, as if he was telling me off for being so dim. 'You can see she needs him.'

I had to laugh. 'Yeah. And weren't you there when I had this chat with Mum?'

'Yes,' he replied. 'I've also tried to ask your amma and abba about it.'

'Let me guess — every time you mention his name, they either talk about what a great son he is and how he's 'finding his feet' or they just change the subject.'

He brought his hand up, resting his chin on his fist, sighing. 'They're getting old. I know what it's like when this happens — it's harder to face up to things when you have such set ideas.'

'And what are they meant to be facing up to?' I said.

What exactly did Malik know about Jay, anyway?

'He is your brother. A man in the family. He should be here to help look after you. And I know Farah must miss him. Mustafa was always telling me how fond she is of him.'

I felt a twinge somewhere in my gut. She always did do anything for Jay. When you're twins surely the person you're meant to look out for is each other? It's the two of you against the world. Not Farah. She was too busy fighting against the world for Jay. Covering for him, telling him off, giving him money, advice, comforting him. And he never came to me the way he did to her. It didn't matter, though, because I wasn't going to stick around in this place and I had my art — poring over abstract images, somehow feeling more at home when reading about these than anything else.

'An only brother will always have a special place in his sister's heart,' he said. 'Just like an only sister will have a special place in her brother's,' he added, thoughtfully.

'Too bad if he doesn't deserve it,' I replied.

Malik leaned in closer — I noticed a small cut from when he must've shaved this morning.

'Bubblee, you don't seem to think any man deserves your sister's attention.'

I scanned past his shoulder — Mum and Dad were looking at us as Fatti glanced our way too. I made a mental note to tell her that she can have him.

'He's a wash-out, Malik. Do you know what that is? Well, it doesn't matter, because aside from that, he never once thinks to do what normal people do: work hard for their money. Forget money — have a passion that at least contributes to the world around you.' I scoffed. 'No, he wants everything handed to him on a silver plate — and you can thank your kala and mama for that,' I added, looking over at Mum and Dad. Because let's face it; spoiling someone doesn't exactly kick their arse into gear.

Malik frowned. 'Your amma and abba said that he's doing some real work now. They said that Mustafa was helping him.'

Since when? They were probably making it all up.

'If you believe that,' I said, 'you'll believe anything.'

★　★　★

'I vote Fatti,' said Mae.

Fatti looked like a deer caught in headlights. The three of us had gone outside to get some fresh air and decide who'd be the one to call Jay.

Mae put her arm around her and said: 'You're the eldest. He has to listen to you.'

Fatti looked at Mae as if she was unsure whether she was taking the mickey or not. I wasn't sure myself. Mae looked serious enough, though.

'Why not Bubblee?' asked Fatti.

Mae flung her arms around and put her hands on my shoulder. 'Because our Bubs is not the most level-headed of people. And everyone

81

knows he's not about to listen to me, his kid sister.'

'I hate to say it, but she's right,' I said. 'After Farah, he liked you best. You never talked back to him.'

'And you're likeable. Obviously,' added Mae to Fatti.

'Of course,' I said.

Surely, that was a given?

'Okay,' said Fatti. 'I'll do it.'

She didn't look too sure but it was progress, at least.

'I'll get his phone number from Farah's phone,' I said.

Mae got her mobile out. 'No need. Already have it here.'

Whatever anyone might say about Mae, she is impressive. We stood around, figuring out whether we should call now or wait.

Fatti took Mae's phone from her and said: 'What's the point in waiting? Let's just get it over and done with.'

Mae and I exchanged looks. Since when had Fatti become so assertive? Fatti looked up at us.

'What about Mum and Dad? Shouldn't we tell them? Or get them to call him?'

Mae rolled her eyes and was about to launch into some kind of Mae-ism when Malik came running towards us.

'Quick,' he said, out of breath.

The three of us looked at him as he stopped.

'They've had to take him into surgery,' he added.

My heart began beating faster, a knot forming

somewhere in my gut.

'Hurry,' he said, already making his way through the hospital entrance again.

For the first time in my life, I saw Fatti break into a run.

⋆ ⋆ ⋆

There was nothing to do but wait. All thoughts of calling Jay went out of the window. I kept looking at Farah who stared into space. The doctors said that there'd been some unsuspected internal bleeding and when they tried to take him out of the coma it had an adverse effect or something. They rushed him into the operating theatre to try to stop the bleeding.

Mum insisted we all sit with rosary beads and pray for him, but to be quite honest, I couldn't quite bring myself to do it. It's not like I hate the guy, but when I looked at Farah and thought about the life she could've had, I realised she's still young and pretty. She could come and stay with me in London. There are so many men in London. Bangladeshi men who aren't like Malik or his brother, but evolved and into travelling and studying and learning about the world. Not just making money and having a comfortable life. Comfortable is just another word for dull.

'Do you want a carrot stick?' Mae offered Farah.

Farah didn't respond.

'I can get you Maltesers if you want?' she added.

Farah just shook her head.

'Mae, just sit down and be quiet for a minute,' said Dad.

He looked over at her, seeing her face that looked hurt. Mae doesn't look hurt very often.

'Babba,' he added to her, 'now is the time to be quiet and pray to God for your brother-in-law's health.'

No-one spoke. Fatti was fiddling with the edge of her shirt and for a few minutes we just sat in silence.

'And even if he's not okay,' I said, looking up at Farah, 'you'll be all right.'

It was meant to be comforting — she likes that kind of thing — but Farah's face shot up.

'I can't believe you,' she said.

'I mean it's going to be okay,' I replied.

She brushed back the hair that had fallen on her face and said: 'You mean you don't care if he's all right.'

'I care if *you're* all right.'

I caught Malik looking at me as if he were seeing me in a new light altogether. At least it was going to put him off. A tear fell down Farah's cheek, her face red with anger.

'Without him there *is* no all right,' she said. 'And someone like *you* will never get that.'

What did she mean, *someone like me*? I felt my own face flush too, but now wasn't the time to have an argument with her.

'Just get out of here,' she said, looking at the floor.

I looked around the room — everyone was staring at me.

'Jay's Abba . . . ' said Mum.

'Faru,' said Dad, 'come now. We are all tired.'

She didn't respond but I wasn't about to stay where I wasn't wanted. Especially when I hardly wanted to be there either. Did she think I came for myself? That it mattered to me what happened to *him*? The only thing that mattered was making sure she was okay, and if she didn't understand that I wanted the best for her, then what was the point?

'Forget it,' I said, getting up. 'I know where I'm not wanted.'

I could've taken a photo of my empty brown seat to replicate in the form of a sculpture later. A metaphor for absence — something that's as unavailable as it is unoccupied.

'Bubblee . . . ' said Mum, 'wait.'

But I didn't wait for anyone or anything. I walked out of there because sometimes it doesn't matter what you say, people will always find fault with it.

8

Fatima

This is why I say it's better to keep quiet than say something so, well, *stupid*. I tried to tell Farah that Bubblee didn't know what she was saying, but I think I was lying. In fact, I *know* I was lying. And so did Farah.

'Your sister really does say anything that comes into her head,' said Malik when I came out of the ladies' bathroom. Had he followed me?

I liked the idea of being followed — as if I was important enough for another person to know my movements — but not so much what he was saying to me.

'She's honest.'

He gave a low kind of laugh. 'She doesn't seem to like Bengalis and yet she is so Bengali.'

Is that all he wanted to talk about? Bubblee? I went to walk past him when he held on to my arm.

'Fatima . . . '

He looked into my eyes and I felt my heart ping-pong around my chest — why didn't it want to settle in any one place?

'You are nothing like your sister.'

What a weird thing to say. I must've looked confused as he added, 'You are more like . . . ' He seemed to search for the words just as he seemed to search my face. What was he looking for? Did my face have the answer?

'What?' I asked, my voice lowered unintentionally.

'You are . . . *yourself.*'

My confusion just grew. What did that mean? He let go of my arm.

'Okay,' I replied, unsure.

Because what else was there to say? Just then I saw a flash of Mum's bright-yellow sari as she turned the corner and saw me.

'There you are,' she said, looking between me and Malik. 'Have you seen Bubblee?'

I shook my head.

'She's not always like this,' she said to Malik, but I could tell she was watching the way he looked at me.

'She is fiery,' he said. 'There's nothing wrong with that.'

'And very beautiful, no?' said Mum, looking at him.

He gave a small nod. Every compliment to Bubblee felt like a stab to my heart. Why wasn't Mae here to have a dig at Bubblee? As soon as the thought came into my head I was embarrassed at how ready I was to betray my own sister, just so this man could think more of me than of her. He gave Mum a curt nod and walked away. Mum watched him as he turned the corner and looked anxious. But then she would be, at the idea that one of her daughters might end up being a widow. The very idea made me forget about Malik for a moment.

'Why does your sister not think about things?'

she said in a low voice.

'It'll be fine, Mum.'

'Did you see the way Malik looked at her when she was saying all those things? What must he think of her? So much talking back is not what a man looks for in a wife.'

A rush of fatigue came over me. I just wanted to sit down, on my own, and eat some prawns and cheese. I could then think about what that weird moment with Malik meant, my poor bro-in-law and everything else in between. She put her hand on my face and said: 'My good girl.'

For a moment I wanted to ask that if I'm so good, then how come they don't care about me getting married? Why don't they look for a husband for me like they do for Bubblee? Don't they know she doesn't even need the help and I do? But I'd sound pathetic and needy, and even though I'm both those things, I don't want everyone else to know. I'd rather crawl under a rock than face all their pitying glances. Especially with Malik there to see.

'Listen,' said Mum. 'Farah said she needs some medical insurance papers to call and try to get private treatment. Your abba has stored the family's insurance in the cubby-hole under the stairs.'

I listened to her instructions and of course, because I don't drive, I'd have to get the bus.

'If you see that Bubblee, tell her I want to speak to her. Maybe you can talk some sense into that girl too,' she added.

I don't know why everyone thinks I can talk

anyone into anything.

★ ★ ★

On the bus I looked out at the green grass, the clean pavements, and saw it all through the eyes of Malik. Does he like it here? Why do I even feel as if I want to ask him? Well, I know why I want to ask him, but what's the point? I touched my arm where he held it and a rush of feeling came over me — I wanted to get off the bus and run back to the hospital just to see him again. And then I remembered him asking about Bubblee and Mum mentioning the two of them getting married. As if I'm not pathetic enough, I'm falling for the man Bubblee might end up with. She might say she's not into marriage but I can't believe it. Why would anyone want to be alone for ever? I don't get that. If you had a choice, a real one, wouldn't you just *go* for it? Like Farah did. Although now look at her. What if Mustafa didn't make it . . . ? I had to shut the thought from my mind — as if it might come true just by thinking it. Still, better to have loved and lost . . .

I got off at the bus stop and began the ten-minute walk to the house when I heard a car beeping.

'Fatima!' someone called out.

I looked on as I saw Ash's car pull up into a side road. I approached him as he leaned out of the window.

'Hello, stranger,' he said.

'Hi,' I said, bending down to see him.

'Where are you going? Get in, I'll drop you.'

'Oh, just home,' I said. 'Don't worry, I can walk. I could do with it,' I added, laughing, but he didn't laugh back. He's the only one I crack fat jokes with and the only one who doesn't find it funny. I'm pretty sure the family would like me a lot more if I joked about the size of my thighs more often. But I don't want to be known as *that* girl — *she might be chubby but at least she's jolly*. I'm not going to be fat for ever, after all.

He'd opened the door on the passenger side and told me to get in.

'How's your brother-in-law doing?' he asked as he pulled out into the road.

His sleeves were rolled up and it wasn't the first time I'd noticed that he has quite hairy arms. I told him about Mustafa being in surgery.

'God,' he said, looking at me. 'I'm sorry. Really hope he makes it okay. And I hope his car accident hasn't put you off.'

I paused. 'Not until you just mentioned it.'

He laughed, which made me smile. Ash's not good-looking like Malik — he's a bit short and his nose is kind of flat. He looks like the type of person you'd pass on the street one day and not recognise the next.

'Weird when you think how short life can be,' I said. 'Not that Mustafa's will be short. He'll get through it.' I saw Ash change into fourth gear from the corner of my eye. 'It just makes you think.'

'It does,' he said. 'About all the things you have. And all the things you don't — like a wife,' he added with a smile.

We drove past the park and I saw Bubblee

pacing up and down, speaking on her phone, flapping her arms about. Probably that Sasha friend. In times like this, I wonder who I'd go to. Mae usually cheers me up in her own way but I wouldn't be able to tell her things — flap my arms like that. But then, I'm not an arm flapper.

'What?' asked Ash.

I'd craned my neck, still watching Bubblee as we drove past.

'Oh, nothing. My sister's there.'

'The social media slave or the London-twin?' he asked.

'London-twin. Bubblee.'

'Ah, yes. *Bubblee.* What a name.'

'Maybe we should pick her up. There was a bit of an argument in the hospital. I should check she's okay.'

He laid his hand on the gear stick — my eyes darted towards number five, as it usually does out of fear.

'About what?' he asked.

I began to explain and realised that we were almost home. It was too late to turn back to get her. He pulled up in front of the house and exhaled after I'd finished telling him what had just happened. I waited for him to say something but he just looked at me and said: 'Your destination, Madam.'

I wonder how he manages to be so happy all the time. I don't think I've ever seen him angry, or lose his temper — he's a driving instructor, surely a bit of road rage would be expected. Maybe it's just a front. Maybe he's pretending he's happy but actually he's miserable on the

91

inside. Maybe he and I are alike. He was still looking at me as I unbuckled my seatbelt.

'Going back to the hospital after?' he asked.

I told him I just needed to get some insurance papers from the house. Thank God I'd be alone for five minutes. I could sit for a bit before going back to the hospital. He looked at his watch.

'I don't have another lesson for a bit so I can drop you,' he said.

'You don't have to do that,' I replied, opening the car door.

'I'll let you drive — don't want you getting out of practice. You're almost there.'

Am I, though? Every time I think I'm almost there the goal-post seems to move further away. But it's important to try to be positive. You have to *think* you can do something — *be* something, or it's never going to happen.

'Are you sure?' I asked.

'Of course,' he said, already getting out of the car.

He stood outside the red door, looking our house up and down. A sudden panic rose inside me about the state the place would be in — even though I knew there's no way Mum would've left it messy. And then I realised, I'd be in the house with him *alone*. It felt a bit weird. I was glued to the spot when he looked at me, expectantly. I walked past him to open the door, fiddling with the key in the lock, wishing he'd step back a little. We went inside and I opened the curtains to let some light in as he looked around the living room, some papers cluttered on the coffee table, Dad's rocking chair in the corner, plastic over the remote. He picked it up and laughed.

'My parents do the same thing,' he said, sitting in the chair, rocking back and forth.

I wanted to say that that was Dad's chair and no-one else sits in it, but thought it might be a little rude.

'Would you like tea or coffee?' I asked, going into the kitchen.

'Tea, please. But only if it's no trouble,' he called out.

Putting the kettle on, I quickly put out a tray of nibbles; biscuits, Bombay mix, nuts — anything I could find. In between which, I managed to squeeze some cheese into my mouth. When I took the tray in he looked at it.

'Is there anything left in the kitchen?'

For a moment I thought he meant he didn't want anything I'd brought out. My face must've had a weird expression because he looked at it and laughed.

'Is this how you feed all people?'

I put the tray down as he took his cup of tea, looking at the country-flowered patterns. What else, other than feed people, should a person do to make them feel comfortable? When I said this he replied: 'The person you marry will have to watch his weight.'

Was he taking the mickey? Referring to my weight? I felt my face flush and said I had to go and look for these insurance papers. Opening the cubby-hole door, I popped my head in and took out the grey file Mum mentioned. When I looked up Ash was standing over me.

'Need any help?' he asked.

'No, it should be here somewhere. Thanks.'

I searched through the file but couldn't find the papers. Getting up, I rummaged through the cubby-hole, found another file — nothing there. Where else could it be?

'No joy?' he said.

'It should be here somewhere.'

On the top shelf I glimpsed a cream file. The papers in it looked too old to be the right ones, and I was about to put it back when some of the papers fell out, amongst which was a photo. When I looked at it, I saw it was one of Mum when she was younger, holding a baby in her arms — I considered it closely and all I could see was the top of the baby's head, which had a load of hair. Next to her, in what seemed to be a hospital bed, was Malik's mum. I guess it must've been a photo of when Malik or Mustafa was born. Mum is looking over the moon, while Malik's mum is smiling; drained but content. Maybe that's why Mum and Dad want Bubblee to marry Malik — if the baby's Malik, the way Mum's holding on to him, it looks like she never wants to let him go. I put the photo and papers — letters that were written in Bengali — back in the file and finally found the papers I was looking for.

'Ready?' asked Ash.

He finished his tea and I cleared everything up before we left the house, making sure everything was pristine. Locking the door behind me, I turned around to see Ash dangling the car keys in front of me.

'Let's get you back on the road,' he said.

★ ★ ★

Driving past the park, I looked out for Bubblee but there was no sign of her. When we parked up in the hospital I felt a flush of relief. Not once did Ash have to correct anything I did.

'You *will* pass next time,' he said.

I looked up at the hospital building. 'Stupid to be worrying about that when so much is going on inside there.'

'I know,' he replied. 'But life goes on and this is important to you.'

I switched off the engine and it was weird; as if I had control of things. I felt like a grown-up.

'He'll be all right,' I said, almost to myself. 'He has to be.'

Because if he wasn't then it'd be like it was my fault. I imagined Farah in plain clothes, crying alone in her big house. The idea made my mouth go dry.

Ash unbuckled his seatbelt. 'Sometimes things don't turn out the way we want them to.'

'Do you . . . ?' I began.

'What?'

'Nothing.'

'No,' he said. 'Go on. Do I what?'

'Do you believe in giving people the evil eye?'

He looked at me carefully. 'You're a strange one, aren't you?'

I felt embarrassed at sounding so superstitious and wished I hadn't said anything.

'Sorry,' I said.

'Why?'

'It was a stupid question,' I replied.

95

'No,' he said. 'I like that you can ask a question like that. Most people would be embarrassed in case they thought they sounded silly.'

'But I did sound silly.'

'No. You sounded . . . ' He seemed to search for the right word. 'As if the world hadn't got to you yet.'

'Oh,' I replied.

I wasn't sure whether that was a compliment or not.

'In answer to your question,' he added, 'I don't know. I think the way we think affects what happens to us, so maybe the same goes for what we think about others.'

'But they're only thoughts.'

'Which eventually become actions. Or *inaction*, even.'

'Yeah. I guess so,' I replied.

Of course he was right. It was so obvious when he put it like that. He checked his watch and said he had another lesson soon, so I got out of the car.

'Thanks,' I said.

'What for?'

I wasn't actually sure.

'Making sure I don't forget how to drive,' I replied.

'You're an old hand at it, Fatima.'

He drove away as I walked back into the hospital, feeling a lot steadier than when I'd left.

★ ★ ★

'Thanks, Fatti.' Farah took the papers, flicking through them as she tucked her hair behind her ears. 'What took you so long?'

'Oh, er . . . '

'Are those what you needed?' Malik, who seemed to have appeared from nowhere, asked Farah.

'Yes. This is it.'

There were quite a few other people in the waiting room, along with Mum and Dad — both of whom seemed to be asleep, with their heads resting on the wall behind them. Not sure where Mae was.

'Any news from the doctors?' I asked.

Farah just shook her head. As I sat down, Malik sat next to me.

'We were waiting for you,' he said. 'Did you see Bubblee?'

'No,' I replied, not mentioning that Ash had driven past her.

It shouldn't bother me that he asked about her, but how come it's the people who don't care that end up getting attention? My parents were furious when Bubblee announced she'd move to London, but she did it anyway and it was the only point of discussion for ages. And here's this man who seems to like her and she doesn't even give him a chance. How do you become the person others care about?

'Took me a while to find the papers,' I said. 'I found a picture, I think of you — with my mum and yours. Just after you were born. Could be Mustafa, but I don't know, I've a feeling it's you. Looked like your mum was in a hospital bed.'

He looked over at my parents' open-mouthed faces.

'Really?' he said, leaning in.

'My mum's holding you.'

'We have the *same* picture,' he said, holding my gaze. 'Why is it hidden and not framed or in an album, like all our other family photos?'

I shrugged. 'They probably put it there and forgot about it. I wouldn't even have noticed if I wasn't looking around for the insurance papers.'

It did seem weird though, seeing as Mum liked to have all these old photos in albums, which she looks at whenever she misses Bangladesh. Just then, Mum woke with a start. She looked around as if confused about where she was — then she seemed to remember, looking around for Farah.

'Think she's calling the insurance company,' I explained.

'Did you see Bubblee? Where's Mae?' she asked as Dad let out a snore.

'Kala,' said Malik, 'let's leave Bubblee — she'll come around when she's ready. I have the feeling she's not a girl to be pushed.'

He gets her already. Farah then came in, frowning and looking agitated.

'What wrong, Bhabi?' Malik asked her.

'Nothing,' she replied.

Dad awoke, standing up almost immediately, making everyone in the waiting room start at him.

'Do you want tea?' Mum said to him.

He shook his head. When Malik asked what happened with the insurance Farah looked up.

'Nothing happened. His insurance's expired,' she replied.

'This isn't sensible,' said Dad. 'I've told you children to keep all your things in order.'

Farah sat down, but didn't seem to be paying attention.

'Can't you renew it?' asked Malik. 'Do they have to know what's happened?'

'This isn't Bangladesh,' replied Dad.

Farah was staring at the floor. 'We'll just have to make do with what we have right now.'

I was too busy looking at poor Farah to notice that Dad's eyes were set on me and Malik. As I looked at him he said to Mum that he did want some tea and that she should come with him. Hospitals can make people act very weird. When they left the room I went and sat next to Farah.

'Are you all right?' I asked.

She glanced at Malik, who was flicking through a magazine, before she lowered her voice. 'They put a stop to the insurance,' she said.

I looked at her, waiting for the point she was trying to make.

'Okay.'

'Fatti,' she said, sighing. 'They stopped it because he'd missed three monthly payments.'

'Oh.'

What did that mean?

'I only asked him about our insurance renewal a few weeks ago and he said they weren't due for another six months. Why did he lie to me?' she said, looking into my eyes so intensely, I couldn't look away. 'Why?' she repeated.

★ ★ ★

I wish she could've asked me a question to which I had an answer.

9

Mae

The good thing about being practically invisible is that no-one really cares where you are. Everyone's too busy dealing with their own dramas. I looked through my Twitter feed and read all the messages people had tagged me in as I slipped out of the waiting room to get some fresh air. I took a picture of the front of the hospital building and put it on Instagram — *#Family #Accident #Pray4Mustafa #Hospital*. It was all turning into a bit of a disaster, really. I opened up my Snapchat and made a quick video about what it's like, you know, when your brother-in-law's in a coma and your sister's stormed out because she's had a bust-up with her twin. *#Feud*.

'That's the Amirs for you,' I said into the camera as I jogged on the spot, because with all this going to the hospital I didn't have time to go for my regular runs. 'And there's no excuse for not doing exercise,' I added into the camera. 'Anyway, drama-central. And still no-one's called my brother.'

That's when the idea came to me, because let's face it, it made sense, considering. No-one else seemed to have their head about them, so I might as well. Do Jay and I have the same relationship as he and Farah? No. I was always this annoying little brat who'd get in his way.

When you're little and stupid you see your big brother as this kind of sacred thing to look up to. At the age of seven or eight I'd see some of the other brothers in school look out for their younger sisters. One boy beat another boy up because he'd pulled his sister's ponytail (she's probably going out with that guy now). Not Jay. Yeah, he'd sometimes ruffle my hair and call me 'squirt' but he was always too busy being out with his mates or on the phone to care when I'd ask him to read to me. Fatti would feel sorry for me, settle me next to her, and take his place. And she was good because even if she saw tears running down my cheeks she wouldn't say anything. She'd just put a box of tissues in front of me and look the other way, like a considerate person should.

So, yeah, when Mum and Dad harp on about *Jahangeeeer*, I'm like, whatever. He must've been a better son to them than he was a brother to me. Anyway, I'm not into holding grudges like Bubblee — that's just OTT — and Farah needed him. That was the main thing. Hiding behind a corner outside the hospital, I tapped on his name. It barely rang before he answered.

'Hello?' he barked.

'*Easy*,' I replied.

'Who's this?'

'Your long-lost sister.'

'Bubblee?' he said.

'The other one.'

'Fats?'

'One more strike and you're out,' I said in a fake American accent.

'Squirt,' he answered as I heard some shuffling in the background.

I scratched a bit of the brick wall. The thing is, even though my brother's a waste of space, I still like it when he calls me Squirt.

'That's the one,' I sighed. 'You used to be on your phone all the time when you were at home — would've thought you'd pick it up more often to make sure none of us were dead.'

I instantly thought of Mustafa, still in the operating theatre. Jay gets away with having to deal with none of it. It's not as if I care or anything, but it's unfair, isn't it? *Mae get off your phone, Mae go to your room, Mae be quiet, even though we're always telling you to pay more attention to the family than to your phone.* Talk about having your cake and eating it too. And then there's Jay, probably chilling out on the sofa, not a care in the world.

'Did Mum or Dad tell you to call?' he said, sounding wary.

'What? No. Listen — '

' — *Where the hell is that number?*' he seemed to say to himself. 'I have to go,' he added.

'But *wait.*'

'What?' he snapped. 'God, Mae, I don't have time for a cosy catch-up. I have stuff to do. Adult stuff.'

'Oooh, you're an adult now, are you? That's a first. Anyway, calm down, I called because it's important.'

There was more shuffling in the background as he swore down the phone.

'For God's sake, Mae, unless someone's

103

dying, call back later.'

'*Mustafa's* dying,' I said.

He paused.

'Well, not dying, but he might.'

'What?' he whispered.

I told him what had happened and that, even as we spoke, Mustafa was in surgery and none of us knew whether he'd come out of it.

'*Shit*,' he exclaimed. Then there was silence before I heard a bang — as if something had hit a wall — on his end of the phone.

'*Shit, shit, shit.* Tell me everything; *everything* you know.'

'I just did.'

He paused. 'Okay, okay. It's all right. It's going to be all right. I just have to think.'

I might as well not have been on the phone for all the random things that were coming out of his mouth.

'What are you talking about?' I said. 'I'm telling you so you can come and see us. Be here with Farah.'

'Farah,' he said. '*Shit.* Farah. Okay, Mae, when did this happen? What day?'

I told him. He paused.

'What time?'

'In the evening, on his way home from work.'

'Yes, but what time exactly?'

'I don't know the *exact* time, but some time between five-thirty and six o'clock,' I replied.

'Oh, Mae, I think I've messed up. I think I've messed up big time. How can this be happening?'

He wasn't making any sense and all I could

keep asking him was what he meant.

'I didn't think,' he said. 'I just didn't think. I mean, I called him and he hung up and when I called back, I just . . . I didn't think. He's going to be okay, though, isn't he?'

It seriously sounded like Jay was losing the plot.

'We don't know. That's why I'm calling you. Can you calm down and tell me what you mean? It was an accident. It's got nothing to do with you. All Farah needs is her brother here to support her.'

'You don't get it, Squirt. It *is* my fault.'

'Unless you were the one driving, I don't think so.'

'It was me,' he said.

'You *what*?'

God, some people took ages to explain stuff.

'I was the one he was speaking to when it happened.'

'What?'

Since when did Jay and Mustafa speak? Jay didn't speak to anyone really, apart from Farah.

'*Mae*,' but he didn't say it as if he wanted me to respond. It was like a call of desperation, only my name came out because it was me he was chatting to.

'It's my fault,' he said. 'I think I'm the one who caused the accident.'

★ ★ ★

It's not like I'm easily shocked or anything, but I had to sit down. There were no chairs so I just

105

sat on the ground, leaning against the wall.

'Mae?'

'You did what?'

'It wasn't intentional,' he said, desperation in his voice. 'We had an argument and . . . and, I don't know, he got angry and hung up on me. I called back but it kept going to voicemail, so I thought he'd just switched his phone off to avoid talking to me.'

'What was the argument about?' I said.

He paused. 'Nothing, it doesn't matter.'

'Er, well, clearly it does matter. If you called him soon after he hung up, then he'd have had the accident straight after.'

This pause was longer.

'Oh, Mae. It wasn't . . . I didn't mean for this to happen.'

'Can you *please* explain what the hell you're talking about?' I said.

He wasn't making any sense and I was tired of him not answering my question.

'Hello?' I said.

'I lost all his money.'

'What? What do you mean, you *lost all his money?*'

Why did he even have any of Mustafa's money? How can you lose something that's not yours?

'It was an investment,' he explained. 'Mustafa hired me to help him out with some of his business stuff. I had access to his accounts . . . '

'Right . . . '

'It was meant to be risk-free.'

'But Mustafa knew about it, didn't he?'

106

He paused.

'I didn't know that this arsehole of a supposed friend was going to stitch me up. There weren't meant to be any risks.'

'You didn't tell Mustafa that you were using his money?' I put my hand to my forehead. '*Jay.*'

For the first time I could see why Bubblee was always mouthing off about him. How stupid do you have to be to give someone else's money to a 'mate' who's going to invest it for you, and not even tell them?

'How much?'

After a few seconds, I repeated: 'How much?'

'A lot,' he replied.

'*How much*, Jay?'

'Over a hundred grand.'

It was unbelievable.

'One *hundred* thousand pounds?' I exclaimed. 'And Mustafa didn't even know.'

He paused. 'I told him I was going to make us both rich. I just didn't tell him how. Mae, you have to understand that this was meant to be a risk-free investment. My friend knew what he was talking about. He'd made loads of other people rich. *Goddamn* that bastard,' he shouted as I heard him kick something. 'The whole thing just tanked.'

'Yeah, but Jay. Nothing is ever risk-free, is it?' I might only be sixteen, but even I know that much.

I shook my head in disbelief. It wasn't even money that Mustafa knew Jay had borrowed. It was basically stealing.

'Jay, this is bad. Like, really, really, *really* bad.

Oh my God, he must've been so mad. What did he say to you? How did it end — well, apart from in an accident?'

'I don't want to talk about it.'

I laughed. 'You're joking, right? People are going to want answers and they're not going to be as calm about it as me, trust me.'

'You can't tell anyone, Mae.'

'Are you mad? I'm not about to lie. Don't you see what this all means? Farah has no idea about the money. The business is going to be in trouble and she'll need to know how to handle it.'

He didn't respond.

'Right?' I asked.

'Right, right.'

'Jay, what aren't you telling me?'

He sighed. 'It's just that he took it a lot worse than I thought he would. I mean, I knew he was going to be livid, and I was willing to do whatever to make it up to him, but he went berserk. As in a mad panic. Started talking about monies tied up in other places and that he was already having financial difficulties . . . '

This didn't sound good. It just didn't sound good at all.

'Will you tell me how the surgery goes?' he asked.

'What do you mean? Aren't you going to come? Where are you anyway?'

He explained he was in the city — which I guess meant London because he said he was getting a train to Paris tomorrow.

'Oh, nice little trip for you then,' I said.

'Listen, Squirt. Don't say anything yet. I'm

going to Paris to try to get this money — at least some of it. I've got friends to stay with there. There's got to be a way to sort this out.'

I hesitated.

'Mae?'

'I dunno,' I said. 'You're telling me to lie.'

'No, I'm telling you to keep quiet for a few days. Listen,' he said, softening his tone. 'What good would it do anyone right now, with him in surgery? Who knows how long he'll be out of it, and in that time I might be able to do something about it. Don't you think Farah has enough on her plate without you telling her the reason behind . . . you know. Everything.'

Why did he make sense?

'How will you get this money back?' I said.

It didn't exactly sound like he had a plan.

'I don't know, but I'm sure as hell going to try. But Mae, the last thing everyone needs is more to worry about, right?'

He did have a point, but it still felt wrong.

'I'm just asking for a little time — that's all. I'm going to make this right,' he said.

I paused. 'Okay. But Jay, you have to message me and let me know how you're getting on. All right? Like, I need to know what's happening.'

He breathed a sigh of relief. 'Fine. Of course, Squirt. You just don't say anything for now. All right?'

'All right.'

He said he had to go — that he was trusting me to do what's best for everyone. You had to laugh at that, didn't you? As if he ever thought of the family when he did stuff. But it wasn't as if it was the time to go down that road. When I put the phone down I tapped on my Snapchat again.

'Sometimes,' I said into the camera, 'even when you think you're doing the right thing, you just can't get over the feeling that the right thing is very, very wrong.'

★　★　★

Secrets suck. When I went back to the waiting room Fatti told me about Mustafa's private insurance being cancelled and how he'd lied to Farah about it.

'It's weird,' she said. 'I never thought they had money problems but Farah told me that for a while bills had been stacking up, but she never thought much of it. Mustafa had been dodging her questions or putting her off by always saying he'd pay them today. Except today never came.'

She looked at me with her wide, worried eyes, which didn't really help *my* worry. So now, because of Jay, Mustafa wasn't able to pay his health insurance bills, because of which Farah couldn't switch to private care. I wanted to call him back and shout at what he'd done. Was he mental, investing money that wasn't even his — who does that?

'You can't tell anyone,' she added, going from worried to severe.

I didn't see how hiding things was helping here, but it's not as if people listen to me. I almost told her that I talked to Jay and what really happened between him and Mustafa. I had to stop myself because she'd probably end up crying — Mum and Dad would see and not only would I get cussed for upsetting Fatti but everyone would find out why she was crying and that'd be the end of it. Looking over at Farah, it was clear that for once, Jay was right. I hoped to God he'd be able to recover at least some of that money.

With all this commotion, I went outside again to try to call Bubblee. I wasn't sure what she'd be able to do but it only felt right that she should at least be here.

'I'm not coming back to where I'm not wanted,' she said.

People are so stubborn. It's like, sometimes it's not about *you*. It's all great that she lives in London now, being into art and that stuff, but she's no Tracey Emin. Of course, I couldn't tell her that or she wouldn't ever speak to any of us ever again. It's not like there wasn't enough to worry about.

'People say stuff they don't mean,' I explained. 'Farah was just upset.'

'Well, I meant every word.'

'Yeah, and when Farah's husband's under the knife it's the perfect time to tell her you think it'd be great if he snuffed it. Well done.'

She paused.

'I didn't mean it like *that*. I mean, I do feel that way sometimes but . . . oh, I don't know.'

Bit rich when my sisters tell *me* to think before I speak. It's hardly an Amir family speciality.

'Listen, do you want him dead?' I asked.

'*No*. I'm not a vile person. I just think that if

111

something like that happened, it'd give Farah the opportunity to finally *do* something with her life.'

'What? Live in a poky flat in London and make clay pots?'

'Mae — it wouldn't hurt if you, of all people, respected the choices I made.'

'Exactly,' I said. 'And at least I'm not here literally trying to kill your dream.'

For the first time since, like ever, Bubblee had nothing to say to that.

'So?' I said. 'You coming back to the hospital or what?'

★ ★ ★

When the doctor came into the waiting room we all stood up at the same time. I don't think Wyvernage Hospital has ever seen so many brown people in one room. The doctor removed her gloves, wiping her brow with her arm.

'We managed to stop the bleeding,' she said.

You could literally hear everyone's sigh of relief. Farah had her hand to her chest as Malik held on to her arm.

'I told you,' he said. 'He'll be okay.'

'That's the good news,' said the doctor. 'However, I'm afraid that the trauma to the head was severe and the operation sent his body into a state of shock.'

'Oh, Allah,' said Mum. 'What is happening to our family?'

The doctor glanced at her before looking back at Farah.

'He's stable and breathing but he's gone into a coma.'

Farah was shaking her head. 'But he was in one before — he can come out again, can't he?'

'He can, of course, come out of it, but the first coma was medically induced. His body's shut down right now and we can't estimate if or when he might come out of this present coma.'

'*If?*' said Farah.

Fatti grabbed my hand.

'We can't be conclusive about anything, I'm afraid. For now, we're monitoring him and the good news is we've stopped the bleeding. You should probably go home tonight. Get some rest. We'll keep a close eye on him overnight and let you know if there are any changes to his situation.'

Farah sat back down as Dad thanked the doctor.

'I'll stay here,' said Malik to Dad. 'You should take Farah Bhabi home and make sure she eats something. I'll call you if anything changes.'

Dad nodded, patting him on the arm, and all I could think was: *This is Jay's fault.* And he's not even here. Fatti's tears fell to the floor like mini puddles.

'You should go home and eat something too,' said Malik to her.

Fatti just shook her head — it took us all a while to see that Bubblee was standing at the door. She walked towards Farah and sat down next to her.

'Come on then,' she said. 'Let's go home.'

★ ★ ★

Sleeping's never been a problem for me. I can sleep anywhere. I'm pretty sure I slept through my sister's wedding, actually. Guess it was before I'd started recording stuff. But that night I couldn't sleep. I'm pretty sure most of the others couldn't either. Farah seemed to be barely breathing, which just meant she was as awake as me. Bubblee shared with Fatti again, because she might've turned up at the hospital but it was probably best to take things one step at a time between her and Farah — let's face it, Bubblee's the type of person you want to smother with a pillow at the best of times.

I kept tossing and turning, thinking about Jay and what he'd done. It'd been six hours since I'd Whatsapped him to let him know the latest and he still hadn't responded, even though the two blue ticks appeared. Amazing, isn't it? How easy it seemed for him to just ignore things. But maybe he was really trying. I had to take his word for it. He did sound genuine about sorting this out — you can just never tell, though. A person can still fail, with all the best intentions in the world. Twitter feed was full of crap and so I got up, grabbed my laptop and went downstairs to open up my blog page, which I run under a pseudonym because, let's face it, last thing I want is for my family to accidentally read it and find out what I write. My parents will remember the way they never let my sisters leave the house and end up grounding me too.

I began: *Runaway*. It all just came out in this wave of words that wouldn't stop flowing. I don't think I've typed that fast or furiously in my life. I began with the day Jay left home and how Mum and Dad just refused to see that he'd do anything wrong; the way Farah would cover for him. How Bubblee always argued to try and get out on her own and Fatti just lived in her own world. All of this ended up with my brother-in-law in hospital in a coma. I was so tired but there was no going to sleep now — I just typed and typed and typed. It was like my entire history all in one blog — but it was held together by that one common theme: family. Weird, given that I usually just let them get on with their dramas, but then this accident happened and everything's become a mess. When I finished writing I checked it for any typos and pressed the send button — it was like a weight had lifted off my shoulders. As soon as my head hit the pillow, I fell asleep.

★ ★ ★

Nothing much changed with Mustafa the next few days. Every time I'd check my blog so see how many times it'd been shared, or Twitter or Snapchat or whatever, my eyes would flick up to look at Farah. Everyone else talked — even made a joke now and again — but not her. She was either staring at her husband or sitting in a daze.

'The thing is,' she said when we were in the room with Mustafa, alone together, 'I don't actually know what to do without him.'

I looked up and it seemed as if she was talking more to herself than me. I leaned into Mustafa's face and eyed it. His lips were cracked, and I never realised before how big his pores were, but that was the least of his worries.

'He looks better today, you know. Less . . . pale,' I replied.

'He does everything for me; the house, bills, mortgage — everything.'

'That's because you spend your time looking after everyone else,' said Bubblee, who'd just walked into the room. 'Here.' She'd brought some tea for Farah.

'How do you know?' I said to Bubblee. 'You're never around to see it.'

'Because I *know*,' she replied.

I'd got one lousy message from Jay saying he was still working on getting the money back but that he wouldn't be in contact too much because he was busy. I still kept him updated though — just so he knew what was going on. Apart from that exchange, Farah and Bubblee hadn't said more then three words to each other. I left my camera running during the day without anyone knowing. I'd gone past caring about whether it's *appropriate* or not. Don't think that there's much that's appropriate about the whole situation.

The following day we were at home when Fatti stood over me as I was slouched on the sofa.

'Mae,' she said. 'Help me clean. Mum and Dad are resting in their room before we go to the hospital and this place is a tip.'

'What about Bubblee?'

'She's in the kitchen.'

I gave Fatti an incredulous look.

'I know. But she said she was doing something

in there so maybe she's surprising us all with dinner. No-one's allowed to go in.'

'Weird,' I said, picking up my phone and seeing that my blog had now been shared over three thousand times.

'*Get up,*' said Fatti.

'Yes, Master,' I replied, saluting her and ignoring the look that Malik gave me.

What a stick-in-the-mud. It was when I was cleaning the windows, that clattering noises came from the kitchen and I heard Malik say to Fatti: 'Do you have that picture you were talking about?'

I wanted to ask what picture, but he'd lowered his voice and something made me stop myself. After a few minutes of Fatti saying it was too far back in the cubby-hole she gave in and they both went into the passage, closing the living-room door behind them. After a few minutes I heard him say: 'See; I said you and my mother have the same hands.'

What a drip.

'No, don't put it back,' he said. 'Keep it out. It should go on the mantelpiece with all your other pictures.'

There was a pause.

'No, no,' said Fatti.

'Why not?'

Then there was another pause before I heard him say: 'Well, then.'

I crept away from the door before it opened and it was a few moments before they walked through it with this picture in hand.

'What's that?' I asked.

'Mum and Malik's mum — when he was born.'

When I looked at him he was staring at the photo before glancing at Fatti. It's like, make your mind up — do you fancy Fatti or Bubblee? Sure, Bubblee's the obvious choice because she's hot, but the more you look at Fatti the nicer her features become. Maybe it's because she's a bit, you know, *innocent*, as Mum and Dad like to say. You kind of want to pull her into a hug most of the time.

'Oh,' I said. 'Okay. That's nice.'

'Mae . . . ' replied Fatti, as if in warning.

'What? I said it's nice.'

Who cared? It was just a photo. So, I carried on cleaning the windows as Malik put the picture up on the mantelpiece with all the other photos.

'Talk about wheedling your way into the family,' I mumbled.

'Little Mae — did you say something?' said Malik.

Little?

'I wouldn't dare, *Mal Baia*. Silenced by your very presence.' I bowed and threw my yellow rubber gloves on the coffee table. At the same time, we heard the kitchen door open with a bang. We rushed towards it and there was Bubblee, standing in the middle of what used to be our kitchen.

'Take a photo, Mae,' she said, looking around.

What seemed like all the pots and pans we'd ever owned were in a pile in the middle of the floor. The counter was covered in condiments; a bottle of ketchup was tipped over and spilling on to the counter; salt and pepper, oil, desi ghee, you name it, it was all spilling over, dripping on the floor. The cupboards were open, one of the hobs was lit. It looked like the place had imploded.

'What the hell?' I exclaimed.

'Mae,' shouted Bubblee. 'Photo!'

Her hair was dishevelled and she was whipping around. She stepped forward, over a pot, and moved the ketchup bottle an inch to the left. Malik looked like he didn't know what to do and Fatti just stared at our sister, who'd obviously lost her marbles.

'Are you . . . are you *okay?*' whispered Fatti to Bubblee.

I got my phone out and started taking pictures in case Bubblee shouted at me again. After I got ten or fifteen I switched it to video.

'Maybe I was wrong about this place,' she said, still looking at the mass of ruin around her.

Fatti and me glanced at each other. She took a step towards Bubblee, slowly, in case Bubblee lost it and threw the frying pan at her or something.

'What happened here, Bubs?' asked Fatti, quietly.

Bubblee shot a look at her and then at Malik, frowning. Not to be rude about my sister or anything, but she was acting a bit like an animal. One that might need to be put down.

'What should happen everywhere,' said Bubblee.

We all waited for her to continue, but, you

know, didn't want to anger it.

'What?' asked Fatti.

She looked around at us again, but this time a smile played on her lips. The madness was either slipping away or was becoming a whole new level of crazy. She took a deep breath, closed her eyes and said: 'The destruction of domesticity.'

★ ★ ★

These arty types, I swear. They make a mess, call it art and then expect you to clean up after them.

'I think, on some level, it was a call for attention for Farah,' Bubblee said, knitting her brows together.

While she was analysing the reason behind her madness Fatti and I tried to figure out how Mum managed to make all these pots and pans fit into the cupboards.

'The Farah who's not even here right now?' I said.

'We shouldn't have to tidy this just because we're women,' Bubblee replied, raising her voice, I guess so that Malik, sitting in the living room, could hear.

'We're tidying it up because *you* made the mess,' I said, throwing a dishcloth at her. 'And we'd leave you to sort your own mess out if there wasn't enough crap going on already.'

What was she on?

'The feeling just came to me,' she said. 'This *inspiration* just took hold and I knew what I had to do. I don't even remember what I was doing or how I did it.'

120

I rolled my eyes and opened my mouth to say something but Fatti shook her head at me.

'Well,' she said to Bubblee, 'now it's out of your system, let's just tidy it all so it's back to normal before Mum has a heart attack.'

Bubblee picked up the ketchup bottle and screwed the lid back on. 'Normality,' she said. 'It's the curse of us all.'

★ ★ ★

By the time Mum and Dad came down we'd managed to clear everything. Not that that would've made much difference to hawk-eye Mum who knows when a leaf's fallen out of place, but when she came into the living room with Dad her eyes immediately fell on the new photo on the mantelpiece.

'Do you like it there?' Malik asked them. 'I asked Fatima why you would hide such a lovey photo.'

He watched them, pointedly, as their faces began to look shifty.

'Maybe a photo of you as a baby isn't something they wanted to display,' said Bubblee.

I waited for someone to say something but neither Mum nor Dad seemed to be paying attention to their rowdy daughter. Malik stood up and Dad seemed to look even smaller next to him.

'Photo of me?' he said, picking up the picture and looking at it before handing it over to them. 'Yes. Maybe that's it.'

Fatti's gaze flitted between our parents and

Malik, in confusion. Or contemplation. One of the two. Keys rattled in the front door and it was Farah who came in, throwing the daily paper down.

'How is he?' asked Dad.

Malik was looking at him in a way that, actually, was a little creepy and it seemed as if Dad knew it.

'Same,' she replied before walking out of the room and into the kitchen.

This weird kind of silence took place in the room. They say you could cut some kinds of tension with a knife, but I was a bit confused about where this tension was coming from. Malik then just took the paper, sitting down and opening it up. As his eyes began to skim some headline, he furrowed his eyebrows. His head seemed to be moving in pace with his eyes as he leaned forward.

'Wha . . .' he began. He looked up and then down, skimming through the article again. 'Has anyone read this?'

Everyone looked blankly at him as he held the paper up.

'What?' asked Bubblee.

Mum and Dad had sat down and were looking at each other, not really paying attention to Malik's question.

'Social Media, Prize-Winning Poodles and The Man in a Coma,' he said.

We all looked at him.

'The car crash reported on Thursday night — which had an adverse effect on the neighbourhood's prized poodle — resulted in an un-named party being taken critically ill and has taken a surprise soap-opera-like twist,' said Malik, reading from the paper.

My heart began to pound.

'A blog that's had over eight thousand shares on social media platforms brings to light a local family feud in which the victim allegedly gave his brother-in-law access to his business accounts. The brother-in-law then took advantage of this and used an unspecified, but to be believed, large sum of money to invest in an unsecure business venture. The victim discovered the loss of this money over the phone while driving, thus causing a head-on collision, resulting in the victim's hospitalisation where he's still believed to be in a coma.'

I was going to be sick. Actually sick. It couldn't be me, surely — there's no way it could've happened. I used a pseudonym. How can you connect a blog with a fake name to a man in a coma? Everyone was staring at Malik as he continued to read, talking about the need to be stricter on banning the use of phones when driving, the role of social media in catching people who break the law and Mrs Lemington's poodle. When he'd finished, everyone just looked at each other. Calm down, Mae. No names have been named. This could be about anyone. *Anyone.* But even as I kept telling myself that, I felt sick. How did this story get out?

'Give me that,' said Bubblee, snatching the paper from him.

She skimmed over the article and then looked straight at me. She knew. I didn't know how or why, but she knew. Mum kept turning her head, looking side-to-side. 'What's happening?' she said.

'Bubblee?' said Dad.

Bubblee was still looking at me. 'Oh, Mae.'

She dropped the paper in front of me and I saw the URL of my blog page available. I realised my sister follows my life more than I thought she did.

She sat back down, not taking her eyes off me. 'You need to tell us everything.'

10

Farah

My head spun. Or the room did. Someone shifted off the sofa; I fell into it, my legs feeling as if they were about to give way. It didn't make any sense. It was like watching a TV drama unfold, except it wasn't on TV — it was my life.

'I don't . . . I don't . . . what?' Everyone stared at me as if I was on the verge of death.

Maybe I was. Maybe this is what the end feels like?

'Jay caused the accident? He lost Mustafa's money?' I asked Mae again.

Because if I asked enough times, surely the answer would be the right one; the one that was logical. Mae nodded.

'But it doesn't make sense,' I said.

Because how would Jay even have access to any money belonging to my husband? Then I remembered my last conversation with Mustafa. He'd hired Jay to help — because my parents had asked him. Jay had done this? My little brother?

'Why didn't you tell anyone?' snapped Mum at Mae.

'He told me not to because he was trying to get the money back,' Mae replied.

Jay? The one I used to watch as Mum changed his nappies. I'd get him to eat when no-one else

125

could — his chubby little hands holding on to the spoon and dropping half its contents on the floor, which always made me laugh. Mae looked at everyone who seemed to be looming over her, their eyebrows knitted, arms folded. Why wouldn't the room stop spinning? I had to close my eyes. When I opened them again, Bubblee was flapping her arms at Mae.

'How?' she said.

'I don't know.'

'You didn't ask?'

'Look, Mae's not the one who lost the money,' interjected Fatti.

There was a lot of noise. I wanted to put my hands over my ears just so I could hear my own thoughts. Just so I could understand what was happening: Jay lost my husband's money; he told him this while Mustafa was driving; Mustafa crashed his car. And is now in a coma.

'She shouldn't be keeping secrets,' said Mum.

Malik drew closer so that he was standing next to Bubblee. I stared at their arms that were touching. The grey of her T-shirt against the navy of his shirt. Grey and navy go well together.

'How much money are we talking about, Mae?' I asked. Nothing.

'How much?' I pressed.

'A lot,' she replied. 'Sorry, I don't know, but he seemed pretty stressed about it.'

'That's good of him,' said Bubblee.

'I mean — I reckon it means your house . . . it's in danger.'

I watched Mae's little face — her fine nose and her eyes that were squinting at me, as if every word she said gave *her* a jab in the gut. I couldn't even locate my gut at that time.

'Reckon?' I said.

She paused, biting her lip and looking at the floor as she nodded. I put my head in my hands. My husband was in a coma and we were in so much debt I could lose my house. It didn't compute. Surely there was some kind of mistake. My brother couldn't do this to me. My husband couldn't.

'And you're saying that he was on the phone to Mustafa, telling him about this money he'd lost just before the accident?'

'Mustafa hung up and that's when . . . you know.'

'Did Jay know what happened?'

I could feel my voice break. These past few days I hadn't asked about my brother because there were too many other things to think about, but what if he knew? And he still didn't come.

Mae shrugged. 'No. He said he tried to call back.'

'How much did he try?'

Once? Twice? Three times? Why didn't he call every minute of every day and then call me?

'I don't know,' she murmured. 'He probably just thought Mustafa needed some time.'

'Or he was burying his head in the sand,' added Bubblee.

Wouldn't it be nice to be able to do that for a change? I kept thinking I might wake up because it all seemed like too much of a nightmare to be true.

'What are we going to do then?' said Bubblee,

looking at everyone; more specifically Mum and Dad.

'We don't know the full story yet,' said Dad.

'Yes, Abba, we do,' Bubblee retorted, waving the paper around. 'It's right here for everyone to see. If you're willing to see, that is.'

'It can't be this bad,' said Mum. 'There will be an explanation.'

I couldn't sit there listening to them talk any longer. I got up, ran up the stairs and into the bathroom, slamming the door behind me. Looking around, I wondered what exactly I was meant to do in there. It's the only place I seemed to be able to get away from everyone. There was a bottle of Cif that I picked up, along with some rubber gloves and I began scrubbing the bathroom tiles. Barely five minutes passed when I heard Fatti and Mae, hovering outside as I flung the door open.

'Would you *just* get on with what you're doing? And let me get on with what I'm doing?'

So, that's what my voice sounds like when I shout. It's not something I do very often. They both looked at me, alarmed as I slammed the door. Ignoring the muttering from outside, I suddenly felt drained of energy and sat back, leaning against the bath tub, the Cif and sponge laid by my side.

It wasn't my husband I thought of, lying in hospital, or my brother — wherever he was. It wasn't even the idea that my life was in financial crisis and that, potentially, we actually had no money at all. It was me. I was thinking about the person I was and had become. And how it

128

happened. Was I always this trusting? Did I ever question things or did my lack of curiosity come about slowly? Day after day of content marriage? You can't complain about having had a decent life with a man who loves you and who you love, but something happened in between. I wanted children and it never happened — never was going to happen — and so everything just became a blur. I didn't quite get it. Just like I didn't get Jay. Just like I didn't get my husband.

Someone knocked on the door before Bubblee's face peeked through it.

'We're going to the hospital,' she said.

I picked up the Cif, squirted the dusty edges of the bathtub and began scrubbing. She lingered at the door.

'We'll just wait downstairs. Until you're ready.' She waited for me to answer. 'We should see how he's doing,' she added.

'So, now it matters to you whether he lives or dies,' I replied.

Why couldn't everyone just leave me alone? They don't care when Fatti hibernates in her room. Why couldn't I hibernate in the bathroom?

'Jay's just as much to blame here as Mustafa,' she said.

I wondered: how can two people split from the same egg be so different? And why didn't *my* eggs work? If I had twins, I'd bring them up differently — they wouldn't be me and Bubblee because I'd do the opposite of everything my mum and dad did. If I had a boy he'd be on the stage with the rest of them, not on a pedestal, watching the show. The tiredness came in waves and this time it made me want to cry. All I needed was for my twin sister to sit next to me in silence. But people never do live up to your expectations of them. I just never thought mine were so high. Isn't honesty and loyalty the bare minimum of any relationship? I rubbed away at the polished ceramic.

'Can I . . . can I come in?'

I looked up to see Malik standing behind Fatti and Bubblee. There were just too many people in this house, but it's not as if I could shout at him. He was a guest, after all, and not nearly as annoying as everyone else at that moment. He seemed to take my silence as a yes and squeezed past my two sisters as they both watched him standing over me. As he closed the door behind him, Bubblee had never looked so outraged. He perched on the edge of the tub, clasping his hands and pursing his mouth into a sympathetic smile. My graciousness towards him was waning quite fast.

'On a practical level, we don't yet know what this means,' he said.

Looking back on all my conversations with Mustafa about bills and payments, I could tell Malik what it meant — exactly what Mae said it did: that we could lose our home.

'We know enough,' I said.

He nodded and paused. 'I wasn't sure whether to say anything to you before because I didn't know . . . ' He brushed his hand through his hair. 'I didn't know how bad the situation was. The truth is, I spoke to Mustafa a week before his accident and he said he was having some financial troubles. He didn't tell me how bad they were, or the details, and I didn't ask, because it wasn't my place. He needed to borrow money, but I didn't have the kind that he needed.'

The floor seemed to spin and blur. This would've been before Jay had taken Mustafa's company's money. Not only was Mustafa already in trouble, but he was stupid enough to trust Jay with access to the company account.

'I wanted to help him, Bhabi, but he was so vague about it and wouldn't give me any straight answers.'

I took a deep breath and exhaled, trying to calm my nerves.

'I was worried about him, but I thought you would've known. He told you everything,' he said.

'Not everything,' I replied. 'Clearly.'

'I'm telling you all this because when I spoke to him he would say how he wanted to make you happy because . . . '

'Because what?'

He cleared his throat. 'Every couple has their problems.' He lowered his eyes, refusing to look straight at me. 'He just wanted to find another way to make you happy. He kept telling me that he'd create an app and that you'd have so much money, you'd never have to worry about anything again.'

As if money bought babies. As if that would somehow make it all better? Why did Malik think this was helpful? Why didn't he see, that if anything, it made me want to smash every single item in this bathroom; in this house?

'Because cash is a great substitute for a baby?' I said.

He looked at the ground again. 'I'm sorry, I just want you to know that he was only thinking of you. Nothing mattered more to him.'

I sighed and leaned my head back, closing my eyes. 'He's not done a very good job, has he?'

Just then there was another knock on the door as Mae looked in. She didn't take two seconds to fall on to her knees.

'Far, I'm so sorry I didn't tell you, but Jay was right in a way, and I wasn't sure, and Bubblee had left, so it all felt, like, *mental.*'

She glanced up at Malik as if he were spoiling her whole speech, but he didn't move.

'Announcing it like that to the public, though, Mae,' I said. 'I mean, for everyone to see. Everyone to *know.*'

I wondered how long it'd take for our neighbours to find out and for everything in my life, which seemed to be spiralling out of control, to be common knowledge. It probably already was. It's not as if much else happened in this town.

'They didn't mention any names,' she said. 'And my blog's under a pseudonym.'

'Mae, how many people had a car accident last week, aggravated Mrs Lemington's prized poodle, and then ended up in a coma?'

Malik was still perched on the tub, watching the two of us. I did wish he'd leave us alone.

'Stupid poodle,' she said.

'You need to think about the things you say

sometimes, Mae. The things you do. Not everything that happens in life is a potential project for you; something to put online and tell the world about. Especially when that life is someone else's.'

My legs were beginning to hurt from sitting in the same position for too long but I didn't have the energy or will to move. Mae was still kneeling next to me. I couldn't quite see her face that was lowered, probably for the shame she felt. When I turned around I saw Dad standing at the doorway, glancing at Malik before looking away as soon as their eyes met.

'Faru. Come on, Babba. Your husband needs you,' said Dad.

I let out a small laugh. So, Dad, I wanted to say, if the roles were reversed and I'd squandered all our money on some venture cooked up by my brother-in-law and never told my partner about it, would I get the same understanding? Would you say, *Your wife needs you?* Typical. I sounded like Bubblee. I pulled myself off the floor, chucking the Cif and sponge to the side and taking off my pink rubber gloves.

'Fine, Abba.'

With which I walked past everyone so we could go and visit my husband who, I realised, I hardly seemed to know any more.

★ ★ ★

'People make mistakes,' said Dad as we got in the car. Fatti, Mae, Malik and Bubblee left in a separate one.

I gripped the steering wheel as I saw Dad look at me from the corner of my eye. My jaw clenched.

'And you know Mae — how much she exaggerates.'

If it was possible, I felt every muscle in my body tighten.

'Faru,' spoke Mum from the back. 'You know your brother — how much he loves you. Things are harder for boys. They have different characters. They don't think about things the same as girls do.'

Dad was nodding. 'We're not saying he was right, Faru. He's made a mistake and he should've told you.'

'And my husband?' I said, looking at Dad as we stopped at a traffic light.

He cleared his throat. 'You must understand, Faru — a man has to do what he thinks is best for his family.'

Family. When you get married, you're not really a family until you have children. People might not agree, but it's always seemed that way to me. And obviously to Mum too, as she said: 'Wouldn't he want security for when you had children? But Allah knows why you are leaving it so late. And now — who knows?'

Not again, Mum. Please, not again.

'I'm his *wife*,' I replied, levelling my voice in case I ended up shouting at her too. *She doesn't know. How is she to realise that she shatters your heart every time she asks about the children you don't have? The ones you'll never have.*

Looking into the rear-view mirror, I asked

Mum: 'Is this the way it's meant to be?'

It's funny, I never really thought about my parents' marriage. For twenty-eight years you see a thing and accept that it's just the way it is. What was Bubblee always moaning about? Why was she always so angry? I hated to admit it, but I was beginning to see the reason. Why was it okay for me not to know and just accept that Mustafa did things without discussing them with me first — especially when they'd affect us both? Did my being happily married mean I stopped seeing things? If so, now it had come and hit me in the face so hard, everything was a blur and my mind was numb. I let out a sigh. But I never was like Bubblee, with high dreams and aspirations. All I ever wanted from life was contentment. And look what I got.

'Well?' I said, as Mum still hadn't answered.

'Farah,' said Dad. 'You are feeling angry. Better to calm down and then speak.'

The car tyres screeched as I turned into the hospital car park. As we got out Bubblee had also arrived, parking her little Ford next to my Mini Cooper. The only person I really noticed was Fatti — she looked distracted. We were all quiet when we entered the hospital wing until I said, 'Call Jay,' to no-one in particular as I marched on ahead. I turned around to see that they had all stopped and were looking at each other.

'Can someone just. Call. Jay,' I repeated, walking off again as Mae caught up with me.

'What do you want me to say?' she asked.

'That he'd better get here as fast as humanly

possible, or there'll be hell to pay.'

'But he's in Paris.'

'I don't care if he's in Timbuktu,' I replied.

As I marched towards my husband's hospital room the doctor was checking his charts.

'Ah, Mrs Lateef. Glad you're here. We've — '

' — Can you give me a minute, please?' I said.

She looked confused. 'Sorry?'

'I'd like a moment with my husband.'

She looked at him lying there, eyes closed, not a care in the world.

'I'm not su — '

'*Please*,' I repeated.

As she left the room the rest of the family walked in.

'Where is he?' I asked.

'Who?' said Bubblee.

'That *brother* of mine.'

Something began to stir inside me. I couldn't look at anyone in the room without wanting to scream. Mae had her phone against her ear and looked at me after checking a message she seemed to have received.

'He's er . . . he's not available right now.'

It's funny. All your life you stand up for someone, explain them to people, follow on from what your parents say: they have to be right because they raised him.

'Your son, Amma and Abba,' I said, looking at them. 'He sends my husband into a coma and can't even come on the phone to speak to me.'

'He is trying to find the money for you,' said Mum. 'At least he is doing something.'

136

Bubblee scoffed. 'Yeah, he's been *trying* to do things for years.' She stretched her arm towards my comatose husband. 'That's what he's done.'

'And aren't you glad?' I retorted.

'Perhaps everyone should take a minute,' interjected Fatti.

Malik put his hand on her arm. 'Let them, Fatima. It's better to speak about these things in the open. God knows there are too many secrets in this family. Don't you think, Kala and Mama?' he added, looking at Mum and Dad.

Fatti gave him an inquisitive look, but I didn't have time to think about what was going on there. I had my own issues to think about. For the first time, what was happening to me mattered most.

'Malik . . . ' said Dad.

'Mama, don't people deserve to know the truth?' said Malik.

Fatti glanced at Mum and Dad and then Malik, a questioning frown forming.

'Why are you even here, Bubblee?' I said. 'When all you have to offer is your cynicism and negativity?'

She looked hurt, but it was quickly replaced with something stonier. I almost regretted what I said when I saw that look — it reminded me so much of when she was younger; how we used to play together and Jay would come and distract me because he'd spilled something on the carpet or broken a vase. For a moment Bubblee and I just stared at each other.

'Faru,' said Mum, glancing at me and then looking over at Malik.

That's when it hit me: how could I have been so stupid for so long? What do my parents know? They're trying to set up their rebel daughter with a man from Bangladesh in whom she has absolutely zero interest. Who, by the looks of it, she finds repellent. What world do my mum and dad live in? Why can't they see the thing that's right in front of them, rather than what they want to see?

'I wouldn't have bothered if Fatti hadn't insisted on it,' replied Bubblee.

Fatti's eyes were darting all over the place now.

'Don't bring her into it,' said Mae.

'Mae — you shush,' Dad intervened.

Mae flung her arms out before whipping around and charging out of the room.

'Mae,' Fatti called out behind her.

When she didn't stop, Fatti looked around the room and said: 'She's not a little girl any more. You have to stop treating her like a child,' she added, looking at Mum and Dad.

'We know, Fatti,' said Mum. She reached into her bag and handed her a tube. 'Here, have some cheese.'

Fatti seemed like she was in the middle of a war of the wills, her eyes flitting between the cheese and Malik. I was just about to say to Mum to stop feeding our eldest sister when Malik interjected: 'She doesn't need cheese.'

'Isn't that typical?' said Bubblee. 'A man telling a woman what she needs.'

'Bubblee,' replied Malik, taking on a tone that

must've got my twin sister's blood simmering. 'You are not the only one that wants the best for Fatima.'

That's when we all looked at him. It dawned on me that Malik and Fatti had been getting quite close — had he actually fallen for her instead of Bubblee? Surely not. Fatti looked at him with such warmth, it made me think that maybe he had. Mum was still holding out the cream cheese.

'Malik, let me talk to you outside,' said Dad, walking up to him, ready to leave the room.

'No, wait,' said Fatti. She paused, looking at both of them. 'What's going on?'

Mum put the cheese back in her bag. 'Nothing, my daughter,' she said.

'*Something*'s going on,' Fatti insisted.

She was right. Mum and Dad looked shifty and nervous while Malik wasn't paying any attention to Dad, who was trying to get him out of the room.

'It's something to do with that picture,' she said.

'What picture?' I asked.

Bubblee explained the photo that Fatti found of my mum, my mum-in-law and Malik as a baby.

'It's not me,' said Malik.

'Malik, please — go and speak to your mama.' Mum sounded more panicked than I'd ever heard her. And she couldn't take her eyes off Fatti.

'Then who is it?' asked Fatti.

Silence.

'*Who?*' she repeated.

Dad stepped forward and held her by the arms. 'Listen, my sweet child.' He regarded her face, her doe-eyes that looked at him in such confusion, her mouth that always seemed to stay pursed. 'Your amma and I love you very much.'

'*What* is going on?' said Bubblee.

For once, I was keen for someone to answer her question.

'It's you,' said Mum to Fatti, stepping forward and standing side-by-side with Dad. 'The baby in the picture is you.'

I didn't understand why this all mattered — who cared whether it was Malik or Fatti? But something on Bubblee's face told me it did matter.

'But you're the one holding me. Malik's mum,' Fatti said, looking at him, 'she's the one in the hospital bed.'

'That's right, Fatima,' said Malik, coming forward. 'Do you see now?'

'No,' said Bubblee in disbelief.

'Malik, please leave this room,' said Dad.

He didn't move. 'You must tell her, Mama. With me here.'

That's when Mum took hold of Fatti, tears in her eyes. 'You are still our daughter, Fatti. It doesn't matter who gave birth to you.'

Fatti's confusion seemed to melt away at this. What did they mean by 'who gave birth to you'?

'Fatima,' said Malik. 'Do you see?'

She stared at him, a look of disbelief on her

face. Bubblee seemed unable to move from where she was standing.

Malik kept his eyes on Fatima, though.

'Do you?' he repeated. 'You are my real sister.'

11

Fatima

I didn't hear anything or look at anyone, I just ran out of the room — what else was I meant to do? Down the hospital corridors, past the reception and nurses' station, through the doors.

'Fatti,' Mae called out.

For a moment I stopped and considered her — the fact that she wasn't my real sister made me burst into tears, right there and then. I realised she was talking to Marnie, who was standing there with a bunch of flowers.

'Fats?' she said, coming up to me. 'What's wrong?'

You're like my little darling, I wanted to say. *Sometimes I want to lock you in your room and other times I could sit and watch you sleep for hours.*

'I'm sorry,' I said, turning around and running out of the hospital, towards the bus stop.

* * *

What was I sorry for? I didn't know. All my life I've felt like I never did fit in. Even though Bubblee called herself the black sheep, at least she was a sheep — I was like a goat. I'd tell myself all the time: *It's in your head, Fatti. Mum and Dad love you.* I wouldn't admit it to the rest of them, but they always have seemed to prefer me over my sisters. Mum keeping cheese in her bag for me wasn't a new thing. Even when I was little there was always a special 'Fatti' stock that the rest of them would whinge over. I should've felt grateful and superior — got a big head like most people do when they're preferred over others — but instead it just distanced me further from them. It didn't help that I was the eldest and my sisters would eye me suspiciously as if I'd tell on them if they did anything wrong. So, instead, I'd just hide in my room, eating snacks, getting fat, wondering what was wrong with me, and why I didn't belong here. Now I knew. It was because I *didn't* belong here. It made me sound ungrateful: poor Fatti being loved too much and fed too much. But you can't help it if you feel like an extra piece in a puzzle that's already complete.

When I got to the bus stop I realised I didn't know where to go. After thirty years of being alive I had no real friends. When I was younger Mum would always collect me straight after school, and when I was invited to parties or to someone's house I'd have to decline because Mum and Dad didn't like the idea of me mixing with girls that weren't Bangladeshi, and certainly not mixing with boys. And then when I got older I was too shy to really make friends. I didn't like looking at myself in the mirror and so I suppose I didn't like other people looking at me either. If I'd been bullied it might've made me feel as if I was alive, but I was just ignored — as though I didn't exist. That's how I liked it.

Stop feeling sorry for yourself. I wiped my tears and tried to pull myself together, when I saw Mae speeding her way towards me. Before she reached me a bus pulled up to the stop and I got on, with no idea where it was going. Her face looking on at me through the window, confused and worried, just made me cry again.

★ ★ ★

Malik is my brother. That was the thought that hit me like a truck when I got off at a random stop near our town. It made me feel so sick, I almost threw up on an old lady. The way I looked at him. The way I thought he looked at me. When he touched my arm and when he'd meet my gaze I had these ridiculous glimmers of hope that *maybe* he felt something. But it was because he was my *brother.* The heat rose to my face as I shook my head in embarrassment. How could I have been so stupid to think that he cared about me as anything more than a sister? Especially when there was Bubblee around. And how would I ever get over the fact that I had *those* feelings about my own brother? It was too much.

My phone rang and it was Mae, followed by Bubblee, followed by Farah. I ignored all their calls but when the phone rang again I saw Ash's name flash on my screen. I hesitated for a moment — how would I even be able to get any words out? But it would be comforting to hear a friendly voice, speak to someone who didn't know that I'm not really an Amir. Who didn't

144

know that I don't think I'm anyone.

'Is everything okay?' he said as soon as I picked up.

How did he know something was wrong? was my first reaction.

'I've been outside your house for ten minutes but no-one's here.'

I'd completely forgotten I had a lesson with him today.

'I'm so sorry,' I began. 'We were in hospital and then everyone was there and so much happened and I lost track of time . . . '

And I don't really have three sisters and I've never actually met my real mum and dad and I'm alone, alone, alone.

'Oh, I see,' he said, sounding annoyed. 'Don't worry — are you far? I'll come and get you.'

'You don't have to do that,' I replied, looking around, wondering how I'd tell him I ended up here.

'I know — but you sound confused enough as it is.'

So I told him which bus stop I was at and twenty minutes later, there he was, getting out of the driver's seat for me. I looked at my watch before I got in.

'The lesson's almost over,' I said. 'Maybe we can skip the last ten minutes?'

Though I didn't know what the point in him coming was; I couldn't drive and concentrate on not killing myself or anyone else.

'You have to use the time you're given,' he said, getting into the passenger's side.

I got in, put my seatbelt on and steadied the

clutch. Before I was about to turn out, he said: 'Mirrors.'

'Oh, yeah. Sorry.'

I checked the mirrors and was about to turn out again.

'Fatima. Indicator.'

I put my indicator on.

'Sorry,' I said.

'Don't be sorry,' he replied. 'Just vigilant.'

I had to swallow the lump building in my throat and just nodded. As I drove my vision got blurry and I had to wipe at my eyes to see the road ahead.

'Okay,' he said. 'Turn left into the next road. Just pull up here for a second,' he added.

I did as I was told and put the car into neutral.

'You can switch the engine off.'

When I did that he said: 'Okay. Tell me. What's happened?'

I shook my head because I couldn't trust my voice — and I know I cry all the time, but the last thing I wanted was to cry in front of Ash.

'Something happened. Even I know you check all your mirrors as if your life depended on it before turning into the road — courtesy of your dad.'

It was too much. Hearing someone else say 'your dad' made it feel like I had to confess to everyone in the world that it wasn't true — it was all a lie and I was a part of the lie without wanting to be. He wasn't my dad. Where was my *actual* dad? In Bangladesh, pretending to be my uncle, living in a place I hardly remember. He might be sitting in a room right now, thinking about me, just as I'm thinking about him. If I have my mum's hands, then what parts of me do I get from him? As these thoughts whirred around my head, tears fell freely down my cheeks.

'Hey, hey, hey,' said Ash, leaning in to look at me, which is the worst thing you can do when someone's crying. Don't people know you're meant to look away and pretend it's not happening?

'I'm fine, I'm fine,' I said, wiping the tears that continued to fall like some unstoppable force. I switched the engine back on but he switched it off.

'I'll believe that when you don't have snot running down your nose,' he said. 'Fatima?'

'I'm not Fatima,' I said, sobbing through the tears.

He looked confused. 'What?'

I shook my head.

'What do you mean?' he asked.

But I couldn't speak because the sobs wouldn't stop and I wanted to run out of the car and never see Ash, or anyone else, ever again.

'Who are you then?' he said, smiling.

'That's the thing,' I said, finally looking at him, wiping my nose with the cuff of my sleeve. 'I don't know.'

★ ★ ★

I started at the beginning — right at the beginning: from when I was a child and always felt removed from everyone else, to just an hour ago when I was told that the people I thought were my parents had actually brought me home from Bangladesh. That my sister's brother-in-law was *my* brother, not my cousin. Her husband was my brother too. That the reason I felt removed all my life was because I *was* removed. It was all jumbled up, but it was jumbled sense. Ash listened, quietly, nodding here and there, but not saying anything. Once I'd finished he sighed.

'I'm sorry,' he said.

My tears and sobs had stopped and I felt a weird kind of empty calm. I stared at the road that led to a dead-end.

'Your family must be wondering where you are,' he added.

'I can't see them right now,' I said. 'I don't want to.'

He nodded, as if thinking about something. 'Of course you don't. What do you want to do?'

It was the worst question a person could ask. I wished someone could just tell me. What is anyone meant to do when something like this happens? How do you begin rebuilding reality? I shrugged.

'Okay. Why don't we go home, you can collect a few things and stay at mine for a few days? Just until you clear your head.'

I looked at him.

'Don't look so shocked,' he said. 'I understand family troubles. You can stay in the spare room.'

'But you're my driving instructor,' I said.

'Aren't I also your friend?' he asked, smiling.

More tears came to the surface — but this

time they were the grateful kind. Suddenly, the idea of staying with a man in a house, alone, filled me with dread.

'No, I'll stay somewhere else. Thanks.'

But where? I racked my mind for anyone who might take me in, anyone who might also call me their friend. No family and no friends.

'Of course. Tell me where and I'll drop you off.'

'I . . . I don't know.'

'Listen, I'm out most of the day, working. But if you don't feel comfortable, that's fine. I just thought it might be good for you to get away for a bit.'

Why didn't I spend more time out, making friends and going places? Not only did I lock myself away from my family but from the whole world, and now, when I'm in need, I seem to have no-one. No-one but my driving instructor.

'Thanks. Yes, please. If that's okay? I promise I won't be any trouble,' I added.

He smiled and said: 'Fatima — you're the least troublesome person I've ever met. Right, now — make sure you check the mirrors this time.'

So I switched on the engine, found my braking point, checked my mirrors, indicated, and drove home in silence to collect my things.

★ ★ ★

When we stepped into the house it felt so unfamiliar and yet recognisable to me — as if all the memories I'd collected over the past thirty years weren't actually true and yet they weren't

149

fake either. I went upstairs and threw whatever came into sight into a bag. Before going downstairs, I went into everyone's room, just to take a look at the spaces in which they live. It wasn't a goodbye, just looking at something in a different light. When I walked into Mae's stuffy room my gaze fell upon a picture of us. It was taken a few years ago when we went to the park and I accidentally sat on some dog poo, which had Mae howling with laughter. I think Farah took that picture. Closing the door behind me, I went downstairs with my bag.

'Ready?' asked Ash.

I looked at the picture of me as a baby — the day I was given away — on the mantelpiece, walked up to it and put it in my bag.

'Yes. Ready.'

★ ★ ★

I never really imagined what Ash's life was like outside his red Nissan Micra. I knew he lived alone but it's weird how empty a place can feel sometimes. This is what he comes home to every day — but he's probably used to it. Maybe I could get used to coming home to an empty space too.

'You can just leave your bags here,' he said as I followed him into another room.

The living room was small but cosy with vintage brown leather sofas and a modern fireplace.

'Would you like some tea?' he asked.

'No, thanks.'

'I'll order some pizza then,' he added.

Just the idea of eating made my stomach twist in a knot of anxiety. I shook my head. 'Oh no, I'm not hungry.'

I hoped my stomach wouldn't grumble like it usually did when I was famished. I pulled my sleeves over my hands, grabbing on to the cuffs.

'Don't be silly. You probably haven't eaten all day.'

He picked up the phone and began to order.

'You're okay with vegetarian?' he asked. 'No halal.'

I nodded, feeling as if the whole day had just slipped out of my control. But then, I'd never felt like control was something I had in the first place. It was six-fifty in the evening — I wondered where everyone was. Were they still at the hospital? Were they calling me and worried that they were only getting through to my voicemail? I'd texted Mae to let her know I was staying with a friend that night, but I didn't want to see anyone's name come up on my screen, so I just turned the phone off. This was the first night I'd spent away from home in thirty years. Today was a day of foreignness. Ash looked at his watch and put the timer on.

'Over half an hour and it'll be free,' he said, smiling, showing his small and very white teeth.

He sat down opposite me on the single sofa and clasped his hands together.

'So,' he said. 'Have we got used to the idea yet?'

'Hmm?'

'That you're adopted?'

My face must've fallen.

'Sorry,' he said. 'I'm sorry. I make jokes too soon.'

I wanted to say I should go and freshen up — isn't that what people say in films? But I was glued to the sofa — my heart was desperate for me to move but my brain and body had other ideas.

'Don't listen to me, Fatima. Well, only when I'm teaching you to drive.'

I tried to smile, but I think it must've come out more like a grimace.

'Why don't I show you to your room? Maybe you want to rest for a while? I'll knock when the pizza's here.'

He took me to a single bedroom that looked like it'd never been used; just a single bed, a side-lamp and a chest of white drawers next to a wardrobe. It seemed quite sad, even though it looked out into the back garden — just as my own room did.

'Thanks,' I said.

'My daughter's room. When she decides to come and stay, which, as you can tell, isn't very often nowadays.'

'It's lovely,' I said, because I couldn't say it felt cold and empty.

'I've told her a hundred times to do it up as she wants. I don't know, put up posters and pictures — whatever the kids do nowadays. But . . . ' He simply shrugged.

'Where does your son stay?' I asked when it didn't seem like he was going to go.

'His room's at the end of the passage. Much

more lived-in. Maybe because he lives in it. But I didn't think you'd want to be in a room that smells of teenage boy.'

I smiled.

'Can I get you anything?' he asked.

'No, thanks. This is great.'

He looked like he was about to leave when he said: 'You can stay here, or if you want to talk or anything, then I'll be downstairs; just watching TV or reading or doing what I do on any normal day.'

'Thanks,' I repeated.

'Right. I'll leave you to it.'

He paused again for a moment before he left the room and closed the door behind him.

I sat on the edge of the bed, feeling exhausted, so I slid under the covers — just for a quick ten-minute nap — replaying these random memories from years ago: me watching Bubblee, Farah and Jay from my bedroom window while they played hide-and-seek; Mae being born and me holding her in my arms for the first time; Dad doing the gardening while Mum cooked in the kitchen. Mum and Dad. Except they're not my mum and dad, are they? Tears trickled down my cheeks and before I knew it I was sobbing into my pillow, as I fell into a dreamless sleep.

★ ★ ★

When I woke up it was dark outside. Where was I? What had happened? Then, bit by bit, the memory of the day came back to me. I closed my eyes again — they felt raw from all the crying

— and lay in bed for a few moments, wanting to go back to sleep, until the faint noise of voices crept into the room. Opening the bedroom door, I realised it was coming from the television downstairs, so I crept down the steps, wondering whether I shouldn't just stay in the room and sleep until this was all over.

'Hi,' said Ash, looking up as I stood at the doorway. An empty plate was next to him, a half-eaten pizza box on the table, and his feet were up on a footstool. 'I came to wake you up but you were fast asleep. I didn't want to disturb you. Come, sit,' he added.

He went and got me a plate, putting a few slices of pizza on it before handing it to me.

'You *have* to be hungry now.'

Actually, the hunger had gone, but I didn't want to seem rude, so sat with the plate on my lap. Ash lowered the volume on the television — he was watching *Star Trek*.

'How are you feeling?' he asked.

'Fine,' I said.

'Here, I'll get you a drink.'

He came back into the room with some water and handed it to me.

'Thanks,' I said, gulping it down in one go.

'So,' he began. 'Have you thought about what you're going to do?'

I looked up from fiddling with the crust of the pizza. 'Do?'

He nodded. 'Where you're going to take it from here?'

Of course. I'd not been there one night but how long was I planning to stay? Where would I go from here? The idea of going to the same house and sleeping in the same bedroom just didn't bear thinking about.

'Sorry,' I said. 'I'll be out of here tomorrow.'

'Don't be silly. That's not what I meant. You can stay as long as you need. What are spare rooms for?'

I looked down at the white ceramic plate.

'It's too soon, anyway,' he added. 'You don't have to think about anything yet, I suppose. I'm always in a rush to think of a solution.'

'And I never can come up with a solution. To anything.'

It just came out, because it was so true, and never felt truer than it did in that moment.

'Perhaps we can find some middle ground,' he said. 'Until then, maybe you should phone home and let them know you're safe. I'm sure they'll be worried.'

Home. The word made me laugh.

'Listen,' he said, as if he heard my thoughts, then paused. 'It might not be my place to say . . . I don't know your family or what your situation is at home, but it always seemed to me — from the way you spoke about them in our lessons — that they weren't . . . well — '

' — Horrible?' I offered.

'Like I said, it's not my place to say. Feel free to correct me. Or throw your pizza at me.'

I put the plate down. He was right. It's not like I could complain about how they never cared about me — if anything, they cared too much.

'That must've been awful,' he replied when I said that.

How pathetic he must've thought I was, to complain about parents who gave me everything I wanted, even though they never let me out of their sight. Who fed me and clothed me and told me they loved me all the time. How could I explain what living as if you see everything through a glass window felt like? Was that because of what happened and how I came to be an Amir, or was that just *me*? Would I have felt like that even if I wasn't adopted? That word — *adopted* — every time it came to me I thought I might wake up from a bad dream. Why was I transferred from one family to another? Did Malik's parents not want a girl? Couldn't they afford it? Did the people I call Mum and Dad ask for me or was I just given to them — a bundle of burden? Did my brother and sisters know but just never tell me? So many questions were swimming in my head, but who was I meant to ask for answers when I didn't even want to see the faces of the two people who raised me?

'I didn't mean it like that. Sorry,' he said, rubbing his face with his hand. 'I'm not the best person in an emergency situation like this.'

I couldn't quite figure out the way to tell him he was like a Godsend today. I'd have been walking around the streets, aimless, if it weren't for him.

'Why? Do you help out a lot of adopted girls?' I said.

He laughed. So did I.

'No,' he replied. 'You're the first. I'm getting some practice. Anyway,' he added, after a pause, 'you don't have to think about what to do yet. It's a lot to take in, I'm sure. And you can use my phone if you do decide to call home.'

Every time I heard that word, *home*, something tugged at me. What did home even mean?

'Which one?' I said.

He sighed. 'God knows, I don't know. But I suppose it's wherever you feel the safest — the most comfortable. Where you can be yourself.'

'Is that how you feel here?' I asked.

'Sort of,' he replied. 'Most of the time. I'm certainly comfortable,' he added, patting the little pouch that was his belly. It was such a little pot-belly that I hadn't noticed it until then.

'Do you like living alone?' I asked.

He seemed so content with everything — with life — that I had to ask. People talk about being alone as if it's the worst thing in the world but I've always known that I prefer being alone. Or maybe that's just me not being brave enough to be around people, because it's not like I didn't want someone by my side. It's not as if I wasn't lonely. Maybe preference is just another word for safety.

'I'm used to it,' he replied.

'Yes, but are you *used* to it, or do you actually like it? I mean, if you had a choice, would you have it another way?'

He smiled and closed the pizza box. 'We're getting into serious territory here.' He looked up at me. 'But then I suppose it's a serious situation.'

I waited for him to answer as I put a small

piece of pizza in my mouth.

'It's not something I really like talking about,' he said.

'I'm sorry. That was a bit personal.'

Why was it okay for me to suddenly ask him questions he didn't invite? Maybe it's because through understanding what another person's like you can understand a bit of yourself. Or maybe find yourself in them, making things a little bit better — as if you're not the only person in the world who feels a certain way.

'Well, since we're here, I can tell you.' He took a deep breath and looked into the fake, unlit fireplace. 'You get used to things because you have to. Not because you like it, just because that's how things are and so you make the most of it.'

Maybe I didn't prefer being alone — maybe I'd just become used to it.

'Can't you change things?'

He smiled as he looked at me. 'Yes, Fatima. You can.'

I inched forward. 'Sorry, I don't mean to sound rude or anything, and it's only because you've been a good . . . well . . . friend, I guess. But . . . why don't you?'

For a moment his face darkened and I thought I'd made him angry. This is why I keep my mouth closed, because who knows whether what I say will hurt a person or anger them? He then seemed to look into the distance.

'I don't know, Fatima. Old age; complacency. Same tired excuses.'

'You're not old,' I said.

'Maybe not in age, but in years lived, trust me — I feel it.'

I sat back, putting my plate on the table.

'Well, with it's come wisdom, hasn't it?' I said.

'I'm not so sure about that.'

'If you could change something,' I asked, 'what would it be?'

He looked at me so closely I began to blush.

'*Hmm. What would I change; what would I change?*' he muttered, seeming to give the idea a lot of thought. He clapped his hands so loudly it startled me, as he said: 'Pretty much everything.'

'You're not being serious,' I said, picking up my plate again and taking another bite of pizza.

'That's because even if I knew what to change, I wouldn't have the first clue how to do it. I'm a creature of habit. Anyway,' he added, 'this isn't about me, it's about you. Tell me, what are you thinking?'

'Why someone's parents would give them up like that. What must be wrong with someone that their own parents didn't want them any longer?'

'Hey,' he said, coming to sit next to me. 'You can't think like that when you don't know the facts — it could be a number of reasons. And you know,' he paused. 'I hate to say it, but you know that having babies for a sister happens a lot in our families. You should speak to your parents,' he said. 'Or you'll start thinking the worst when it probably isn't even true.'

What could be worse than being adopted? And how could I trust what they had to say, anyway? If my brother-in-law hadn't been in hospital and Malik hadn't come to London and I hadn't found that photo, then would I have just died not knowing who my birth parents were? No matter which way I looked at it, everything felt like a lie and a betrayal.

'I don't want to hear anything they have to say right now,' I replied. The idea of speaking to Mum and Dad made my body stiffen.

'Well,' he said. 'What about your aunt and uncle? Your birth parents?'

I looked up at him.

'You can call them,' he suggested.

But suddenly this place seemed too small for me. Not his house, but Wyvernage itself and everything in it. The sameness of it all made me angry and stifled, and an urge rushed through me.

'Or I could go to them,' I said, almost to myself.

'Hmm?'

I looked up at him. 'What if I went to Bangladesh?'

He stared at me.

'That's where I was born and handed over. I don't even know what the place looks like. I barely know what my birth parents look like.'

In that moment I didn't think about the fact that I'd never left the country on my own, that it'd involve me travelling alone and seeing the people who gave me up, alone. It was crazy. Of course I couldn't go. I was angry with them too, of course. But it wasn't the same kind of anger — it was like anger removed. Perhaps because I knew them less, it hurt less. It was a stupid thing to think I could do.

'You know,' said Ash, 'that doesn't sound like an awful idea.'

'Really? But I've never . . . '

'What?'

How could I tell him that I'd never travelled alone? That I never did anything alone? But I'd run out of energy to think of a lie, or a diplomatic way to say it.

'I've never done anything like this before. Travel alone.'

He smiled. 'Fatima, you'll find that in life, there's a first time for everything.'

161

12

Farah

We sat at Mum and Dad's, all in a bit of a daze. As I looked around the room at everyone's sombre face, each person lost in their own thoughts, I tried not to be reminded of it looking as if a funeral had just taken place. I tried calling Fatti a hundred times but it kept going to voicemail so I could only leave her messages. I couldn't quite get my head around it — she was my sister *and* my sister-in-law. I thought of Mustafa, lying another night in his hospital bed; how we might lose everything, yet how he was unaware that he had also just gained a sister. For some unknown reason, in that moment, my love for Fatti seemed to multiply in a way that might make my heart burst. If only I could tell her.

'You never told us. Any of us,' I said, looking at Mum and Dad.

Dad rubbed his eyes — he looked pale and tired. Mum didn't look much better.

'All this time, and she's not actually our sister,' I added.

Mae's head shot up. 'Of course she's our sister.'

Her eyes sparkled with tears that wouldn't fall.

'I know; that's not what I meant,' I added, sighing, looking at the ground, wondering what it'd be like if it swallowed me up.

162

'Poor Fatti,' said Bubblee. 'As if a woman doesn't feel displaced in her life enough.'

Oh, God. Why can't my sister let a person feel what they feel without attaching social issues to it? Everything was another type of patriarchal oppression, everything was a female experience. Why couldn't it just be a *human* experience? What was more disconcerting was seeing Mae nod in agreement. When I shot a look at her she just said: 'What? She has a point, you know.'

'We love her like our own,' said Mum. 'She is our first.'

'Mum,' said Bubblee. 'I'm sorry to say it, but you don't lie to the people you love.'

My dad looked up, eyes flashing in pain and anger. 'When you have children, Bubblee, then you will understand what a parent goes through.' He raised his finger at her. 'Until then, don't tell your amma and abba what they should or shouldn't have done.'

Bubblee retreated on the sofa.

'They said I couldn't have babies,' said Mum. When she looked up she stared right into my eyes — it was so intent, I wondered whether she knew. 'If I couldn't have a child, then what good was I as a woman?'

Bubblee scoffed. 'Wow.'

'Not now, Bubs,' I said to her, sighing.

I've grown up so used to seeing Mum shouting out rules, telling us what to do, what to wear, what *not* to wear — and it was fine, because she was our mum and you let some things go — but it was so strange to think that as we cooked together in the kitchen, or as I helped her repaint the living room or we did the gardening together, she was carrying around this secret. This weight of a hidden past. Did she ever want to tell me? Were there ever moments when she wanted to just sit down with me and say: *Faru, I have a confession to make.* Just like I sometimes wanted to tell her that I couldn't have babies. Because it would be a relief — it would be out there for everyone to know and I wouldn't have to carry it around inside me like some terrible burden.

'Things are different for you now,' said Mum. 'You have choices. But even if I had a choice, there's nothing I wanted more than to raise a child as my own,' she added.

My heart seemed to tighten and push tears to my eyes. I could understand *that*. If I adopted a baby, what would I do? Raise it so it knew that I wasn't actually its mother, waiting for the day it turned around and said it wanted to go and find its real parents? Or bring it up as my own and have something like this happen? Lies have a way of coming to the surface. It all felt a little too much like a baby factory — Mum's sister giving birth only for Mum to take it home with her, but I wondered what I'd do if Bubblee offered to have a baby for me. The extraordinary thing was that Mum ended up having all of us, one after the other, not two years after they went to Bangladesh to get Fatti.

'Fatima was a miracle because when she came into the house you all followed,' she said. 'She's the reason you're all here too.'

'I thought it was God that did all that, Mum?'

164

said Bubblee, raising her eyebrows, condescension in her voice.

Mae sighed and rolled her eyes. 'What's he going to do? Come down and hand babies over to people? He uses people as blessings for others. Loser.' She looked down at her phone and mumbled, 'Anyone can tell that Fats is obviously a blessing.'

'Try her mobile again,' said Bubblee to Mae.

She did but it went to voicemail again.

'Where can she be?' said Mae. 'It's not like she's got millions of friends.'

'Oh, Allah. Keep our baby safe,' said Dad.

'She's a thirty-year-old woman,' said Bubblee. 'If she needs her space then we have to give it to her.'

'London has hardened your heart, Bubblee,' said Mum, but without the usual indignation. Just sadness.

There were too many things going on in my head — Jay, husband, coma, baby, Fatti — all whirring around. I had to close my eyes and think. But thoughts weren't coming to me, just feelings; a mixture of sadness, anxiety and God knows what else.

'It's late. Let's all get some sleep,' I said.

'How can we sleep when we don't know where she is?' said Mum.

'Mum, please. Bubblee's right. Fatti's a grown woman. She said she's staying with someone tonight, so we're just going to have to wait to hear from her.'

Although, even as I said it I didn't quite believe it. She might be the eldest, but with Fatti

165

you never know what she's thinking. As much as I hated to admit it, was she even capable of looking after herself?

'Whatever,' said Mae as she stalked off to bed.

I didn't have the energy to ask what this particular *whatever* meant.

'At least we've got rid of Malik,' said Bubblee, also getting up and stretching her limbs.

He'd gone to stay with a friend who lived in Manchester, not least because Mum and Dad were furious with him.

'Well, whatever you might think of him,' I said, also standing, 'he's our sister's brother.'

★ ★ ★

Of course, I couldn't sleep. My hand kept on resting on my stomach — the place devoid of a baby. Now, with my husband in a hospital, how could we even try? How could we discuss the possibility of adoption with him lying in bed, fighting between life and death because of my brother? Because my husband lied to me. What was Fatti thinking and feeling right now? Did she know we still loved her? Who cared whose blood ran through her veins? She was still our Fatti who ate too much cheese in a tube and walked around trying to do nice things for people. Even though her mind and what she thought were a mystery, she was our mystery and it was up to us to solve her.

And where was Jay at this time? Would he even care that she was adopted? For years I'd made excuses for his lazy ways and that sometimes he didn't seem to feel things the way people should — but I thought it was down to being the only boy, maybe; feeling lost. But I felt lost too, and I was still here, wasn't I? I didn't run away, take someone's money, lose all of it and then not even face the consequences.

I got out of bed and walked into the passage, a dim light coming from Fatti's room. For a moment I thought she'd returned, but when I opened it, it was only Mae, on her phone.

'What are you doing here?' I asked.

She put her phone down and tucked it under the pillow. 'Nothing. Felt like sleeping in here. Just in case she came back. You know.'

'Get some sleep,' I said.

Just as I was about to close the door, Mae said: 'What they did was wrong, you know. Keeping it from her and all of us. But I get it.'

'You do?'

She straightened up in the bed and looked at the lilac paisley duvet cover. Lilac's Fatti's favourite colour.

' 'Course.' She looked up. ' 'Course you can lie to the people you love.'

Our little Mae — so much like a bird; tiny and fluttery, learning how to fly.

'You do whatever you can to keep them safe, right?' she added.

I nodded. Mae was still so young and had so many disappointments to face in life, but if I'd decided on one thing, it was that I wouldn't hide from the truth any more, or hide it from someone either.

'That can be true,' I replied. 'But sometimes

you have to ask: are you keeping them safe, or yourself?'

★ ★ ★

I woke up early the following day, thinking no-one else would be awake, but I heard faint voices coming from downstairs. Creeping down the stairs, I looked over the bannister to see Mum and Dad, sitting in the living room. Their relationship has always been so functional and connected to us that I found it odd, seeing them together like that, talking quietly.

'I should go out and look for her,' said Dad. 'Who knows how she slept.'

Mum sighed and replied: 'Maybe Bubblee is right. Let's be patient.'

Dad rubbed his eyes. 'What's happened? When did our daughters become the ones who we listened to? Has Jay phoned?'

Mum shook her head.

That bloody Jay. I sat on the steps. How come the two men I loved the most have been the most disappointing? All I've done my whole life is look after that brother of mine, and trust my husband. Have I been utterly stupid? Maybe Bubblee's had it right all this time — attach yourself to no-one and nothing, and at least you're free from this feeling of betrayal. As I sat on the steps, thinking about these things in a kind of daze, I thought about our home.

'I can sort the mortgage,' I'd say. Or, 'I can pay those bills.'

'No,' he'd reply, snatching away letters from

me, laughing. Then he'd hold on to me and say: 'I'm looking after you, for ever.'

When I told Bubblee she practically sneered, and I never understood how she didn't find it romantic. Fatti got it — she knew how lucky I was. Why did my twin sister think I was being locked in some kind of cage when I was being freed from all burdens? Ones that I needed to take up when I found out I couldn't have children, just for something to focus on.

Without Mum and Dad seeing, I got my keys and made my way to the home my husband and I made. As I pulled up to my home I saw Alice, peering from her window. She walked out of her front door in her pale-pink dressing gown, her red hair tied up in a bun.

'Farah,' she said as soon as I came out of the car.

The fresh morning air had already given me the shivers.

'How are you? How's our Mustafa doing?' she asked.

'He's the same,' I replied, not able to look her in the eye.

There was something about Alice's demeanour that was hesitant. She tightened the bow around her robe.

'You tell me if you need anything?' she said.

'Thank you,' I replied.

'It . . . whatever's happened. You know, in your family. I'm sure you'll all sort it.'

Oh, God. She knew. Everyone now knew.

'We all have our problems, after all, don't we?' she added.

I nodded as she gave me a sympathetic smile and walked back into her house.

★ ★ ★

It was funny how cold and empty it felt when I walked through the door. I went straight to the filing system in his study, flicking through folders, picking up various invoices: car insurance, health insurance, personal bank statements. I began trawling through all the statements in the past year — ridiculous outgoing payments, investing in the next thing he wanted to invent. I shook my head. There were a few payments to one J. Amir. One dated as far back as eleven months ago. That was soon after we'd found out about not being able to have children. Why had Mustafa kept Jay's working for him a secret from me for so long? I was mourning over the mother I'd never be and my husband was secretly giving our money to my brother. Every time we talked about babies, or I cried, he was throwing away our future.

I heard something come through the letterbox. There were more cards that had come through from neighbours and friends, but it was the red letter that caught my eye: *Final Notice*. I licked my lips that had suddenly gone dry as I opened the envelope. Skimming through the letter, I could barely compute what it said: *late mortgage repayments, arrears, bank loan overdue.*

Please be advised if payment isn't made in the next 60 days your house will liable for repossession.

I had to sit down, but there was no seat

nearby. Everything was happening all at once — it couldn't be possible that we'd lose our home in sixty days, surely. Not that soon. Not like this. I read the letter again, this time poring over every word. My heart seemed to catch in my throat. I rushed up the stairs, into his office and looked for the file with our mortgage details. *Statements, statements, statements.* And then I saw it. I couldn't believe it. Mustafa had re-mortgaged our house.

'No,' I said to myself, shaking my head. 'This just can't be true.'

I looked around as if expecting someone to be there, someone I could say this to; say *anything* to. But the house resounded with emptiness. And it was all his fault — my stupid husband who was on the brink of death and now destitution. He'd taken out another loan on *our* home and not told me. Another lie. Another secret. Making a fool out of me all over again. I grabbed my keys, rushed out of the house and sped down the quiet roads towards the hospital.

As I marched into his room, Bubblee and Mae were already there.

'We'd been looking for you,' said Bubblee. 'You left your phone at Mum and Dad's.'

But I hardly looked at my sisters. I just stared at my husband, lying in bed, without a care in the world, while mine was falling apart.

'*You!*' I shouted, grabbing on to the bed-rail and shaking it.

'Farah . . . ' began Bubblee.

'You unbelievably *stupid* man.' Tears of anger surfaced as I glared at his unperturbed face.

171

'Who does that? Who fritters away thousands and thousands of pounds without telling their *wife*? Who takes out another mortgage on their home without telling the person they're meant to be sharing their life with? I'm your *wife*,' I exclaimed, stabbing at my chest with my finger. 'Didn't you *think*?'

'Faru, what's happening?' I heard Mum's voice in the background, but I didn't turn around. I was too busy staring at my husband, anger rising that he wasn't waking up and fixing this.

'You'd better wake up,' I exclaimed. '*Hey!*' I shouted, leaning into Mustafa's face. 'You wake up and you fix this and you be my husband again, or I swear to God I will sell your organs to keep our home.'

'Faru,' I heard Mum's voice again. 'He's in a coma.'

I felt someone's hand on my arm, but I pushed it away.

'Did you hear that?' I spat at him. 'Your kidneys. Your lungs. I'll sell your eyes and your liver and even your scraps of flesh if they're worth anything. And all the bits of you that remain, I'll make a korma out of them and feed it to the dogs — I swear to God I will if you don't wake up. I'm not joking around.'

'Far, maybe — '

'As for your heart. No, I won't sell that. I wouldn't even give that to the dogs. I'll throw it out of this window,' I said, striding up to the window, pointing out at the grey skies. 'Creepy crawlies can nibble at the veins because *you . . .* '

172

My voice began to break. 'You *promised* you'd always be there.'

I couldn't help it; the tears were streaming down my hot, flushed face.

'And if you promise something you'd better keep it. We can't have a baby, we've almost lost our home, I will *not* lose you too.'

That's when I lost my words to sobs and my body weight to someone who'd enveloped me in their arms.

'Shhh,' came Bubblee's voice, brushing past my ear. 'You're okay, Far. You're okay.'

I felt myself being moved and settled into a chair, in which we both just about fitted.

'He'd better keep his promise,' I gasped, voice muffled against Bubblee's shoulder.

'He will,' she whispered, stroking my head. 'Of course he will.'

I stayed like that, sobbing, gasping in her arms. When I was finally able to breathe properly, I lifted my face from Bubblee's shoulder and found the room was empty, apart from my husband, still lying in bed. Could he hear what was happening? Did he have any idea at all?

'What do you know? You don't even like him,' I said.

'Just so we're clear,' she replied. 'I faulted you for marrying him, not him for loving you.'

I hadn't realised there was a difference.

'I've lost everything, Bubs.' The lump in my throat came back. 'Everything.'

'Not everything,' she replied, tightening her grip around me.

We were squashed together, unable to move, maybe even unwilling — the last time we were this close was probably in our mum's womb. The crying had given me a headache and the warmth of her arms somehow helped soothe that pain.

'Has anyone heard from Fatti?' I asked, barely able to look at Bubblee.

'No. Not yet,' she replied.

'Are you worried?'

'I don't know yet.'

She'd handed me a tissue with which I cleaned my nose as I sat up. I took a deep breath, trying to even out my breathing.

'Where'd everyone go?' I asked.

'Are you all right?' she asked.

I rubbed at a mark on my trousers. 'Maybe you were right,' I said, licking my thumb, attempting to get the stain off my trousers. 'I've spent my married life relying on him, and now look.'

We both glanced at my husband's bed.

'The house . . . ' I said.

'What?' Bubblee put her hand on my leg, covering the stain.

I looked at her. 'How could he have told such a lie for so long?'

'Unfortunately people make mistakes,' she replied. 'And plenty of them.'

I stared at the grey lino. 'Like Mum and Dad. Mustafa gave Jay that job for their sake and they didn't tell me either.'

'I don't know. Maybe they thought that despite the fact that you always stuck up for him, you knew it'd be a bad idea.'

Of course it would've been a bad idea! My husband *and* Jay? The former too trusting and the latter . . . well. I thought about all these lies I'd been told and then about Fatti. My lies might've stretched over a year, but the lies Fatti was told stretched her entire life. How must she be feeling now?

'Far,' said Bubblee. 'What did you mean when you said that thing about not being able to have a baby?'

I couldn't really remember half the things that came flying out of my mouth. Then it began to come back to me — yes, I'd declared in front of my entire family, for the first time, that I couldn't have a baby. I told Bubblee what the doctors had told Mustafa and I last year.

'Oh, Far,' she whispered, putting her arm around me. 'Why didn't you say something? My silly, stoical sister.'

My tears were making another appearance.

'You'd have thought it was just another hindrance in my life, anyway,' I replied. But without malice or anger. Just fact. That's who Bubblee is.

'All I want is for you to be happy,' she said.

I was, though. I really thought I was as happy as I could be, without being a mother, but now it felt like even the idea of happiness was impossible.

'It's just hard, you know,' she said.

'What?'

She paused. 'I want all these great things for you. For you to be out there and, I don't know . . . just *out there*. Living this amazing life.'

'I'm not like you, Bubs. I don't have all these grand ideas about life and art and things. It's always been the simple things: a home, a family. Being there for Mum and Dad.'

'I guess you're a better person than me,' she replied. 'Me and my errant ways.'

I put my hand on her leg and gave a laugh. 'You make us more interesting, at least.'

She looked at me, but it was hard to tell what she was thinking.

'We'll fix this,' she said. 'I don't how but we'll get Fatti back and sort all of this out. I promise.'

It wasn't me being negative, but I couldn't see how it was possible. Still, I didn't want to be the one to curb Bubblee's optimism — positive thinking didn't exactly come naturally to her, and so I simply nodded. In that moment I might not have had much else, but at least I had my twin sister.

13

Mae

'You didn't think.'

Mum was all over me, wagging her finger at me while I sat and looked at the ground. Jeez, Farah completely lost it in there. I've never seen anything like it — what with her being the 'together' one. I felt bad for her, but not as bad as I felt right now, with Mum towering over me and Dad standing next to her as she shook her head.

'Give me this phone,' she said, putting her hand out.

My head shot up.

'Come on, give it to me.'

'But I . . .'

So, my reflex is to say 'But I never did anything,' except this time maybe I did. Not that I meant to. It was all an accident, obviously. And why was I being punished for it now? I took the phone from my back pocket and gave it to Mum.

'No more videoing. See your sister in there?' she added, pointing down the corridor. 'All because of this phone.'

'But —'

' — Listen to your amma, Mae,' said Dad.

'What trial Allah is putting us through,' said Mum.

At least they didn't see me roll my eyes.

'Mae — just because you're the youngest, it doesn't mean you don't have to think about things.'

Which was rich, considering the fact that my parents had spent the past thirty years lying to Fatti. I'm only sixteen.

'What's your excuse?' I mumbled.

Mum leaned in. 'Hmm? See,' she said, looking at my dad. 'No respect for anything because she's been given everything.'

'Mae,' said Dad, taking the seat next to me. 'You must know how much all this has hurt your sister.'

I looked at him. 'And what about how you've hurt Fatti?'

Dad looked up at Mum, who'd not taken her eyes off me, as she added: 'No phone, you come straight home after school — '

' — But — '

' — You don't see your friends on the weekend.'

'Maybe — '

' — No,' said Mum, not letting Dad finish. 'Until she begins to think about what her actions mean, she will do as I tell her.'

All I did was tell the truth. It's not like I wanted Jay to tell me what happened — I was only trying to sort stuff out, and this is the thanks I get. How was I supposed to know that the stupid local paper would somehow find out about my blog and print a story about it? It's mental. I stayed sitting there as Mum and Dad went back into Mustafa's room. Responsibility? I didn't see anyone else going on about what Mum and Dad did, or what Farah's husband did, or what Jay did. Talk about hypocrisy. A few minutes later Bubblee came out.

'She all right?' I asked.

Bubblee stood over me, just like Dad. 'God, Mae. What a mess. On top of which, thanks to you the whole town knows what's happened.' She shook her head at me. 'You just have to say what you're feeling, don't you?'

'Oh my God,' I exclaimed. 'It was an accident. And you say stuff all the time.'

'I say it to people's face. I don't go online and broadcast it to the world. Honestly, social media will be the demise of our society.' She looked up and down the corridor as if searching for something to do — some way to start fixing all these messes. 'Have you heard from Fatti?'

I crossed my arms and fixed my stare on the meningitis poster in front of me.

'Mae?'

'No. Dad's taken my phone, hasn't he? And why would she even want to call us? Now at last she has an excuse to get rid of us. Who can blame her?'

'You're being a brat.'

'And you're being a cow.'

She paused. 'One day, Mae, maybe you'll see that not everything is about you.'

Since when? Nothing is ever about me.

'Anyway, come on. I'm taking you to school. You've missed enough days.'

But I was too angry to move.

'Mae. Get up. I don't have time for this. Our

179

sister's missing and another one's about to lose everything.'

Our sister? As if she cared about Fatti more than I did. As if she had any idea about who she was or the things she felt. What a joke.

'Whatever,' I said as we made our way out of the hospital so I could finally be in school; a place where at least I wasn't ignored.

★ ★ ★

It's not like paranoia was ever my thing. Fatti was insecure enough for all of us. Who cared what people thought or said? But when I walked down the school corridor, the break-time bell having just rung, I swear everyone's eyes were on me; people covering their mouth to whisper things, staring then turning away as soon as I looked at them.

'Oi, Amir,' someone called out.

I turned around to see Anabelle at the end of the corridor, her skirt hitched up to her arse.

'Your family not in jail yet?' she said.

She sauntered up towards me, her bestie by her side, chewing gum, looking like a skank. That's what happens when you live on e-numbers. Eat a salad now and again, for God's sake.

'You've got to be real thick to end up giving your family secret away in the newspaper — got too big for your plimsolls, didn't you, Miss I-have-five-thousand-YouTube-subscribers.'

'Don't come too close,' I said. 'Your breath stinks.'

'Says curry-breath.'

Up close I could see her freckles, the pock-mark next to her nose, her green eyes wild with what I'd call too much sugar.

'Original,' I said.

It wasn't, but it still made my face flush because everyone was watching, their lips curled into a smile. I'd spent most of my school life being mediocre — not too popular but not exactly worthy of being picked on — despite the fact that I'm one of about seven brown people in the school — but it didn't seem that way any more with this pack of wolves. Annabelle stepped towards me and it was all I could do not to take a step back, when a teacher came walking down.

'What's happening here then? Ah, Mae.' Mrs Brown looked at me with a tight smile, her wrinkles etched in her skin. 'Good to see you back in school. Annabelle, will you please pull your skirt down and wear your tie straight.'

Everyone dispersed as Mrs Brown looked down at me with her withered face.

'Now, how's your brother-in-law?' she asked.

'Still a human log,' I said, which might've sounded mean, but it's not as if she really cared.

'Mae — I really wish you wouldn't sound so *irreverent* all the time.'

But what were the options, eh, Mrs Brown? Sit there and cry like my sisters, Farah and Fatti? Or be a rage-against-the-world machine, like Bubblee? You'd have thought that at least my teachers would appreciate me putting my energies towards being creative. Turns out they're as bad as my family.

'I realise you must be going through a very difficult time right now,' she continued. 'But if you need to talk about anything, or tell me about any . . . ' Her eyes flicked towards a crowd of girls I could hear behind me. ' . . . *unsavoury* behaviour, then you should know you can come to my office. Okay?'

She peered at me over her black-rimmed glasses.

'Yeah. Thanks, Miss.'

Maybe she did care. Maybe hanging around with Bubblee too much has worn off on me.

'It's yes, dear. And not to worry. Now, off you go to class. Off you *all* go to class,' she added to the people behind me.

By the end of school, it was clear that everyone thought my family was some kind of blight on Wyvernage.

'All right, Kelly?' I said to my friend of three years in science, who then moved her stuff and sat with Anabelle and her cronies.

I guess it was my first lesson in wolf-pack mentality. What a waste of a human being, I thought, tears stinging my eyes. Is this how Fatti felt? Isolated from everyone? Even though no-one gave her a reason to feel that way, you can't help feelings, can you? That's the point. All I heard the entire lesson was snickering with eyes darting towards me, no-one taking the seat next to me.

Lunch wasn't much better. I sat with a bunch of people from media studies and suddenly someone had to use the bathroom or had detention or whatever. I shook my head at how unoriginal people were. And yet, I looked at my quinoa salad and wanted to cry because it was like I had no-one. No friends, no family — not any that were speaking to me, anyway — and no Fatti.

'What idiots.' Sarah came and put her tray down, taking the seat opposite me. She looked over at Annabelle and her minions. 'In ten years she's going to be stacking shelves for a living.'

I looked at Sarah, her blonde hair in a high pony as she picked up her sandwich.

'It's my penance,' I said, feeling so grateful I could've leaned over and hugged her. 'Serves me right for thinking it was a good idea to pour out my feelings on social media.'

'Are you joking?' she said. 'It's the most exciting thing to happen around here in decades. We should all be buying you drinks. Except you don't drink.'

'Do you have any idea what it does to your liver?'

'All right, Amir?' Sanjay came and sat next to me. 'Don't think I like you or anything. My mum said I have to be nice to you because she's friends with your sister.'

'I'm utterly grateful,' I said, bowing my head towards him.

'There, there, Babba,' he replied, putting on an Indian accent as he patted my head. 'Good girl.'

I noticed Sarah blush as he smiled at her. Great, that's all I needed, Romeo and bloody Juliet.

Still, it was mental how everything outside

these school gates had changed but everything inside was just the same. Students really do live in their own little bubble. I wondered where Fatti was. I get her being annoyed and all, but didn't she know that we'd be worried? Didn't she miss *me*, at least?

'Your brother sounds a bit wild,' said Anne, who'd come scampering to our table and sat next to Sarah. 'Is he single?' she asked, her eyes widening.

I took a sip of my smoothie. 'He's a waste,' I replied.

My whole family was actually, but it was too depressing to tell everyone that.

'Still,' she said, leaning over the table, 'that was a good blog.'

'It was all right, you know,' added Sanjay, loosening his tie. 'I read the whole thing without falling asleep.'

Sarah laughed as I mumbled a thanks.

'I mean,' Anne added, 'I was like, *Mae should be a writer.*'

'She takes cool videos,' replied Sarah. 'She doesn't sit at her laptop writing stories.'

'Yeah, but imagine if she did both,' said Anne.

It was almost as if I wasn't there.

'You get these two arts and you stick them together,' she added, clamping her hands together.

'Oh, yeah? How'd that work then, genius?' replied Sarah.

'I don't know. She's the one with all that creative stuff going on.'

Anne might be a little dim sometimes but at

184

least she's nice. She made me smile, anyway.

'Thanks,' I said.

'Oh my God,' Anne exclaimed as Sarah had to lean back. 'You could get famous and we'd be like your groupies.'

Sarah started laughing. 'Sanjay could be our minion.'

'I've got better things to do with my life, thanks,' he said.

'What do you mean?' said Sarah. 'You can roll out the red carpet wherever we go. Prostrate before us, like the humble servant you are.'

'I'm leaving this table,' he said, about to take his tray before Sarah stopped him.

'Please take your leave first, lowly one,' she said.

Sarah and Anne laughed as I glimpsed Anabelle scowling at our table.

'Stop it!' Anne said, holding on to her legs. 'I'll wet myself.'

'My mum seriously owes me,' he added, shaking his head.

The idea of Anne wetting herself made me and Sarah laugh. For a moment, looking at Sarah, Anne and Sanjay, I forgot there was anything wrong, then I remembered Fatti and the thought entered my head: when was the last time I laughed like this with all of my sisters?

* * *

As I watched the clock on the classroom wall tick I wasn't sure what was worse — staying in school or being home. I looked out for Sarah, Anne or

185

Sanjay as everyone flooded out of the school gates but couldn't see any of them.

'Yeah, with any luck he'll be put in jail for taking money from his own family,' I heard Anabelle's raised voice as she pushed past me down the road away from the school. *What a waster.* I ignored it because it's not like anything intelligent ever came out of her mouth. She was into riling people and getting riled isn't really my thing; like I've said before, I leave excessive emotions to the rest of my family. When her pack laughed at her remark, it might've been useful if I had my phone — just to pretend to have something else to concentrate on.

'It's a disgrace, really,' she continued. 'But not exactly surprising when you think about where they come from.'

I bit my tongue, told myself to cool down and not get worked up over words from a loser. I wanted to push ahead — I could walk faster than any of them, but their crowd was too big and I'd have bumped shoulders with someone, for sure. It's not like hyenas need an excuse to attack.

'People who use their family dramas to get more followers are beyond disgusting,' she added, looking back at me. 'I mean, talk about desperate. A bit like her fat sister.'

She could've called me all the names under the sun and I'd have just rolled my eyes, but those words; mentioning *my* sister. Something boiled inside me that didn't bother to check with my brain or logic. I lunged at Annabelle from behind, gripping her around her neck, pulling her back as we both fell to the floor.

186

'You take that back,' I shouted, pulling at her hair. 'You take that back!'

'Oh my God, *fight!*' someone called out.

'Get off!' she exclaimed, pushing at my chest to try and knock me back.

The more she wrestled, the angrier I got, and it turns out I'm a lot stronger than I look. Fat sister? *Fat* sister? I pulled her hair again, and some of it ripped out.

'My hair! The stupid cow's gone and torn out my hair,' she cried, grabbing her head as I sat on top of her, her locks in my hand.

Before I could throw her hair back and hit her, I felt someone grab me from around the waist and pull me up.

'That stupid cow! Call a teacher,' she cried.

I kicked my legs in the air as I was turned around and dragged through the crowds, away from the fight scene.

'Stop kicking,' said a voice that was only now beginning to compute. People were still staring at me, but maybe because it looked like I was being kidnapped.

'What the . . . ?' I looked back and it was Malik. 'What are *you* doing here?' I said, practically shouting still.

Malik let go of me as he looked around. He smiled at a few students who'd probably missed the fight because they didn't look like wild, excitable dogs.

'Calm down, little Mae,' he said, putting up his hands. 'Come on, let's walk.'

I was too angry to argue but angry enough to stomp with him, especially since he called me little Mae. I mean, if that's not going to get your goat, what is? We walked in silence for about ten minutes. I wanted to go back and punch Annabelle in the face. I wanted to rip *all* of her hair out. She can say what she likes about me, but my *sister*? I was still thinking of ways I could get my revenge on her when we got to the park. Malik made me take a seat on a bench before sitting down next to me. My breathing was still coming in short gasps as I felt the adrenaline pumping through me. If Annabelle were in front of me now, I'd lunge at her again.

'Here,' he said, 'have some water.'

I saw a bottle of water appear under my nose but ignored it. 'Okay,' he added.

That was how we sat for a while until it got a bit ridiculous. I snatched my bag and made to walk home.

'Wait,' he said.

I stopped.

'Sit back down. Please.'

I did, because like I said, I was too angry to argue, but it's not as if I wanted to hear what he had to say. Forget Annabelle. He's the reason Fatti had run off somewhere.

'What are you even doing here?' I said.

'I was worried about you,' he said.

'Why?' I asked, looking at him for his ulterior motive. As if anybody ever actually worries about me. Not that I care, obviously.

'Because my sister worries about you.'

'*Your* sister?' I said.

That was rich, wasn't it? Talk about jumping on the Fatti bandwagon.

188

'She is my sister,' he replied, calmly. 'We have the same blood; the same parents.'

'Blood doesn't make you family.'

He smiled and looked at the grass peppered with daisies. 'But it makes you something. It creates a bond, yes?' I shrugged. Whatever. 'Things aren't going so well at school?' I shrugged again.

'Mae, come on, you can put this sullen teenage act on, but you're better than that. You're a bright person — talk to me as if I understand that.'

I just wanted to storm off and shout: *What the hell do you know about anything!* Because it can take a lot out of you; being all *whatever*. More energy than people can guess.

'It was nothing. It was my first day back, and turns out my school is full of ignoramuses,' I said.

He looked confused.

'Stupid people,' I said.

'Ah, yes, yes. Students are never easy.'

He paused as we both looked at some children running around in the distance, playing with a Frisbee.

'Listen,' he continued. 'I'm sorry the way things happened. I didn't think she'd run away like that.'

'It's like, you could've given her some warning. Or Mum and Dad some warning,' I said. 'A hospital room where our brother-in-law's lying in a coma isn't exactly the best place to be all: *Yeah, by the way, let's tell everyone the truth about who's really in the picture. Oh, and*

189

look. You're adopted.'

'I know, I know. But it was so frustrating for me. The truth is, I'd only found out about Fatima days before the accident.'

I looked at him. 'Really?'

In all the mental-ness of comas, adoption and running away, I realised we didn't actually know about how Malik knew. It was pretty obvious Mustafa wouldn't have known because there's no way he'd have kept it from Farah. Though, given he lied about other things, who knows?

'Really,' he replied. He blew out a puff of air as he shook his head. 'I was very angry with my parents. When I told my brothers in Bangladesh they were surprised and asked about it but weren't angry like me. But then I'd always wanted a sister.' He nudged me as he added: 'I was always jealous of your brother Jay for having four. Anyway, I'd tried to get hold of Mustafa but he was busy, not happy with me because I couldn't lend him money he'd asked for, and he kept saying he'd call me back. When we got the call from your parents, after the shock of finding out about Mustafa's coma, I thought maybe this was fate. Maybe my brother's accident is a way for me to finally meet my sister.' He rested his arm on the back of the bench and looked at me.

'What did your parents say?'

He paused. 'I don't think now's the time to talk about that.'

'Malik . . . oops, sorry. Malik *Baia*, of course — I think we all know there's never a right time for anything.'

He smiled and looked at me like you might

look at a puppy. Fondly. It was annoying but not so annoying that I wanted to tell him to go and do one.

When he didn't speak I said: 'So tell me what you said to them.'

He considered it for a moment. 'You know your amma couldn't have babies?'

I nodded. 'Crazy, isn't it? Considering what came after.'

'I didn't think it was a good enough reason,' he replied. 'Passing around a baby like this, without thinking about the consequences. Maybe if it hadn't been done in the family it would've been more understandable.'

'How?' I asked. 'Don't get me wrong, it's not like I think it was a genius idea, but don't you think if you're going to adopt a baby it's better if it belongs to someone you know rather than, like, a complete stranger?'

'Don't you English people have the saying: too close to home?'

I nodded, thinking about this. 'I suppose. So,' I added, 'your parents didn't say much?'

I wanted to know what they thought, how they felt.

He paused before answering. 'You'll find out in life that people disappoint you in a hundred different ways, Mae. And don't be fooled,' he said, looking at me and raising his eyebrows. 'You'll disappoint people just as much. But disappointment in your parents is a pain very different to anything else.'

'Yeah, I get it,' I said, nodding. 'It's like, they're the people you want to love the most, but then they can make it the most difficult. I mean, it's whatever, because you're going to love them anyway, but you just wish they were more what you wanted them to be. Like, you wish they could see you. Or see themselves,' I added, taking the bottle of water he'd put down between us.

I took a sip as he nodded. 'You are wise, Mae. Make sure you remember that.'

I snorted through the water. 'I'm just a kid. What do I know?'

'More than a lot of people. I think even you realise that. I hope when you're older you will have the confidence to know it.'

I screwed the lid back on the water. 'Thanks. So,' I said, handing the bottle back to him, 'do you fancy my sister, Bubblee?'

He got up. 'Time to go home now, I think.'

'Who could blame you?' I replied, putting my bag over my shoulder. 'She's hot. I mean, you know as well as I do, Mal Baia, that she's a handful, but maybe you like that.'

I considered him. Sure, he had that accent, but he was all-right looking — kind of manly with the whole angular feature thing going on.

'Maybe with time you'll also learn to not say everything that comes to your mind,' he said as we walked towards home.

'I mean, you could try to tame her, but it wouldn't go down very well; plus, you'd need like a proper thought-out plan for that, which just makes the whole thing creepy. Not to mention oppressive. And she'd see through it in seconds, because let's face it,' I said, keeping up with his quick steps, 'you're not her favourite person on the planet.'

'Here, have some more water,' he said, handing me the bottle. 'And maybe you can focus your ideas on how to find my sister.'

I shot him a look.

'Sorry . . . *our* sister,' he said.

'Aren't you going to come in?' I asked when we stopped at the end of my road.

'I'll come soon, but for now will stay with my friend.'

'You can't ignore my parents for ever, you know.'

He smiled. 'I know, little Mae, but let's all take one step at a time.'

'All right. Can we begin with you not calling me *little Mae*? It's weird.'

'Oh,' he said, looking embarrassed.

'Don't worry, Mal Baia. You'll get used to being around lots of women. One day.'

* * *

When I got home I went straight to my room. No-one was home anyway. Not having my phone was like missing a limb or something. I got all fidgety and I'd reach out for something, only I'd realise what I was reaching out for wasn't there.

I opened up my laptop and went into my video file. There were tens of hours of videos on this thing. I flicked back to the video, right before Mustafa's accident and the day Fatti failed her twenty thousandth driving test. I laughed at her eyes shifting around as she's trying to make sure no-one sees her squirt cheese into her mouth. There's another bit with Mum and Dad looking at her; Mum's laughing and Dad . . . I zoom into his face. He's not exactly a laugher, but there's this sparkle in his eyes. I forwarded a bit to where I come into the shot because I've let the camera rest on the mantelpiece and Dad's explaining a bit of maths homework to me. There's Farah, kissing him on the top of his head before she ruffles my hair. Another clip and Bubblee's in the room, frowning while Fatti and me are trying to suppress laughing at her. Then there's the bit where we're all in hospital — everyone's face as grey as the hospital walls. I look at the time on the video. We all sat in the same place for five hours. I don't even think we said much to each other. Just Dad bringing in tea for everyone; Mum counting her rosary beads; Bubblee probably texting her friend, Sasha. Mum leans into Dad's ear and he looks over at Bubblee and nods while Mum seems to say a prayer and looks up at, I reckon, God.

'Mae,' comes Fatti's voice. 'Put the camera away. Now's not the time.'

I smile at her serious tone. As I jump from clip to clip there aren't that many moments that I'm alone — that Mum isn't asking about Farah, or Bubblee isn't wondering about Dad, or Farah isn't mentioning Jay, and I'm not being sent from one person to the next. There's Malik, taking over tea duties. *As if* he doesn't fancy Bubblee, the amount he looks over at her. This weird feeling fleeted in my chest. It's not the best, always being told where to go or what to do, but then, looking at these clips and frames, zooming in and out of their changing faces, at least I know I always will have somewhere to go and something to do.

That's when I opened my Gmail tab and emailed Fatti.

★ ★ ★

I hadn't expected her to write back that quick, so when I saw her name pop up on-screen, I almost leapt at my laptop.

From: Amir, Fatima
To: Amir, Mae
Subject: Re: Where are you?

All right. Let's meet.

I breathed an internal sigh of relief, but after the initial relief, I thought: she could've written more. I'd asked how she was, where she was, what she was thinking. I told her what's going on at the house and that everyone's worried about her, but no response to that. Maybe she didn't care any more? I let her know that I didn't have my phone, but that I'd see her at the park the following day, after school. Whether I'd make it through school was something else.

After my chat with Malik in the park, I went back into school completely prepared to apologise to that sorry excuse for a human, Anabelle, for, you know, ripping her hair out. I didn't see her until she pushed past me so hard I

195

fell on my knees in the middle of the corridor. Everyone laughed as I tried to pick myself up, but I stumbled because I think I did something to my knee as I fell.

'Where you belong,' she sniped as she turned around and gave a disgusted look.

So, I decided I'd apologise to her when hell froze over, which according to Mum, is never going to happen. It was pathetic, really. I hoped Sarah or Anne or Sanjay would be around somewhere to help me out. But no — people just stood around snickering, not even offering a hand. It was humiliating, and for I think the first time in my life, I felt lonely — as if there was nothing to protect me or help me, and I missed Fatti so much, I couldn't wait to see her. It was the only thing that got me through the day.

I rushed to the park after school and waited at the benches near the swings, just like we'd agreed. Fifteen minutes passed. Then another ten. Before I knew it I'd been waiting for forty-five minutes. It wasn't like her not to turn up when she promised. Not if she promised *me*, anyway. Was I no longer her sister just because we didn't have the same parents? I had to hold back the tears that stung my eyes because I'd have expected it from anyone but Fatti. I'd been waiting a full hour as I looked around for her again and I began to realise that maybe she wouldn't come after all, and that I wasn't sure when I'd see her again. But when I stood up, there she was, fiddling with her hands near the sycamore tree, gazing at me.

'Sorry I'm late,' she said, when I walked up to her.

I wasn't sure whether to hug her. We're not really the hugging type in our family — but then these weren't normal circumstances, and I was so relieved to see her I wanted to just wrap my arms around her. Just so she knew she *was* still my sister, and just so I could see if she felt the same way. She folded her arms.

'I was about to leave,' I replied. 'I should've known you wouldn't stand me up.'

When she didn't speak I asked where she'd been staying.

'At a friend's.'

'What friend?' I said, sounding more unconvinced than I'd meant to.

'I *do* have friends,' she said, reddening.

'Yeah, yeah. Just wondered. That's all.'

There was no point in making her feel crappier than she already did.

'Listen,' I said, matter-of-factly, because, let's be honest, Fatti and me never have done emotional, 'when are you coming home? Mum and Dad are going berserk, Farah's losing the plot and Bubblee's even more annoying than usual.'

'What do you mean, 'losing the plot'?' she asked.

'You know. Like, mental. Shouting at Mustafa when he can't hear a word and going off on one about selling his organs and making a korma out of them.'

'Farah? Shouting?'

'Exactly,' I responded.

'What do you mean, selling his organs?' she asked. I recreated the scene at the hospital for Fatti, who looked at me in shock.

'Properly crazy,' I summed up.

'Don't say crazy,' she said. 'She's been through a lot.' The wind rustled the leaves in the trees. It was a little cold in the shade.

'Yeah, well — looks like she and Bubblee don't hate each other as much, at least,' I said.

'Really?' she asked as she smiled.

I nodded. 'So have you thought about it then? Coming home?' I said.

She looked at the ground. I wondered if she was crying but when she looked up she didn't even look upset.

'I can't come home,' she said.

I folded my arms. 'What do you mean?'

She looked around the park, up at the sky, lost in some thought. 'It's not . . . it's not really *home* is it?'

What was she talking about?

'Of course it's home, you idiot. What else is the place where you've lived and grown up?' I said.

'Idiot?' she said.

'What, now you're going to act all older sister on me?'

She started wringing her hands. As she slouched, I noticed her stomach bulge and I suddenly thought of that Annabelle. It made me want to pull out the rest of the hair on her head.

'Look, come home and Mum and Dad will explain everything. It was all mental and they know they should've told you but they made a mistake. People make mistakes, don't they?'

She shrugged.

'You know that Mum couldn't have babies?' I said.

She looked at me — clearly it hadn't occurred to her before.

'But she had all of you afterwards?'

'Yeah, Dad said you were the miracle that made us possible.'

Her features softened then, her eyes becoming watery with tears.

'So I was given up to her?' I nodded.

'I don't know how someone could do that,' she said, looking at the ground.

I realised that she didn't know that Farah couldn't have babies. It seemed like the right time to tell her, so I did. She looked so mortified at the fact that it was as if someone had told her *she* couldn't have babies.

'Oh no,' she said. 'That's . . . that's *awful*.'

'I know,' I replied.

She looked out into space. 'All this time she was hiding it from everyone. And I . . . '

'What?'

She shook her head. 'Nothing. Just that I thought she had it all.'

We sat in silence for a while before I said: 'What are you going to do then?'

When she didn't reply I couldn't help but get annoyed.

'*Say* something then,' I said.

Maybe I should've been nicer to her but everything was making me angry. She needed to see the videos I'd taken, she had to see that it didn't matter if she was adopted or not.

'I've got something to show you when you come home. You'll see for yourself,' I said.

'Mae,' she said. 'I'm not coming home.'

'What do you mean not coming home?' I asked. 'Where else are can you go?'

'I'm going to Bangladesh,' she replied.

'*What?* Bangladesh? As in the country?'

Then she explained that she'd already booked her tickets and was going home to see the people that had given birth to her.

'To meet my family,' she added.

'*Family?* Just because you share DNA? And what are we? Chopped liver?'

'You don't get it, Mae. I always felt like the odd one out, and now I finally understand why. It's a relief. For so many years I thought there was something wrong with me, but actually, it was because I wasn't in the right place. I never did belong here.'

'Right,' I said. 'So you belong in a place you haven't visited for, like, twenty-five years, with people who you don't know from Adam?'

'I don't expect you to understand.'

I didn't understand. It's not as if I didn't get that the whole thing was a shock and that she should be angry. Of course she should be raging. And she should come home and shout at our parents and throw things to show her rage, like a normal person. She shouldn't get on a plane and look for a new place to belong, though. What about the rest of us? What about me? She was going to leave the people who loved her for these people who'd decided to give her away.

'No, it all makes perfect sense,' I said.

'Mae . . . '

'You don't even have your passport or anything.'

'That's what I needed to ask you. I need you to go home and get some things for me. And you can't tell anyone what I'm about to do. I'll tell them myself.'

Great. More lies for other people. As if I hadn't got in enough trouble the first time around.

'Please, Mae. I need you to do this for me.'

She looked at me with those puppy-dog eyes she gets sometimes, which makes it impossible to be angry at her.

'When will you be back?'

'I don't know.'

I heard some kids shouting in the background as a dog was chasing a ball. The sky was getting overcast and I wondered: *Why is everyone just getting on with life as if everything is normal, when it's all changing?*

'Are you even coming back?'

Tucking her hair behind her ear, she replied: 'I don't know.' She paused. 'I mean, what would I be coming back to?'

'But . . . but, you have to pass your driving test.'

It was the first time she laughed. It kind of made me laugh as well.

'I've waited this long.'

I went to sit down, leaning against the bark of the tree. She came and sat next to me as I picked up a twig.

'Don't be angry,' she said.

'Don't act like a brat, you mean.'

I felt her arm around me. 'You were never a brat.'

She was the one who was meant to cry, but tears came to my eyes. I should've been the one comforting her. I *was* a brat. Bubblee was right. But with Fatti gone, who'd be left to tell me otherwise? How was I meant to tell Fatti that I needed her more than she realised? More than *I* realised.

'I'm not angry, Fats.'

We both sat in silence for a while before she asked how my assignment was going. I just shrugged, said it was fine. I couldn't explain to her what it felt like when I watched back all those clips — you had to see it to feel it. And I wasn't about to tell her what was going on at school. She'd end up worrying about me, and actually, sometimes it's best to save the people you care about from getting upset.

'Aren't you worried about what's going to happen to Mustafa?' I said. 'Your brother?'

The words didn't come out very easily.

'Of course, but me being here or in Bangladesh won't make a difference.'

'And what about Malik?'

She picked at her fingernails, and I had to smack her hands.

'Gross,' I said.

Fatti sat on them instead, but she didn't look at me.

'He's not staying with us any more, you know. He's at some friend's house,' I said.

When she didn't answer, I added: 'Listen, I know it's gross because you fancied your brother. I mean, seriously *vom*.'

'Oh, Mae, don't,' she said, screwing her face as if she'd throw up.

'But it's not like you knew.'

'I don't want to talk about it,' she replied.

'Fine,' I said. 'Mum and Dad will be upset, you know.'

She nodded. 'I know. But I need to do this.'

You can't argue with needs, can you?

'Oh, here,' I said, reaching into my bag.

I handed her the tube of cheese. She laughed and finally those tears made an appearance — she was still the same Fatti.

'See?' she said. 'If you really were a brat then you'd have got me celery sticks.'

She looked at me and pulled me into a hug. That's where we sat for the next half an hour, in silence, watching the clouds pass over us.

14

Fatima

You know that moment, the one you've waited for forever? The one you've seen in films and witnessed in other people's lives — while you're eating cheese or failing another driving test — where people realise: *This is it. This is where my life begins.* Sitting on the aeroplane, looking out of the small window as we travelled down the runway, ready to leave England behind, was that moment for me. It was the first time in weeks I didn't feel sad. Maybe it was the first time in thirty years. My life was finally going to begin. I wasn't just watching things change for other people while I looked through some kind of glass window.

Mae kept calling me to try and change my mind. She told me that she'd spoken to Malik and he said I should wait. That he'd come with me to Bangladesh because I should have some kind of support, and we just needed to see first how much longer it might be until Mustafa came out of his coma. What if he never came out of it, though? Plus, the idea of spending a whole plane journey with Malik made me feel sick. All those feelings I had when I first met him came back with each memory, except in reverse form. It'd take me a while to get over that. Anyway, hadn't I waited enough already? I had to explain to

Mae: when you're born it's just you and your mum and that's how I wanted it to be. I was going to be born again.

She told me to come to the house to speak to Mum and Dad about what I was about to do. Dad was pacing the garden alone when they weren't all at the hospital. Mum did nothing but pray. Even when they weren't saying anything, Mae said you could tell they were thinking about me. I didn't want to seem ungrateful, but I couldn't bring myself to look at them. If I looked at them I knew I'd feel guilty — as if I was betraying them, even though, really, they'd betrayed me. I'm not pitying myself, I'm just stating the fact. If I looked into Dad's eyes, or Mum's concerned face, my resolve would've wobbled. I didn't want to be the Fatti that wobbled. I wanted to be like Bubblee — unapologetic. And I could see myself apologising to them the minute I told them I was leaving to go to Kadi Pur, Sylhet, Bangladesh. So, I called them instead.

'Fatti, my daughter,' said Mum with a tremble in her voice, so I knew she was about to cry. 'Where are you, Fatti? Come home. I have cooked so many nice things for you. I'm buying your prawns every day in case you come home.'

It should've been nice to hear, but it just annoyed me. *I don't want to be the Fatti who eats prawns and cheese from a tube any more.*

'How's Mustafa?' I asked. 'Is there any progress?'

'He is the same. Everything has changed but he is the same,' said Mum.

205

Dad's voice then came on the phone.

'Babba, how are you? Are you okay? Where are you? Tell me and I will come pick you up. Your amma and I have been so worried for you. You should come and see your brother-in-law. He might be sleeping but he will know who is and isn't there.'

'Please, don't, Ab — ' I stopped myself because he wasn't really my dad, was he? Even though the sound of his voice made me want to snuggle into his arms like I did when I was a child. 'I mean, I'm okay. I'm safe. I promise. As for Mustafa, tell Mum I'm praying for him.'

This time I wasn't lying — I was actually praying for him. What else could I do from a distance?

'When are you coming home?' he said. 'Your sisters, your amma, they all miss you. *I* miss you.'

Imagine if I heard that in person? I'd never have left. I could hear Mum in the background, who kept on asking questions. So I told him where I was going. He passed the message on to Mum.

'What do you mean, you're going to Bangladesh?' said Mum, taking over the phone.

'I need to meet them. The woman who gave birth to me. She's your sister,' I added.

'My sister,' replied Mum. 'Who is she now? I don't know. It's been so many years since I've seen her.'

I suppose now I understood a little better why. Perhaps it was too hard for my biological mum to keep in communication with the woman she'd given her child to. Maybe regret led to distance.

'Think about this,' said Mum. 'We are your family, Fatti. And how are you going to go, all alone?'

'Malik's told his parents and someone will pick me up from the airport — and anyway, I'm an adult,' I added. 'I'm able to travel alone.'

There was some muffling as I heard Dad's voice again. 'At least come and see us once before you leave.'

I paused. 'No, I'm sorry.'

'When will you come back from Bangladesh?' he asked.

'I don't know.'

I heard him sigh. 'Fatti, when did your heart become so hard?'

It was too much. *My* heart was hard? What did they expect? For me to be angry for a little while and then just forget they'd lied to me? Did they think I wouldn't want to know who I really was? Who my parents really were? Did they think I wouldn't want to speak to my biological mum and see how much of her was in me? Or that I'd not want to sit and listen to my biological dad and figure out how many characteristics we shared? Whether we liked the same food or music or *whatever*.

'When I found out the people I thought were my parents lied to me,' I said, and without waiting to hear another word, I gently put the phone down.

When I turned around, there was Ash. I hadn't heard him come into the house and wasn't sure how much of my conversation he'd heard.

'Sorry,' he said. 'I should've knocked.'

'I'm sorry,' I replied. 'It's your house. You shouldn't have to knock. My parents,' I said, holding my phone up.

'Ah.'

'Told them I was going to Bangladesh.'

'How'd they take it?'

I put my phone down and sat on the sofa.

'That well?' he asked.

'Why are they so shocked that I want to do this? All this time you think you know your parents and actually, you realise, you might not have been living in the same world.'

'I think that can be true of a lot of relationships, to be honest,' he replied, taking the seat next to me.

I know it's his home, but being so close to him felt weird — I wished he'd sat on the sofa opposite.

'You talk as if I'm the one in the wrong,' I said, lowering my voice and gaze.

Sometimes it just feels as if no-one's really on your side. And the ones that are, like Mae, aren't there to offer the comfort you need.

'Hey,' he said, putting his hand on mine. 'You have to remember I'm a parent, not a person who's discovered they were adopted.' He sighed, holding on to my hand that I involuntarily pressed into his. 'I'm not saying you're in the wrong. I'm just saying that right now they're scared they're going to lose you.'

'I can't not meet my real parents just to make my adoptive parents feel safe. *They're* the adults. They're the ones who should've seen this coming. They shouldn't have lied to me all this time.'

'Would your decision have been different?'

He rubbed my hand with his thumb and I wanted to lean into him; just to rest my head against his shoulders.

'Maybe not, but at least they'd have been honest.'

'Hmm,' he said, nodding. 'Well, I'll tell you something, being a parent hurts. Even when your children are happy and things are going well there's always this fear of what might go wrong and how you're going to protect them from it if it does. And then there's the disappointment in yourself when you know you can't. The pain of having to see these little humans you brought up with so much love and care go through something you can do nothing about. Even if you didn't believe in God, you might turn to him out of desperation.' He looked at me. 'You're not their only child, but it seems to me they've loved you just as much as the rest. No?'

It wasn't something I could disagree with. I looked at him and shrugged. 'Maybe love isn't enough.'

He looked at me, confused. 'That doesn't sound like the Fatima I know.'

'Maybe I don't want to be that Fatima.'

He took a deep breath. 'Well,' he said, pursing his lips as if in sympathy, 'that would be the most tragic thing out of this whole situation.'

What did that mean? I closed my eyes, as the plane took flight, trying to forget about what was past so I could focus on the future. I just knew it was going to be different. I could feel it in my very bones.

★ ★ ★

As I stepped out of the plane I hadn't realised how the heat would sweep the air from my lungs. But there was no time to catch my breath, as a woman with her family behind me told me to move faster.

'Sorry, sorry,' I said, desperately trying to walk down the stairs of the plane with my hand luggage while making sure I didn't trip on my long kaftan. My parents would see: I was Western, but I'd retained parts of my culture — parts of *them*.

I'd wanted my arrival to be a surprise, just to see the look on their faces: that surprise, mixed with disbelief, followed by relief that their daughter had finally come home. Mae had called me from a number I didn't recognise and before I knew it, she'd handed the phone over to Malik.

'Fatima. How are you?'

'Oh. Fine. Thanks,' I said, wanting to hang up immediately.

'Good. That is very good. Now listen, I've already told my parents you'll be coming to Bangladesh.'

'Oh.'

'It's better this way. Families don't like surprises,' he said. 'Now, are you sure you want to go alone?'

'Yes. Definitely,' I replied. 'What did they say when you told them? How did they sound?'

210

Because no-one gives away a baby just like that. I thought of Farah and whether I would do the same for her: if I had children and could make her happy by giving her one of them, would I?

'You will see when you meet them,' he replied. 'And you are comfortable, where you are staying?'

'Yes. Ashraf's been a good friend,' I said.

'Hmm. Fatima, I don't think it is proper for you to be spending so much time with a man who's not family.'

I looked over at Ash who was writing out a cheque and drinking his tea. He smiled at me as I smiled back. It felt ironic that Malik should be telling a girl who was given away at birth about what's proper or not, but I suppose this is what having a brother who's actually there, as opposed to Jay, is about.

'Take care of yourself,' he added.

'Thank you,' I replied.

I wanted to say more, but I wasn't sure what, so I just said bye and put the phone down.

I didn't understand the bustle here; why people had to shove me out of the way, why no-one was queuing. I wiped my brow with the scarf I'd placed over my head as I left the plane, but I'd only walk another step and beads of sweat would be forming on my upper lip and forehead again. All the while my eyes were darting everywhere, looking for something familiar. The faces in view confused the pictures I'd seen of my biological parents — everyone seemed to potentially be my mum and dad. It didn't help that my heart was beating so fast I thought it might burst through my chest. *Settle down, settle down.* But it's hard to settle anything in clamour. I stood in the middle of the airport, turning around, waiting to be recognised.

'Affa?'

I whipped around to see who'd called me sister. It was a young boy, no more than seventeen, holding a sign in Bengali. I recognised a few of the letters — it seemed to spell Fatima.

'Fatima Affa?' he added.

I nodded, looking over his shoulder, wondering who he might be with.

'Come with me,' he replied, taking my bags.

He didn't give me much of a chance to ask who he was before he led the way, the veins in his skinny arms protruding as he carried my bags and weaved effortlessly through the crowds. Even without the bags I was stumbling and breaking into a semi-jog just to keep up. We came into the open where people seemed to scatter but the sun's bright light was the next thing to accost me. My footsteps stopped at the sight I saw: skeletal, elderly men and women, begging for money; malnourished children, holding out their hands for coins. For a minute I thought I'd entered into a film set — it was so different to where I'd been just under ten hours ago. It took a few moments before my brain managed to tell my feet to begin walking again. I passed each person as they held out their hands to me. Was I meant to give them money? It seemed rude to walk by and just ignore them.

The more I looked at each person the more they pleaded. I got my purse out and began to hand over notes to whoever I passed until I realised if I kept doing this I'd have nothing left in my wallet. When I looked around I'd also lost sight of the boy. I had a flash of panic, thinking that he'd taken my bags and that coming out here alone was the stupidest thing to have done. Then I saw him, metres ahead of me. I clutched my chest with my hand. *Thank God.* I breathed a sigh of relief. Mae's right. I do worry too much. He'd stopped by a small, battered-looking beige car and opened the boot. When I walked up to it I looked at its scratched surface and the dented door on the passenger's side. To be honest, it didn't look very safe and this boy barely looked old enough to drive. He threw my bags in the boot and slammed it shut. There was the tiny possibility that I was the wrong Fatima Affa, wasn't there? I cleared my throat.

'Excuse me . . . '

He'd already walked over to the driver's side and was getting into the car, so I had to get in too.

'What's your name?' I asked, keeping the car door open because I wasn't ready to leave a crowded space with a man I didn't know. Plus, the heat in the car was so intense I wondered how we'd manage to breathe in it.

'Raja,' he replied, putting on a little cap before he leaned over me, grabbed the door handle on my side and slammed the door shut.

I barely had a chance to register before he was already honking at the minivan, crammed with people, in front of him.

I went to put on my seatbelt before realising that there wasn't one. It had been cut out of the car.

'What happened to the seatbelts?' I said.

This was apparently funny because he laughed out loud and adjusted his cap, beeping at the rickshaw that was now in his way.

'Where are we going?' I asked, watching the streets that were lined with all kinds of stalls: fruit, vegetables, fresh juices.

Raja pushed his hand on the car horn again and this time kept it there as he replied, 'To your home, Affa.'

The nerves I had were untangling themselves. Someone must have told him who I really was — maybe even what happened. Perhaps there was going to be a gathering of people to welcome me back to the place where I was born.

'And who are you?' I asked.

'A neighbour,' he replied as a plume of dust wafted into the car. 'No AC, Affa. Old car.'

'That's okay,' I replied, trying to wave it out of the way just as a blast of what could only be described as sewage-smell blew into the car as well. I grabbed my scarf to cover my nose in case I wretched. I wasn't sure what was worse, being in a hot, stuffy car, or having hot, smelly wind in my face.

'How well do you know the family?' I asked.

'Auntie and Uncle? Oh, my family has known them since I was born.'

He must know.

'I do little jobs for them, like this, to earn

214

some money.' He leaned in a little. ' 'What use is having money if we can't help our neighbours?' ' he said, as if impersonating someone. 'And then Uncle gives me ten takas for three hours' work, as if that will pay my school fees.'

'Do you mean my uncle?' I asked, thinking it was probably a bit early to call him my dad.

He nodded and gave a toothy grin as he put the car into fifth gear, shooting down the road that was getting smaller and bumpier. Men and women ambled by on the side-streets, carrying various things on their heads. There were many buildings covered in scaffolding and we passed a tea garden every so often. It was like chaos on the street — still so many beggars and tooting horns, people shouting through windows at cars overtaking one another. Raja didn't look into his mirror once and indicating here looked like it might just be a novelty.

'Careful,' he said, as he drove over a pothole, causing my head to knock against the roof of the car. 'Don't tell my parents I said that about Uncle. They say I should be grateful I get to do work for them, but you shouldn't talk about having money and helping, and then paying me nothing.'

'They're well off then?' I asked.

Not that it mattered, but I wanted to know everything about them; all the ins and outs so I could understand who they were. We'd never really talked about them in the family, and even if my parents, or Mustafa and Farah did, I hadn't paid attention. Raja shrugged.

'They have five sons. And one of them lives in

England. Married his cousin there and he makes lots of money.'

Raja obviously had no idea who he'd just collected from the airport. I wondered when was the last time Mustafa managed to send money home? Were my biological parents' financial states tied up to Mustafa as well? I was about to tell Raja exactly who I was when he continued: 'And Malik Baia is doing well too. Top accountant. All the girls are after him but he just works, works, works. So, Affa, when you have sons who are all making money, then you can't be poor, right?'

'What about the other sons?'

He told me about the other three brothers who perhaps hadn't done as well as Mustafa and Malik, but who at least had jobs, and apparently that was impressive enough when considering how poor the family was when they were growing up. Was that why they gave me away? They couldn't feed another mouth? Was it a coincidence that that mouth happened to belong to a girl? I didn't want to think like that, though. How did I know what they were going through when they gave me away? It's just that with five brothers, how come it was the girl that was given away?

We drove the rest of the way in quiet as I looked out at the landscape. Somewhere along the way the roads had become narrower and narrower. There were vast fields of rice on either side. Raja slowed the car down as he had to let oncoming traffic through. Whenever he had to stop he pulled up so close to the side that every time, I thought we'd topple over and I'd meet my end with a face full of rice. The wind didn't feel fierce on my face any more though, because he drove slower. Resting my head on my hands as I leaned out of the window, I knew I was alone — except for Raja, the stranger in the car — but for perhaps the first time in my life, I didn't feel lonely. I thought about Farah and how Mustafa was doing — Malik and Mae promised to keep me updated. I saw Mae once more before I left.

'Dad's gone quiet and Mum hasn't shouted at me once the whole week,' she said when she brought me my things. 'Apart from when they found out I'd seen you and I hadn't told them.'

When I looked at her I didn't really hear what she was saying. All I kept thinking was: how is it that my little sister isn't actually my sister? When I think of her face as she spoke to me, my feeling of contentment wavered — as if something wasn't quite right. I never did feel like I could say what I was thinking or feeling — apart from with Mae. Partly because you just never knew if she was listening, with her attention always glued to her phone. But I think she did.

'Don't you wonder how Mum and Dad are doing?' she'd asked.

I thought of them and wished I wasn't still angry with them. For a minute I even thought that maybe I'd go and see them, but in the end I wasn't sure I'd be able to do it without walking out of the house and never being able to return again. When I told Mae no, I didn't mean to sound selfish or heartless, but I guess that's how it must've sounded.

'Almost there,' said Raja as he drove through a muddied field, looking right and left. 'Uncle will kill me if he sees me do this again, but who can go through all those windy roads when this way gets you home so much quicker?'

He pulled up in front of a small gated house and beeped the horn. The gate opened with a rumble as Raja hopped out of the car and took my bags out of the boot. With a tap of his hat he'd got back in the car and was driving away, leaving me to stand looking at the stranger who'd come to the front of the house. Was he a servant there? A family friend? My dad? I couldn't tell.

'You are here,' he said, beads of sweat forming above his grey brow.

I nodded. I needed a glass of water. The man called for someone, who popped out of the house and took my bags in.

'Come inside.'

As I walked up to him he looked at me, inspecting my face, my blue kaftan, the bag that was hanging from my arm. I expected him to say something but he just nodded as he led me into the house. I didn't expect the ceilings to be so low, or the room to be so dark with the light so bright outside.

'Come, sit,' he said, smiling for the first time, showing his stained orange mouth.

I took a seat on one of the beige sofas, looking around the room. The bare walls had some cracks in them, though the paint was white and clean. On the table next to my sofa I observed small, porcelain figurines of cats and rabbits placed in front of pictures of, I was assuming, the rest of the family. I recognised Malik and Mustafa in one of them. And there was a small one of Mustafa and Farah on their wedding day.

'You don't recognise your abba?' he said when I looked back at him.

My heart raced. Did he actually call himself my dad? His eyes were blue-rimmed from old age, his wispy grey hair looking greyer against his dark, shiny bald patch. I nodded, feeling as if I might tumble into his arms if only he moved a little forward. He just smiled at me. Before I could say anything he looked up at a woman who'd stepped into the room from the back door. I stood up, though I don't know why. Her face was familiar; there were more lines on it, the scarf of her orange sari exposing strands of henna-dyed hair. I recalled the picture I'd held in my hand — the woman lying on the hospital bed, smiling as she looked up at the woman who was going to be my mum.

'It's your daughter,' he said to her.

I glanced at him as she walked up to me. She was so frail I thought I'd break her when I bent down to hug her. Was this really my mum? I thought she'd hold on to me for longer — but then I suppose she wasn't used to doing that.

'Was your flight comfortable?' she asked as we both sat down.

'Yes. Thank you,' I replied.

'I've sent her bags to her room,' said her husband.

'You've met your abba?' she asked me.

An image of Abba in England flashed past me;

him putting his arm around me; him standing in the garden, overlooking the flowers; his face when I found out I was adopted. I hesitated.

'Yes,' I replied. What else was there to say?

Before I got here I'd assumed there'd be a conversation, with them explaining what they did and why before they referred to themselves as my mum and dad. For a moment I wished Mae was here. Even Farah or Bubblee. Maybe even Jay. The woman who gave birth to me gave me a sad smile and I remembered that her son was in England in a coma, and here I was, thinking about myself.

'Baia is doing okay,' I said, putting my hand on her leg and then looking at her husband.

I didn't know if this was completely true, but it felt like the right thing to say. Tears surfaced her eyes.

'We are far away from our children and can only pray that God looks after them.'

Her husband was staring at me when he said: 'Show Fatima to her room. She must be tired and want to rest. Dinner will be ready soon.'

Rest was the last thing on my mind but his wife had already stood up and I was obliged to follow her, up the concrete staircase to the room that had been prepared for me.

'It's Malik's room,' she said, opening the door to a room that was even more dimly lit than downstairs.

'We will call you when dinner is ready,' she said as she left and closed the door behind her.

I sat down on the bed that was so low, I had to straighten out my legs on the rough, blue carpet.

I heard a distant sound of sheep bleating. Looking at the bare walls and shelves, I wondered how much room had been made for me. It didn't seem as if anyone had ever lived in here. There were so many ways I'd imagined meeting my birth parents for the first time. It had included tears — on both sides — long hugs, lots of questions and answers. I imagined my birth mum grasping my hands, apologising for what she did; my birth father taking me into his arms, calling me his beti. Something seemed to open up in the pit of my stomach. But I had to give them time — it must be a shock for them too. Already I heard Bubblee's voice in my head: *Shock? For them? What about you?* And maybe she'd have a point, but it's not always about how you feel; sometimes it's about how another person might feel. Bubblee's never been able to put herself in another's shoes — that's the problem. Except that they didn't seem shocked. How could they be when they were already referring to themselves as my mum and dad?

I got my phone out to text Mae and tell her about the weird openness of my meeting with them, but instead I just wrote that I got here safely and told her to let everyone know. I asked how Mustafa was doing. All these years being around him and I never knew he was my brother. I tried to look back and think about a special connection I might've felt with him. I thought of all the times we'd talked and spent time as a family, and whether he ever knew I was more than just his sister-in-law. Looking around the room again, I thought about Malik. Perhaps I should've taken him up on his offer to join me here. But, no, that was the old Fatti. *I've made the decision to come here alone, and I'll see it through. Hopefully, unlike my driving tests, it won't be a failure.*

★ ★ ★

All I did was rest my head for a moment and I fell asleep, to be woken by the call to prayer that was so loud, I almost fell off the bed. For a moment I thought I was back home, only everything around me had changed, so maybe I was still dreaming? When I looked out of the meshed window I realised this was reality and I was in Bangladesh. I lay my sweaty head back down and stared at the ceiling.

'Just don't expect them to . . . '

I remembered Ash's face before I left to go to the airport. He'd offered to drop me, but he'd already done so much, I didn't want to trouble him any more.

'To what?' I asked when he paused by the door.

He smiled. 'Nothing. You're an optimist. That's what I like about you.'

He looked at the ground before adding, 'Don't be afraid to ask the difficult questions. They owe you answers.'

I sat up on the bed and shook my head, trying to wake up my foggy brain. I got a whiff of my underarm odour and thought it best to take a shower. Mum's voice came into my head: *Always say bismillah before you start anything.*

'Bismillah,' I muttered, standing up and walking into the bathroom.

After freshening up and having a shower — which was weird enough, because I had to sit on this stool and use a bucket and wash myself with cold water — I went downstairs. My birth dad was reading the paper while my birth mum was nowhere to be seen.

'Salamalaikum,' I said, entering the room.

He peered over his paper. 'You're up. Are you rested?'

I nodded, even though I didn't feel rested. The brain-fog had been replaced with this feeling of separateness — though that wasn't exactly new to me.

'Your amma is getting the food ready.'

The word jolted me again. Perhaps this was their way of making me feel welcome, to show that they acknowledged who I was — wouldn't it have been worse if they didn't?

'Should I go and help?' I asked.

'No. You are our guest,' he replied, putting his paper down. 'Your amma from England called for you.'

'Oh.'

Didn't he find it weird that he'd referred to two different women as my mum within the space of a few minutes, without batting an eyelid?

'You should call her back. Mustafa bought us an iPad and you can use Skype. Doesn't your family use Skype? This is how everyone communicates now.'

I told him that Mum was old-fashioned and

223

hadn't yet got her head around technology.

'Maybe I'll just let her know that I'll call her. When I'm ready,' I said.

He didn't seem to take much notice of this. I watched him as all these feelings I had came to the surface.

'It's nice to be back. In the place I was, you know . . . born,' I said.

When he stared at my face I couldn't help but gaze back — I think I have his eyes. His skin is darker than mine, but that's because he works out in the sun a lot. A moment passed before he smiled, still staring at me.

'All that really matters in life is what you remember,' he said.

I paused.

'No. I mean, yes, but no as well.' Beads of sweat had formed on my forehead. 'It's important to know where you come from. Isn't it?'

My stomach felt like it'd been tied into a knot, because even though I'd hardly eaten since I got here, something was giving me heartburn. He leaned back and put his hand out, looking at nothing in particular.

'These are foreign ideas,' he said.

I thought they were just human ideas. I didn't say anything, though, because I felt my face flush. Was that what he saw me as? A foreigner?

'Anyway,' he added. 'You're very welcome here.'

Thank God his wife came in when she did because I wasn't sure what else I could say to him.

'Are you hungry?' she asked, serving up rice-and-fish curry, chicken curry and hookti.

'She's a healthy girl,' said my birth dad, looking at me.

Perhaps my outfit didn't quite hide enough of my fat.

'Your sister has looked after her very well, hasn't she?' he added with a laugh, looking at his wife.

She laughed as well and replied: 'The England air, you know. It is healthy for everyone.'

I smiled, but I didn't quite understand what was so funny about it. The whir of the fan felt very loud as we sat at the dinner table.

'Tell me more about my sons,' she said, putting some hookti on my plate. 'I am praying every day to God that he is better. And what about Malik? Is he eating okay? He always forgets unless I remind him.'

'You worry too much,' her husband replied to her. Then he turned to me. 'But this is what I said when Mustafa went to England to settle with your sister. A man shouldn't leave the place he was born for a woman he thinks he loves. All these films you children watch. It spoils the head.'

I watched him as his mouth moved around, chomping on the dhal.

'They've been married for five years. They're very happy,' I replied. '*Mama*,' I added, pointedly.

There was no thinking about whether Mustafa loved Farah. He definitely did. Anyone who knew them could see that.

'You must call me Abba,' he said.

'Haan, Beti,' added his wife. 'And call me Amma.'

I couldn't quite get my head around it. Was I meant to say yes and then pretend to be happy families? Why didn't they feel embarrassed? I felt embarrassed and I wasn't the one that gave away a child.

'Oh, I . . . hmm.'

It wasn't exactly an answer but I wasn't sure how to respond without seeming rude, because they just seemed so *relaxed*.

'You should try to come to England,' I said. 'To visit. I know it's hard for you to travel.'

He gave a low laugh, looking at his plate. 'England,' he said, shaking his head as if just the idea of England was ridiculous.

'Tst. You shouldn't listen to your Abba, Fatima Beti. People risk their lives to go there,' she added to him.

'They're people who don't love their own country enough to stay in it.'

Any hunger I'd felt was dying, as I could barely put the food in my mouth.

'Your Abba's health is always up and down,' she said, pouring some water in my glass too. 'Has Malik been helpful to the family?' she asked.

'Yes. Very.'

'He's a good boy.'

I glanced over at my birth dad but caught a glimpse of my birth mum's hands and it made me smile.

'You know, he told me you and I had the same

226

hands,' I said, putting mine out to show her.

She took my hand in hers and turned it over in her palm, squeezing my hand as she gave it back to me.

'They are more like my sister's,' she replied.

'Hmm,' said her husband who observed the hands that had been given back to me so quickly.

I tried to think of something to say; anything so I could listen to something other than the whirring fan and the food squelching in everyone's mouths.

'This is delicious,' I said.

'Best-quality dhal,' replied my birth mother. 'Our boys do well for us. Is food expensive in England?'

'Hmm? Oh, well, I don't know. I suppose it's not cheap.'

'Yes, things will seem very cheap to you here. Pound is strong,' said her husband.

'Do your other sons live quite close?' I asked.

I was told they did and that I'd meet them all tomorrow.

'We have twelve grandchildren, mashallah,' she added. Then gave a list of all their names, mixing up their ages and spending a good five minutes trying to remember their birth dates but forgetting. 'But no grandchildren in England,' she said. 'Farah has waited a very long time to have babies, and now . . . ' She looked down at her plate.

I shifted in my seat. It wasn't exactly my place to tell them about Mustafa and Farah's personal life. I wanted to give some words of consolation, like: they'll have them once he's out of the coma, but knowing what I knew, that would've been a lie. I put another mouthful of dhal in my mouth.

'This is what I mean,' said her husband. 'Women there are forgetting their values and purpose in life.'

I paused, about to speak, but then thought better of it. Except what he said just felt all *wrong*. Farah might not be a mum but she *has* value and purpose. I tried to think about what it might be. For example, she helps Mum in the kitchen. And I know Mum and Dad go to her whenever they need an appointment fixing with the doctor or something. Also, I can't remember the last time I did a grocery shop — when Dad doesn't do it, Farah does. In fact, thinking of it, I began to see just how much Farah did for the family, even though she no longer lives with us. Really thinking about it, I began to see how little *I* did. Is that because I'm always in my room? Why had I never really noticed this about Farah before?

I tried to open my mouth, but found the words weren't coming out. As I finished my food, my birth dad put more chicken curry on my plate and told me to eat more.

'I'm full, thank you.'

'No, no. Are you on a diet?' he asked.

I shook my head, feeling my face get hot.

'You can diet when you go back to England.'

Meanwhile my birth mum had already put more dhal in my small bowl.

It wasn't as if they were mean or unwelcoming exactly, but there was this feeling I had that I couldn't put my finger on. When I went to bed after dinner all that fizz I felt while on the aeroplane had gone flat. I wondered how everyone back home was — what they were doing, whether they'd be at the hospital still or on their way to the house. Replaying the evening in my head, I tried to remember any questions my birth mum and dad had asked me. They talked about Malik, about Mustafa, about England and Bangladesh. And Farah. It occurred to me that they hadn't asked about my parents or my sisters except in a vague, 'How is everyone?' way. And apart from everyone else, weren't they curious about the life I had, growing up — how Mum and Dad had brought me up, what my likes and dislikes were?

I hadn't realised how much I was looking forward to telling them about that; about school and things which always felt so insignificant, but would be made significant by them wanting to know. I went to sleep with a strange emptiness inside me, praying that tomorrow would be better.

It had to be. Coming out here would make no sense, otherwise.

★ ★ ★

'You're telling your parents what they should or shouldn't do.'

I hovered at the door when I heard my birth dad, speaking into his iPad. He must've sensed me there as he turned around, mumbled a goodbye and hung up.

'Salamalaikum. You missed Malik on Skype,' he said.

Which wasn't exactly correct because he could've handed me the iPad.

'How's my . . . ' I hesitated. 'My brother Mustafa?' I added, with a little more conviction.

'The same,' he replied, rubbing his eyes.

Of course my expectations of them had been too great. Their son was not only in a coma but in a foreign country. How would my parents feel if they couldn't see me if I were in that state? My *adoptive* parents.

'Malik asked how long you were thinking of staying,' he said.

'Oh.'

'You are welcome for as long as you want,' he added, as if he were reading from an autocue. 'Think of this as your home.'

'Thank you, *Mama*,' I said.

Because surely they should know that I can't just call them something they haven't really been to me. Maybe further down the line I'd be able to — but for now I could only call him Uncle.

'Okay. Mama,' he said. 'Whatever you prefer, Babba.'

I was still standing in the doorway, unsure of whether to sit on the sofa or go through to the dining room for breakfast. I just smiled and nodded as I made my way into the kitchen. My birth mum was at the stove, stirring what looked like tea in a pot.

'Can I help with anything?' I asked.

'No, Babba. You sit down. Did you sleep okay?'

'Yes. Thank you,' I replied, even though I hadn't managed to sleep properly all night. I kept tossing and turning, trying to shut out the negative thoughts from my mind and having weird dreams. I stood there, looking around the kitchen for something I might be able to help with so I didn't have to keep thinking of what to say or ask next.

'You must miss your sons,' I said.

A faint smile spread on her face. 'You raise your children, they leave and you wonder if they think about the sacrifices you made for them. But boys are independent — it is their nature.'

If only she met Bubblee or Mae. The question that came to my mind was inevitable, but how was I to ask it without even more awkwardness? But then what had I come for, if not answers? I suppose I was afraid of hearing ones that I didn't want to hear.

'Do you miss . . . ' I paused. ' . . . not having any girls with you?'

She looked up from the stove and I searched her face, looking for something that might remind me of myself.

'Girls are good for their mothers. But the worries of getting them married . . . ' She looked at me and smiled. 'Doesn't my sister worry that you're not married yet?'

It was a bit like driving a kitchen knife through my stomach.

Even though I don't think she meant it in a rude way — she was just asking — but it left me a little winded anyway.

'Things are different in England,' she added.

'Here, look.' She went and opened one of the kitchen cupboards and pointed inside. I wasn't sure what I was meant to be looking at.

'New dishes,' she explained. 'Mustafa sent them to me two years ago and I still haven't used them. We're waiting for special guests.'

I smiled, something like hope filling my heart as I thought she was about to take them out, but she just closed the cupboard doors and went back to the stove.

'I'm sure my sister has many dishes like this in England.'

'Yes,' I said. 'I suppose she does.'

I wasn't quite sure about the importance of this conversation, or where it was going.

'She always liked nice things. You can tell her when you go back that I also have nice things now.'

She poured the tea out in a teapot and switched the hob off. 'I just pray my son is better soon. You're travelling. The prayers of a person who travels are always heard. Have you been praying for him?'

I nodded. Of course I had been.

'Malik isn't looking for a wife there, is he?' she asked.

'What? Oh. No. He's there for Mustafa,' I explained.

She nodded. 'I don't mind — he is such a clever boy, he would make more money there, but you've seen how your uncle would feel.'

She started telling me about my other brothers — the word just slipping out of her tongue with such ease — who we'd visit.

'You can tell Farah how nice their children are,' she said. 'Then maybe she will have some of her own.'

It was odd — I waited for her to be embarrassed at mentioning women having babies in front of the daughter she gave away, but she just continued stirring the tea, and getting the breakfast ready.

'Mubeen's wife is nice but the other two are very cunning,' she said.

Mubeen was the youngest. Apparently all her daughters-in-law had her sons wrapped around their little fingers.

'None of them will be getting my beautiful dishes when I die,' she said.

She got out a plate and filled it with thick biscuits that looked a bit like toast.

'Remember: you can start your diet when you go back home.'

The whole conversation felt warped; as if it were taking place in a parallel world, or that I'd floated outside my body and was watching it, and myself, thinking: *What the hell is going on?*

'Do you miss your sister?' I asked.

I had this urge where I wanted her to feel bad, guilty, *something* other than just smiling serenely at me as if I were just another house-guest.

'We each have our separate lives, and we are living them. She moved to England so many years ago now.'

With which she shrugged.

'It's nice to have you visit. Maybe next time you can bring her too.'

For a moment, I had to ask myself: did she

233

even remember what she had done thirty years ago?

'I thought I'd stay here. For a while,' I said. She paused and smiled at me.

'It'd be nice to learn about the place where I was born.' It took all my courage and strength but I gathered my nerves. 'Before I was given away.'

'Yes, Babba, you must stay as long as you like. With Malik gone, it'd be nice to have someone else here. Can you cook? I can teach you some recipes. But my sister would have done that, no? Babba, you are right — how nice it would've been for me to have a daughter.'

That's when I had to question whether I was in the right household and she was the right woman.

'You had *me*,' I said, watching the tea in the saucepan simmer and bubble. 'You chose to give me away.'

She wiped her hands and took three tea cups out of the cupboard, putting them on the tray with the teapot and plate of biscuits.

'You were a very cute baby. And my sister wanted one so badly — what greater thing can a sister do for another but give her a child?'

But I wanted to ask: didn't you *feel* things? Didn't your heart break when you handed me over for the last time, not knowing when you might see me again? That your sister would be raising a baby that was yours? I looked at the floor because I couldn't be sure tears wouldn't surface. And then I thought, who cares if they do? She should see them, since in some ways,

234

she's been the cause of them.

She picked up the tray and indicated for me to follow her. 'But just think — how would we have paid your dowry?' And she laughed at the idea as she set the tray down where my birth dad was already sitting. He rubbed his hands and put a biscuit on my plate before taking one for himself.

'Dowry?' he said. 'Look at our daughters-in-law, what did they bring with them?'

He bit into the biscuit, taking a sip of the tea and said it needed more sugar. My birth mum went and got some more from the kitchen.

'But still,' he added when she'd come back, 'we should be grateful.'

It was another meal time I managed to lose my appetite.

★　★　★

After breakfast I said I'd go and rest in my room for a while. As soon as I shut the bedroom door I burst into tears. I sobbed so hard, lying down in my bed, clutching the covers and scrunching them up in my hands, that I gave myself a headache. It was worse than them not caring, it was *indifference*; as if what happened was the most normal thing in the world. Is this why Malik wanted to come with me? Because he knew what his parents were like? My breath came back in gasps as I thought of my own parents, and realised that since I'd found out about being adopted, it was the first time I'd thought of them as *my* parents again. Was it just because my birth parents were such a huge disappointment? If they'd been wonderful, and everything I wanted them to be, would Mum and Dad have mattered to me less? I was still angry with them but in that moment I wished Mum was there to give me my stupid cheese and prawns, and Dad was there to say, 'Now, now. It's okay.' Just then there was a knock on the door. I sat up and wiped away the tears that had been streaming down my face. God knows how I must've looked.

'Here's some water for you,' said Malik's mum, who came in and stared at my face. 'Have you been crying?' she asked. 'Look at your eyes — so red.'

'I'm fine,' I said.

'Why are you upset?' she asked. 'Do you feel ill? You foreigners have very sensitive stomachs. Shall I get your uncle to get some medicine for you?'

How could she be so nice and yet so uncaring at the same time? I didn't understand.

'No, thank you. I think I just miss home.'

'Oh, yes. A girl is very sad when she's away from home and her family. Don't worry, I am here,' she said, putting her arm around and me and hugging me. 'Why don't you get ready and we will go and see your cousins. You will like to see nieces and nephews, won't you? Since you don't have any of your own.'

She poured some water in a glass for me and handed it over.

'Do you know, when Mustafa was little he always wanted to go to England,' she said. 'I should've known then he would leave us.'

I watched her as she stared at the floor, probably thinking of Mustafa and what would happen to him, and I thought, maybe she doesn't get it. Maybe she doesn't understand that you're not meant to tell someone they should forget about dieting while they're staying with you, right after commenting on how well fed they look; or talk about the dishes you've been sent by your son when your daughter is standing in your kitchen waiting for an explanation about why you gave her away; or keep making digs at your guest's sister for not yet having children.

'He'll be okay,' I said, taking her hand.

'Yes, and then I'll tell him that he must look for a husband for you. Why have your parents left it so late?'

I shrugged. 'Our town is small. Not a lot of Bangladeshis.'

'Maybe someone here?' she suggested. 'You know how many men want to go to England? They will be lining up for you.'

The idea of men lining up to marry me was nice, but the reason why they'd be lining up wasn't. I wasn't sure why that'd be a good prospect for me. We sat there for a while, talking about nothing very significant, but as I carried on listening to her I began to make mental notes of the differences between Mum and her. I could see the similarities — straightforward, maybe a bit too blunt at times, kind to guests. And then there were the differences. The main difference, really — and I'd never be entirely certain of it — but I did think, if this woman couldn't have had babies, I wonder if she'd have raised someone else's with as much care and love as Mum had raised me.

★ ★ ★

It took a while to get my head around it. Every day I'd wake up and think maybe today it'll be different, but it never really was. After a few days I got used to the routine of having breakfast with them after the call to prayer in the morning, resting for a bit, reading, then having a second breakfast and going to visit their friends and family. Everywhere we went I was introduced as the 'niece' from England, but I realised that this word was interchangeable with 'daughter'. I watched people's gaze and wondered what they were thinking; did they think it odd? Normal? It didn't seem to be a secret and yet it wasn't really talked about.

When I visited my brothers I didn't know what to expect. Before I got to Bangladesh I thought maybe they'd be like Malik, but having met his parents, I had to wonder. I could imagine Bubblee being horrified at the way everyone came in and out of each other's homes. The children who'd be passed around for babysitting when another brother needed to do an urgent job. The wives of these brothers all kind of merging into one.

'As if we were just made to reproduce and play maidservant to husbands,' I could imagine her saying. It made me smile and almost reach for my phone to text her. I didn't. But I wanted to.

'Ah, Fatima,' said one brother, looking me up

and down. 'Look how big you are.'

It was the common phrase for me whenever someone met me for the first time. I was told so often not to worry about dieting that I realised it seemed like it was exactly the thing I should be worrying about. Remembering Mum and the way she never once would mention anything like it, I just smiled, answered questions and took hold of a baby when I could to keep myself distracted from all these people. What was weird was how little each person seemed to think about Mustafa lying in a hospital bed in a coma. I'd have to be dead to not worry about any of my sisters if they were in the same situation — no matter where in the world I was. Even though my conversations with the family didn't go beyond the small talk of *How are you?* and *What's England like?*, they loved having photos taken: family photos, individual photos, selfies, one with me and all the children, me with one sister-in-law and then all the sisters-in-law, me with all the brothers. I tried to tell them I wasn't very good in photos but that didn't seem to matter. And for all the excitement these photos brought on, I couldn't help but want my own bedroom to escape to, even if it was just for ten minutes.

It was one day, when I came down the stairs and overheard the two of them talking.

'Maybe there is no-one in England who wants to marry her,' I heard my birth dad say.

I stepped back, my heart beating fast, a knot of nerves forming in my stomach. It wasn't right to listen in to people's conversations and yet I knew who he was talking about. I leaned in again.

'It's the parents' duty to find someone,' my birth mum replied. 'There is always someone to marry.'

'It's laziness. Farah hasn't even had a baby. Everything is upside down in that country.'

It didn't make me cry. People talk about being crushed, and it was something like that, but it wasn't me that was crushed, it was an idea I had in my head. A feeling I had in my heart.

'Not everything can be blamed on the country,' she replied.

'Where are those cushions I bought for the sofa?' he asked.

She responded to him and added: 'I'm very surprised my sister isn't worried. But she was always a bit careless. If I was Farah's mother I'd have told her she is a shame to the family for waiting so long to have a baby.'

'Hmm. No, not these ones. The green ones,' he said.

The blood rushed to my face as sweat prickled my skin and I swung the door open.

'Hello, Beti. Which of your uncle's cushions do you prefer?' she asked, holding a green embroidered cushion in one hand, and yellow in the other.

'Farah is *not* a shame to the family,' I said.

They both looked at each other.

'Of course she isn't. We were just talking. Although, it's not normal, is it?' she replied. 'Doesn't matter. These things aren't up to us in the end.'

My birth dad took the cushions from her

hands and put them both on either side of the sofa.

'I prefer the green one,' he said. 'Fatima — you must tell me which you like best.'

It was as if they didn't realise I'd heard them.

'Hmm?' I said.

'Which do you prefer?'

'The er . . . the green one. About Farah — '

' — No, no,' he said, waving a hand in the air, putting another green cushion on the other side of the sofa. 'Forget about that. You mustn't take these things to heart. We love all our daughters-in-law equally. Mustafa's Amma — shall we have chai?'

He turned around and looked at his wife expectantly.

'Yes, but we have to get ready for dinner as well. Look, Fatima, I bought you this suit.'

She handed me a turquoise outfit with little white mirrors all over the shirt dress.

'Oh, thank you,' I said.

'It will look very nice on you.'

I tried to detect whether there was any spite in her voice; a dig, a jibe. But I don't think there was. Her husband was still looking proudly at the new cushions.

'Yes,' he added. 'Turquoise is a good colour for you. Girls should wear bright things.'

They weren't startled when I'd come in. It was as if they didn't care if I heard or not.

'This was the colour dress you wore when you went home with my sister,' she said.

'You looked like a doll,' said her husband.

He looked at me rather fondly as my feelings

softened towards him.

'When we gave you away I said to your . . . *kala*: 'She would have given us lots of happiness.'' He smiled and I felt tears surface my eyes. 'And you know what she replied?'

I shook my head.

''But I am giving my sister happiness.''

★ ★ ★

From that moment something began to shift. Every day, as I visited more family members, and spent time with people that weren't Amirs, that hurt I felt the first few days began to disappear. Visiting everyone's families reminded me so much of back home — the way Farah would come through the door; Bubblee returning from London like a tsunami and then leaving; Mae, quietly going around, being sneaky and taking snapshots of all of us without us realising; Mum peering out of the kitchen window to see whether Dad was trimming the hedges or looking over at Marnie. The mum and dad that raised me. I remembered Ash's words: 'Did they ever make you feel as if you weren't loved?'

My thoughts were interrupted by one of Malik's brothers' wives: 'When do you think you'll go home?'

I smiled and didn't even take offence at the idea that she might only be repeating what my birth mum and dad were talking about behind my back. All this time I wondered why I felt so removed from my family, and the answer came when I found out I was adopted. Coming back here, I thought I'd finally find a sense of belonging. But all it did was make me realise where I didn't belong. Funny — it took thirty years and a flight across an ocean to realise belonging isn't about the family you're born into, but the family you've grown into.

'Soon,' I said.

That's when I picked up my phone and called the airline to ask when the next available flight back to England was.

15

Bubblee

The first thing I noticed when I walked into Farah's living room was the row of cards on the mantelpiece, the side table and dotted around the room. She explained they were from friends and neighbours.

'Who's *Augustus* and family?' I asked, picking up a bright-green card with flowers on the front.

'Remember the little grocery on Rectory Lane?' she said. 'They sold it to a family who now run it.'

'Oh yeah, right. The Greggs used to own it,' I said, putting the card down again.

'Yep. The Greggs are now the Blacks,' she said, throwing her keys on the coffee table.

I picked up a few more cards, skimming the messages written inside.

'That's quite an essay,' I said, reading one in which the handwriting had been squeezed so much it was barely legible.

Farah smiled. 'That's from Pooja — you know, Sanjay's mum? He goes to Mae's school.'

I put the card back. No, I didn't know Sanjay's mum Pooja.

I barely knew who Sanjay was. 'I thought Mae went to an all-girls school.'

'No,' said Farah as if I was slow on the uptake. 'She got the youngest-child treatment and got to choose where she wanted to go. Remember?'

'I almost forgot that. You're right.'

Glancing at the various well-wishes from neighbours, I wondered how many cards I'd get if my husband went into a coma. Just as well that's not likely, given my lack of a husband. Something to be thankful for.

'Right, so first things first — we need to know exactly how much debt you're in,' I said, settling on the floor with papers and files all around me.

Farah stared at the abyss of paperwork.

'It's going to be okay,' I said.

This might've been stretching things slightly because, quite honestly, I couldn't see *how* it was going to be okay. What a god-awful mess. The only useful thing I could think of was how I could use all this paper to make some kind of papier-mâché sculpture. It would be symbolic; the hollowness of the sculpture being a metaphor for our materialistic life. I was going to mention this rather clever notion to Farah but after looking at the expression on her face, I realised perhaps it wasn't the right time. The only thing now was if Jay would come through and be able to recover some of that money. It was her only hope.

'How?' she asked, not looking at me.

'One step at a time,' I replied. 'There's enough despair going around for now.'

Farah seated herself on the floor with me. 'How do you think Fatti is?'

We'd all been banned from calling her by Mae.

'Let her be,' Mae had exclaimed. 'God, even

flying to the other side of the world, she can't get rid of us. She just needs time.'

Mum had called her sister: the look on her face when she was told that Fatti didn't want to speak to anyone was one I'd never witnessed before. I'm used to Mum looking surly, but not heartbroken.

'How are you?' she'd asked, her voice strained once she'd got over the fact that she'd been denied access to Fatti.

I couldn't hear what was being said on the other side. Mum then added that Mustafa was much the same, but everyone was praying for him.

'You will look after my daughter, won't you?' she said after a few minutes of conversation. 'She's a sensitive girl, but very good.'

It was interesting to see how Mum understood that about her. Not that it was rocket science, but you do wonder what your parents pick up on.

'Did Mum eat before we left home?' I asked Farah.

'That's the last thing on her mind,' she replied. 'I tried to feed her something, but she just couldn't seem to stomach anything.'

Hours passed as we went through bills and documents and cheques. We both looked like we'd weathered a storm by the end of it.

'Well, it doesn't look good, does it?' I said.

'Thanks.'

I sighed. 'Sorry.'

Just then the doorbell rang, which Farah got up to answer.

'You put the casserole in the oven at a low heat,' I heard.

A few seconds later Farah entered the room with Alice, who was apparently her next-door neighbour.

'Oh my,' she said, putting the casserole on the table and barely able to suppress her excitement as she looked at me. 'You must be the glamorous artist twin sister from London.'

I tried to get up from the mountain of paperwork and had barely managed before I was taken into Alice's arms and held there for much longer than was comfortable or necessary.

'You are every bit as beautiful as Farah said you were,' she said, holding on to my arms and looking at my face. The only thing I noticed were the freckles that were scattered all over her face.

'Shall I put the kettle on?' asked Farah.

'Oh, no, thank you. I have to get going. What's all this?' Alice said, looking at the paper-covered floor. Before either Farah or I could reply, Alice was already looking out into the garden, having put the floodlight on.

'Right, dear, I'll ask John to come over tomorrow to mow your lawn. I mean, you don't have time for it and it's a shame to see it so, well, *run down.*'

'Oh, no, you don't have to do that,' said Farah. 'Really.'

'It's not a problem,' said Alice. 'All the things you do for us.'

I had a feeling that Farah could've protested until Mustafa came out of the coma and she'd still have lost the argument. It seemed as if Alice was a regular occurrence in this house and yet I'd never heard of her. But then it's not as if Farah and I talked on a regular basis. I wondered if Alice knew the whole story about me: the twin who didn't like her sister's husband and wasn't happy with the marriage?

'Now, the Neighbourhood Watch meeting — '

' — God,' interrupted Farah. 'I'm so sorry — '

' — Don't be silly. Of course you can't have it here now. Dan's already offered to have it at his.'

'But he did it last time.'

Alice waved her hand as if to shoo away my sister's ridiculous comment.

'And of course you can't come to it,' added Alice, 'so we'll take notes and Pooja said she'd send those to you.'

In another flurry of conversation, casserole instruction and garden assessment, Alice was about to leave when she said, 'Oh, it's chicken, by the way, but *halal*.'

She lifted her shoulders as if this was the most novel thing she'd heard all week.

'I had no idea we had a halal butcher's here!'

Farah leaned in and hugged her tightly. When Alice left I said: 'She seems . . . excitable.'

'Stop it,' said Farah. 'She's lovely.'

She sat down next to me and picked up a bunch of papers, sighing. I don't think tragedy is necessarily a bad thing — it can show what a person is made of, and that adage — whatever doesn't kill you makes you stronger — I believe that. In some ways I think tragedy can even be good, but looking at Farah in that moment, I guessed not everyone had the same feeling.

'How are you?' I asked.

'How do you think I am?'

'I was going to say that Jay might come through and find a solution to this, but we both know that's not going to happen,' I said.

Just another failure in the line of all his failures. It wasn't one that Farah could cover up this time, either.

'Don't say that. He's my only hope right now.' She paused and then looked at me. 'Is it my fault? Did I have this coming to me?'

I shook my head, trying to organise the papers by invoices and statements, as well as dates. 'I don't think many people deserve to have their husbands in a coma,' I replied. 'But our actions . . . obviously they have consequences.'

She looked at me in amazement. 'I just can't believe the things you say sometimes.'

'Far, I'd be lying if I didn't think you covering up for Jay all the time's hardly helped, but to be honest, that's our parents' fault more than yours.'

'Everyone's to blame for something, then. What about you?' she said. 'Or are you just able to sit back and judge all of us while you're let off, scot-free?'

I leaned on the sofa. She was upset and so I wasn't going to get into an argument about it — not after what happened last time — but I wasn't about to lie just to make her feel better, either. I did wish I could take her out of this nightmare, but we're all adults; we should be able to handle the truth.

'I never covered up for my brother. He's

249

always been havoc and the sooner Mum and Dad realised, the better it'd have been. Anyway, like I said — they're the adults and should've behaved liked it.'

'And you leaving home and never actually asking about your family helped, did it?'

'I'm entitled to have my own life,' I replied.

'So entitled that you forgot about the one you lived for twenty-three years before moving out.'

It was ridiculous, her equating me moving from home — which any normal person should do as an adult anyway — with covering up for Jay and letting him be the disaster he is.

'But Bubblee,' she said in a much smugger manner than suited her, 'everything has consequences. Right? You weren't here to solve family problems; help Mum and Dad when they needed it. You weren't *here*, full stop.'

'Let's not argue,' I said. 'It's not the time.'

'But it's time to dish out responsibility and yet take none of it yourself? You living your great, liberal life in London, not caring what goes on back here, and thinking you've evolved beyond us?'

'I'm here now, aren't I?' I said, holding up papers.

She gave a hollow laugh. 'Yeah. It only took a coma. I might've messed up with Jay, but at least I cared enough to be around to mess up.'

Fine, I'd been eager to get back to London after just a few days of being here in the beginning, but that didn't mean I didn't *care*. Of course I cared. I just had things to get on with. My family don't understand the kind of commitment and time it takes to succeed if you're going to be an artist.

'And have we ever told you otherwise?' she asked when I said that to her. 'I know Mum goes on about you moving back home and getting a *proper job*, but has she forced you? Really?'

'Well, no but, God. It's as if wanting to do something outside of the family's a sin,' I said. 'I mean.'

'No-one said you had to *stay* here. But a few more phone calls, just asking how everyone is. I mean, you'd forgotten Mae was in a mixed school and you had no idea who Alice was, even though I know I've mentioned her to you over the past month. You just don't seem to think anyone's life, other than yours, is important.'

I could feel my face flush. She didn't understand. I didn't have time — I was busy. I didn't need the day-to-day humdrum of who did what; the latest concern in Mum's life about Fatti's driving, or Mae's school work, or Farah's lack of having any babies, to clutter up my creativity. Sasha told me that I needed to focus on myself and try to achieve my dream. Farah was already looking over some papers again. I did wonder — when was the last time she thought about herself before others?

'I didn't realise anyone missed me,' I said, getting back to the papers too.

After all, I was the black sheep, with all these odd ways and *ideas*. Who even cared about my opinion when it's always so different to everybody else's? As if not having me call was a huge loss to anyone. Of course my family loved

251

me — most families love each other just because they have to — a weird tic in the DNA — but there are levels of love and I don't think mine ranked very high. Farah looked up at me and shook her head.

'For someone who thinks she sees people for what they are, you can be really blind sometimes.'

★ ★ ★

I stayed that night at Farah's. She said she shouldn't get used to staying at Mum and Dad's. They were worried about Fatti and there were only so many problems we could all deal with at one time — so we were delegating them. I stayed up in bed for a long time, thinking about what she said about me not being in touch enough. I knew there was truth in it, but I'm not about to apologise for wanting to do more in life than just get married and have babies. Still, perhaps I could've called home more often, listened, even if I didn't really hear what was being said. Maybe I was too caught up in my own life to care about what was happening in everyone else's. But their problems were just so *provincial*. Did this make me a snob? Is that how they saw me?

I didn't sleep very well that night and then the doorbell rang far too early the following morning. When Farah didn't answer, it rang again. Not knowing where Farah was, I went to see who it was, still wearing my shorts and vest top.

'Oh.' It was Malik. 'Sorry,' he said, staring at me.

'For what?' I asked, because if you're ringing a person's doorbell then you expect someone to answer.

He looked away, fixing his eyes on the welcome mat. 'I . . . er, it's very early still, isn't it?' he said, glancing at his watch.

'Yes,' I replied, blocking the doorway. If he wanted to come in, then he'd have to ask.

'Is Farah in?'

I nodded.

He waited a moment before adding: 'I'm like a vampire — you'll have to invite me.'

He smiled. His wit wasn't really amusing but I couldn't stand and block his way forever, so I let him in.

'*Farah!*' I called out, wondering where she was.

'I'll let you get changed,' he said as he walked in and took a seat at the kitchen table.

'Why? Haven't you seen a girl in shorts before?'

It was preposterous: a man coming into *my* — well, my sister's — house and telling *me* what to wear. If he was uncomfortable then that was his problem, not mine. The colour in his cheeks rose as his dark hair flopped over his eyes and he stared at the table.

'I don't know what's worse,' he said. 'A woman who knows how beautiful she is or one who doesn't.'

I paused, not sure what to say, but still annoyed just at *him*. He looked faintly embarrassed.

'As if it matters,' I said. 'It's hers to guard or

253

show, as she pleases.'

I waited for the usual tropes about modesty and expectations and was ready for an argument, because God knows I could do with some kind of vent.

'Yes,' he said, looking up. 'You're right.'

I paused.

'But?' I asked, folding my arms.

'But what?' he replied.

'There's always a but.'

He smiled at me as if I'd said something amusing before he looked over my shoulder.

'Sorry, I was in the shower,' said Farah, coming into the kitchen.

He stood up and said hello, before sitting down again. 'I wanted to let you know that I've spoken to Fatima and she's coming home in the next few days.'

'Oh, thank God,' said Farah, putting her hands to her face.

I breathed an internal sigh of relief but it was annoying that he should be the one to bring us news of our sister. She might be his sister by blood, but that doesn't make them family.

'You could've told us over the phone,' I said.

'Bubblee . . . ' said Farah.

'But then I would not have been here for our charming exchange,' he replied.

I glanced at Farah who was suppressing a smile. 'How did she sound?' she asked.

He paused. 'Okay, I think. It was hard to tell. The connection wasn't very good. She sounded a lot better than I thought she would; considering.'

'What do you mean?' asked Farah.

He ran his hands through his hair, as if searching for the right thing to say. 'My parents . . . sometimes they don't know the things they say.'

'That's hardly a surprise,' I spouted.

They both stared at me.

'I meant that aren't all parents like that? Some of the stuff that Mum and Dad come out with . . . ' I added, looking at Farah.

'They're always fine whenever I've spoken to them,' she replied to him, ignoring my comment.

He looked at me briefly before looking at Farah. 'Yes, well, knowing someone through speaking on Skype and living with them your whole life are different. Anyway, parents are human. We love them anyway.'

Farah smiled and nodded.

'I'll collect Fatti from the airport,' I said.

'You don't have to do that,' replied Malik. 'She said someone's already collecting her.'

'Who?' said Farah and I in unison with perhaps a little too much force, because Malik looked taken aback.

'I don't know. A friend, she said. I think the same one she stayed with.'

'You know? Who was it?' I asked.

'You probably don't think patience is important,' he said, looking at me, 'but you'll have to wait and ask her yourself.'

There's nothing more presumptuous than someone claiming to know something about you. Perhaps the look of disdain showed on my face because Farah interrupted what I was about to say by asking how Malik got here. He apparently took the bus. When he said he'd be on his way and that he'd see us at the hospital later, she insisted he stay. He looked at me as if to ask for permission.

'It's not my house,' I replied. 'Stay. Leave. It's up to you.'

Farah hit the back of my head and smiled at him. 'You'll have to get used to her.'

'Would you wish that on a person?' he replied, leaning back into his chair.

I went to put the kettle on — as if I was the type of person to find that faux reverse-psychology flirtation charming.

'Can I help you with anything here?' he asked, looking at the papers we'd left on the floor the night before.

'Not unless you can tell us how to pay off all your brother's debts,' Farah said, her mouth tightening.

Malik sighed. 'I'm sorry. This isn't what a husband is meant to do.'

I had to scoff. 'That's the problem.'

'Oh, Bubblee, give it a rest,' said Farah.

'It's true. Assigning expectation to gender is part of the problem.'

Malik held up his hands. 'Your sister likes to argue about everything,' he said to Farah.

'Her sister is standing right here,' I replied.

He stood up and came into the kitchen area as Farah went to tidy the papers.

'You are right. Again.'

I wasn't sure what was worse — saying stupid things or giving in so easily.

Lowering his voice, he added: 'But isn't honesty all that matters between husband and wife?'

I had to lean back. I smelt the fresh scent of his aftershave and noticed how long his fingers were. He was far too close for my liking and I wasn't the kind of girl that quivered at the sound of a man lowering his voice.

'All that matters,' I said, looking pointedly at the lack of distance between us, 'is space.'

This time, I didn't care that he looked embarrassed. He stepped back and nodded, taking his seat at the table again. Just because a person's good-looking, it doesn't mean they have the right to expect you to respond to their vacuous banter, no matter how nice they smell. The doorbell rang again and when Farah came back in, her neighbour John was also in tow.

'You really don't have to do this,' she said as he made his way to the garden.

'You're doing me a favour,' he replied. 'Get out of that damned house.'

He fiddled with the patio door until he managed to unlock it.

'Are you going to help?' he shouted.

We weren't sure who he was speaking to because he was looking at the lawn. A few moments later he turned around and looked at Malik who put down his paper and joined John outside.

'Are we women incapable of mowing a lawn?' I said.

'Be my guest,' Farah replied, opening her arm up towards the garden where it seemed Malik had been instructed to weed the flower beds.

'Your neighbour seems charming.'

He was battling with the lawnmower and I'm quite sure he emitted more than a few expletives. Farah laughed as she looked at him.

'I know. I found him terrifying when I met him. Thought he hated us because we're brown. Turns out he just hates everyone, equally. But you know Mustafa,' she said. 'He wins people over when he puts his mind to it.'

She must've seen me look away.

'Well, most of the time anyway,' she added.

She looked out into the garden again. 'John's a bit rough around the edges, but I don't know what I'd do without him or Alice. And anyway, you're one to talk about being charming. The hard time you give Malik, it's a wonder he hasn't pushed you into my begonias. You really should give him a break.'

I watched her as she got some bread out and put it in the toaster.

'He tries so hard, though. It's nauseating. I just don't like the way he's turned up and shaken everything around. You've got to admit, that was such an unnecessary scene he made at the hospital. And the way he goes on about Fatti as if she's more his sister than ours. I mean, it's intrusive at best.'

'Well, at least she has a brother who's alive and well and who doesn't swindle people for their money either.'

I gave a low laugh. 'I don't know. He rubs me up the wrong way, looking at me with his puppy-dog eyes. I'm not interested — get the picture?'

'Carry on like that and no doubt he will,' replied Farah, watching him in the garden.

'Would you both like some breakfast?' she called out.

They just wanted tea.

'We have cereal as well,' she said to me.

'Why do you even need to know your neighbours, anyway?' I said. 'Your family just lives a five-minute drive away. Isn't it a bore having to deal with so many people ringing your doorbell all the time?'

She shook her head at me. 'I never understood why you didn't like people.'

'I like people.'

She raised her eyebrows. 'Who?'

I paused. 'You guys.'

'You have to; we're family.'

'Well, you know, there's Sasha. And Edgar,' I added. 'Mila. Juan.'

'Apart from Sasha I don't recognise any of those names. And I actually listen to what goes on.'

'You're just trying to prove a point,' I said.

'The family isn't going to make sure no-one burgles me when I'm out with them at a wedding or something. Or call the police when there's a racist attack.'

'Which must be really helpful when the police themselves are racist.'

She rested her hands on the kitchen counter. 'Bubs, I love you, but aren't you exhausted?'

'Of what?'

'Of *always* seeing the worst in people and circumstances? Don't you, for once, just want to see the good in people?'

I poured the boiling water into four mugs. It's not that I see the worst in people, it's just that generally people tend to show their worst sides when it comes down to it. And if you expect the worst, then at least you're not disappointed further down the line. If Farah had been a little more discerning about her husband, then this whole situation might at least not have come as such a shock.

'I know what you're thinking,' she said. 'Fine, maybe I turned too much of a blind eye to what Mustafa did. Maybe I should've been a bit more like you, but Bubs, if you could be just a little bit like me too, I'd like to see you be as happy as I've been. Whatever the outcome is now — I *have* been happy. Don't you want that?'

'I don't want to be made a fool, Far.'

'Is that what I am to you?'

I took her hand, because I didn't want to argue, especially after last night, but she had to understand. 'That's what most people are.'

'You know it catches up with you,' she said.

'What?'

'Foolishness. There's not enough cynicism in the world to prevent it.' She looked out into the garden, Malik wiping his brow already. 'But first of all, why don't you go and put on a robe.'

I gave her an exasperated look.

'You're not in London any more, Bubblee.'

I took out the teabags from each mug, glancing outside, and replied, 'We're not in Bangladesh, either.'

We got to the hospital and Mum and Dad arrived half an hour after us, Mae dragging her feet behind them. Farah sat in the room with Mustafa as I told the rest of the family that we should give them space.

'Er, yeah, because *he* really needs it,' said Mae as we all exited and went into the waiting room.

Malik smiled and ruffled her hair, which — I don't know why — annoyed me. Especially since Mae didn't do her usual disgusted face, but instead laughed, while telling him to get off. I took her by the arm and told her we could go and find her a kale smoothie from somewhere.

'Please,' she replied. 'Do you know how much sugar and preservatives they put in those drinks?'

She took one out that she'd made at home, and another for Malik. When did this unlikely friendship take place? There were still curt nods exchanged between Malik and Mum and Dad, but according to Mae he'd apologised to them. I guess it might take a while for them to forgive him. Quite right too. As I watched Mae telling Malik about the latest docu-film she'd watched, I decided to leave them to it and see how Farah was doing. I stopped at the door and saw her holding Mustafa's hand.

'I'm still so angry with you,' I heard her say. 'And I *will* sell an organ of yours.' She lowered her head so her forehead was resting on his hand. 'I'll just make sure it's not one you can't live without.'

I had to swallow the lump that had formed in

my throat. She then started telling him about the kind of casserole that Alice had brought, and how John was fixing the garden, and the cards they'd received. I suppose this was the life they'd built together, with Mum, Dad, Fatti and Mae and all these friends and neighbours — all these commonalities they shared. If I had a pencil and paper at hand in that moment I think I'd have drawn a picture of the way Mustafa's wires pressed into his skin, and the way Farah's fingers were interlocked with his. In that moment I prayed, for the first time, that Jay would somehow at least be able to save their home for them. Then I turned around and decided to phone Sasha.

'If I was in a coma, do you think people would send me cards?' I asked.

'But you'd be in a coma, so what would be the point?'

'It's hypothetical,' I said.

'Even hypothetical need grounding in some form of reality.'

I gave an exasperated sigh. 'For God's sake, Sash.'

'You know I'm right,' she replied. 'What's wrong? You're not having an existential crisis, are you? Small towns can do that to a person.'

'No.'

'Good, because the one thing I rely on you for is clarity.'

'Really?' I asked.

'Of course. Are you missing home? It's so dull here without you.'

I thought of my little flat, around the corner

and the coffee I was missing, getting the papers in the morning and walking around London, finding the newest exhibition.

'I've been able to catch up with the family,' I said.

'Hmm. That doesn't answer my question.'

I wasn't sure what home even meant any more. Perhaps I had spent too long here. I told Sasha that Fatti was returning in a few days, about Malik's unwanted attention but his inextricable link to us now — a cousin we could've ignored, even if he was our sister's brother-in-law, but we can't ignore as Fatti's brother.

'I miss *you*,' I said.

'I could be there tomorrow if you want?' she answered.

'Sash,' I began. 'Do you ever get . . . lonely?'

She laughed so hard, I had to move the phone away from my ear.

'Bubs,' she exclaimed, still sounding amused. 'I'm *dying* of it, obviously. We *all* are. And don't let anyone fool you into believing otherwise,' she added.

In all the years I'd known her, I don't know why we'd never had this conversation before. We talked about all sorts of things: the world, art, social disparities, the patriarchy, but never that one thing that can drive you into a metaphorical hole, shut you up inside a room like it did Fatti, linger in your bones even when you're in a crowded place. Sasha just always seemed so together and in charge of who she was and what she did. She and loneliness didn't make sense. I suppose you can never know how someone feels until you ask them. Maybe that's what Farah meant by me never calling — it showed too much of how little I cared.

'You're lonely? Really?'

'Of course I am. Aren't you?' she asked, shocked at the notion that I might not be.

I turned around and looked into the room at Mustafa and Farah, Dad in front of the vending machine in the corridor, Mum, Malik and Mae probably inside the waiting room — all these people who'd sent Farah those cards. Sasha was right, obviously — loneliness is par for the course. I just couldn't help but think that some of us are less alone than others.

16

Farah

It's the not knowing that's the worst part. When Mustafa and I were trying for a baby and it just wasn't happening, there was a time when we were both in denial, refusing to believe there could be something wrong with either one of us. The minute we came out of the denial and decided to have tests to find out, that period of waiting almost felt as difficult as the previous two years of attempting to make a baby. We only had to wait a week. It's been almost a month since Mustafa's accident and there's no obvious improvement, no more information as to whether he'll come out of it, except that the longer he's in a coma, the less likely it is that he will. This thought sends me into such a panic that I stay glued to the spot because I'm not sure I wouldn't fly into a frenzy. I can feel myself on the brink of falling apart when Bubblee might ask what a certain invoice was for, or a neighbour might come over with more casserole, or Mum will need help in the kitchen. It sounds selfish but in some ways Fatti's absence has been good, because Mum and Dad are both so worried that I'm too busy calming them down to have time to be concerned about my own problems. Even though their problems are my problems. That's just the way it works.

I came home from the hospital and Bubblee insisted she come with me again, but I wanted to be on my own. Perhaps she was offended — I don't know, but as helpful as she'd been lately, I needed to not have to speak, or listen, or argue, or get my point across. I'd just lain down on the sofa for a moment when the doorbell rang several times. I looked at my watch and it was almost eleven o'clock at night. I crossed into the front room to peer out of the window and see who it was. A tall, dark figure loomed outside — the person had their back to me and my heart began to race. I dropped the curtain as he turned around. Should I call the police? There was urgent knocking on the door as I ran into the kitchen, grabbed a knife and came back out into the passage.

'Who is it?' I asked, briskly.

There was no answer. I got my phone out, ready to dial 999.

'Open the door,' came a voice.

'Who is it?' I repeated.

'Far,' said the voice. 'It's me.'

Surely it couldn't be. I must've been hearing things.

'Jay?' I said.

When he didn't respond I opened the door and there he was: my little brother — the reason my husband was in a coma and I might lose the very house I lived in.

'Hi,' he said, his brown eyes lacking the sparkle they usually had.

I wasn't sure whether I was dreaming or not when he added: 'Can I come in?'

Something in me hardened. This was the boy I'd protected my whole life, whose faults I hid from my parents, my sisters and even my husband. If I'd not always covered for him, would Mustafa have trusted him with the company accounts the way he had?

'Let you in?' I said. 'Let *you* into my house?'

'Far —'

' — I wouldn't let you into within an inch of this country, if it was up to me.'

'Listen —'

But before he could finish the sentence I'd slammed the door in his face, grabbed my car keys from the kitchen counter, before opening the door again and dragging him by the arm into my car.

'What are you doing?' he said. 'Where are we going?'

'To the police station,' I said, buckling up my seatbelt.

'What? No, wait —'

' — I've waited long enough.'

I stepped on the accelerator and the car tyres screeched as I turned into Mum and Dad's road. Of course I wasn't going to take him to the police station, but it was good to see he had the fear of something in him.

'Get out,' I said when he saw we'd parked outside our parents' house.

'Far, can we just talk? Just you and me. Please?'

I couldn't look at him, his shoulders slouched, because if I did then I might be inclined to hear him out and he didn't deserve that. I got out of the car and when I walked into my family's home he at least had the decency to follow me.

'What are you doing here?' Mae was sitting on the sofa, flicking through the TV channels when she looked over my shoulder. 'What the . . . ?'

'Hey, Squirt.'

Mae's eyes flicked towards me and Jay.

'Do you have a death wish?' she said, looking at Jay.

'Where are Mum and Dad?' I asked. 'And Bubblee and Malik?'

'In bed,' she replied, sitting up and switching the television off.

'Aren't you going to give your big brother a hug?'

She got up and went to hug him, half-embarrassed.

'That's more like it,' he said, tightening his grip around her, glancing at me.

'Mae, go to bed,' I said.

'What?' she said. 'No.'

'Mae. *Go to bed.*'

She shook her head slowly as she repeated 'No,' enunciating as much as she could. I didn't have the energy to argue with her.

'That's all anyone tells me to do,' she said, looking at Jay, who watched her in amusement. ''Go to bed, Mae. Get me tea, Mae. See what your sister's doing, Mae.''

'What is all this noise?' came Dad's voice as he walked down the stairs.

He stopped as soon as he saw Jay.

'Fatti's Mum,' he called out. '*Fatti's Mum.*'

That was the first time I'd heard Dad call

Mum that since before Jay was born. He was still stood in the middle of the staircase when Mum emerged, asking what was going on. Then she saw him.

'Oh, my son,' she exclaimed, almost knocking Dad out of the way and rushing down the stairs. 'My son, my son, my son, my son.'

She held his face in her hands, staring at the lines on his brow, the droop of his eyelids. Why do our parents seem to have selective memories? By the time Mum's dramatics had finished Bubblee and Malik had also come downstairs. Bubblee accidentally bumped into Malik on the way through the door but he ignored her as she said sorry.

'Well, you've got a nerve,' said Bubblee to Jay.

She glanced at Malik whose brows were furrowed in contempt. Jay rubbed his hand over his face as we all looked at him. I thought of when he was a child with his mouth covered in chocolate, his little finger placed in the dimple of his chin because he said he liked to make sure it was still there. He looked around at us but his eyes rested on me.

'I'm sorry,' he said.

'*Sorry?*' said Bubblee. 'Do you realise what you've done? Do you ever think of anyone but yourself?'

She went on for a few moments with this train of questions. Jay didn't seem to have an answer for any of them. He sat down on the sofa, his eyes flitting from person to person.

'Where's Fatti?'

'Adopted,' replied Bubblee.

'What?'

'My sister's in Bangladesh,' said Malik.

'*Your* sister?' Jay's face creased in confusion.

'*Our* sister,' corrected Bubblee.

'You have a lot of catching up to do,' I said to Jay, folding my arms.

But I was thinking, *He's back. He's recovered some of the money. Things might just be okay.* The consolation of this let me cling to the anger rather than giving way to despair.

'You must be tired, Son. Why don't you rest tonight?' said Dad.

'*Tired?*' exclaimed Bubblee. 'She's the one who's tired.' She flung her arm towards me. 'Her husband's in a coma, she's about to lose her house, everything, and *he's* the one being offered a rest.'

Dad looked at Mum, but she was staring at Jay.

'I have some explaining to do,' he said. 'I know.'

'Did you manage it?' asked Mae, looking at him, smiling in encouragement.

Hope doesn't seem to last very long in this house. His crestfallen face said it all. I gasped without any tears escaping. It was the only thing that could've helped and now, whether I got Mustafa back or not, we'd lose our home.

'You haven't recovered any of the money?' I whispered, clutching to what was left of my sanity.

'I'm sorry, Far,' he said, looking me straight in the eye. As if to say, *Hey, I gave it a go. It didn't work. At least I tried.*

Nothing. He had nothing. He explained how he'd got into some trouble and that he no longer had any money at all — no place to stay, no friends to help him. He wasn't here to save me; he was here to save himself.

'Uncle, Auntie,' said Malik. 'I'm sorry to be so frank, but this is the son you've put so high on a pedestal, when your daughters . . . ' He looked at the three of us and paused. 'How proud you should be of *them*.'

Mum shook her head as tears ran down her cheeks. 'How much we've worried for you, Jahangeer. How much I've prayed for you and asked God to bring you back to me safely, but see how much damage you've done?'

'I'm sorry, Amma. Abba,' he added, looking at Dad.

'Okay,' said Dad. 'Let's all go to bed and we will talk about everything tomorrow.'

Mae brought down sheets and a blanket for Jay who'd sleep on the sofa while I shared with Mae and Bubblee. I could feel his eyes on me as I left the room and walked up the stairs.

'Good night, Far,' he said.

I wasn't ready to wish him a good anything.

★ ★ ★

The following morning Dad knocked on our bedroom door and asked Mae and Bubblee to give us a minute. He looked at me for a while as Bubblee pushed Mae out of the room.

'He ruined everything,' I said to Dad as he closed the door behind them.

Dad sat down and patted my hand. 'He was always a very naughty boy.'

'*Naughty?* Is that all? I hope you're not here to make excuses for him, Abba, because honestly — '

' — Ssh, ssh, ssh, Babba.' He put his arm around me and I rested my head on his chest. 'I'm here to say sorry to *you*.'

I looked up at him.

'There are times when a father has to think about how he's raised his children. You were always a very good girl.'

'Not your favourite,' I said.

'Parents don't have favourites.'

I raised my eyebrows.

'Fatti is something special,' he added. 'She came to us when we had no hope of having any children. Still, each of you has a special place here.' He patted his chest. 'But when Jahangeer was born we thought God had heard all our prayers. This would be the man who would look after our family when we grew old. He would protect his sisters from harm.'

I shook my head at the very idea.

'Maybe it is our fault. So much expectation on one person — how can someone ever live up to it?'

'You're making excuses for him *again*. He's an adult,' I said.

'He will feel his mistakes, Faru. But because of it, I must feel mine too.'

I looked up at his brown, freckled face.

'Will you forgive me?' he asked.

I put my hand in his and nodded because I

didn't have the energy to be angry any more. It was costing too much, and my parents were worried enough about Fatti as it was. Anyway, hadn't they tried their best, bringing up five children in a foreign place, wanting to fit in and yet wanting to maintain the culture they loved? Yes, I had things to blame them for, but the things I had to be thankful for far outweighed those. Mum opened the door and saw us, sitting on the bed.

'I'll make your favourite breakfast,' she said to me.

That was probably the best apology Mum could muster. It was hard to believe that she'd gone through what I was going through, wanting to become a mum. But here she stood — with a very problematic but equally present family. For me, just then, she was hope.

★　★　★

We were all in the kitchen and for a room crowded with people there wasn't a lot of conversation, apart from Mae, who gave Jay some kind of nutritional information on the sweet, thick tea he was given to drink.

'How long are you here for?' Jay asked Malik.

'As long as it takes for Baia to wake up.'

'Do you want some water?' Bubblee asked Malik.

'No, thank you,' he replied without looking at her.

Mae had made a smoothie, which she put in front of him. He picked it up and observed the contents. 'What is it this morning?' asked Malik. 'This is very green.'

'That, dear Baia, is me making you a healthier person,' she replied.

'Ah,' he said. 'If only all of your sisters tried that,' he mumbled.

Bubblee's face went a shade of red. Jay was too busy playing with his breakfast to notice anything. It was only when I stood up to get ready that he got up too.

'Can I speak with you? In private?' he asked.

I couldn't bring myself to say yes, but when I went up the stairs and into Mae's room he walked in behind me.

'This place looks the same as when I left it,' he said. 'Remember this was my room for years?'

I began folding some of Mae's T-shirts, just to have something to do.

'How long will it take for you to forgive me?' he asked. I turned to him.

'Is this troubling you — not having your naïve sister cover for you? Now Mum and Dad can see you for who you actually are?'

He stepped closer, his under-eyes dark from lack of sleep.

'I could say sorry a thousand times, Far, but it wouldn't matter. I just want you to know that I'm going to do everything I can to help.'

'How nice of you.'

He paused. 'I've made a lot of promises in the past so I won't make any now. You'll see it from the things I do this time.'

Then he stepped up to me, kissed my forehead

and left the room. I sat on the bed, holding on to Mae's T-shirt, wondering what it was he could possibly do to bring my husband back to me.

When we all got to the hospital I watched Jay look at Mustafa and wondered what he was thinking. How sorry was he? His face seemed blank, as if he was there because it was the right thing to do, rather than because he actually wanted to be there.

'That's your handiwork,' I said to him, looking at Mustafa's inert body, wondering if I'd ever feel his arms wrapped around me again.

Mum and Dad didn't try to defend Jay. He continued to look at Mustafa as he nodded.

'It should be me in a coma,' he said.

'Don't say things like that,' said Mum.

'Yes, it should be.' I watched Jay, waiting for a reaction. He stood with his head bowed low, maybe taking all I was saying as a kind of punishment. 'But it's not,' I said, sighing from the tiredness I felt in my bones. 'It's not.'

When I was in the room with Mustafa, alone again, I took his hand.

'What's going to happen to you?' I asked him.

There was a piece of fluff on his cheek that I removed. I took some ice I'd got, wrapped it in some tissue and placed it against his parched mouth.

'What if you don't wake up and I lose our home?' When I put my hand in his I missed his fingers clasping around mine. 'But if you do wake up, don't think I'll forgive you just like that. That's not how it's going to work. Because ... ' I paused. What if he could hear me? I leaned in closer, looking at the crease in his neck, tracing it with my finger. 'I *can* live without you. I've realised that. I just don't want to.'

* * *

'Any room at the inn?' said Mae as she walked into my house that evening with Bubblee. 'I've been chucked out of my room for the prodigal son.'

'Ugh. I don't know how you can be polite to him after everything,' said Bubblee to her. 'I mean, the nerve of him, just turning up and expecting to be forgiven.'

Mae took her phone out and laughed at a message she'd received.

'What's so funny?' asked Bubblee.

'Malik,' she replied.

'Aren't you two just the best of friends?'

Mae looked up and scrunched up her nose. 'Yeah — he was kind of annoying at first, wasn't he? But he's all right, really. Comes out with some funny stuff. And it's not his accent I'm laughing at.'

'You're such a racist,' I said to her. 'Mustafa sounds similar to him.'

Mae and Bubblee both looked at each other, trying not to laugh.

'Yeah, we know,' replied Mae. She put her hands on Bubblee's shoulders. 'If only you weren't such a miserable cow you might see that he's funny too.'

Bubblee took her wrists and handed them

back to Mae as she went into the kitchen and put the kettle on.

'Did you see Mum rush down the stairs like that?' she said, shaking her head. 'As if Jay hasn't ruined the whole family?'

I told them both about Dad's apology to me.

'What does that even mean?' asked Bubblee.

I shrugged. 'Maybe they see him a little clearer now.'

'Well, it's a little late, isn't it? The damage is done.'

I turned to her. 'Bubs, go easy on them, will you? Do they really deserve the same kind of contempt you show everyone else?'

She looked away as the kettle began to boil. Mae was still on her phone, typing a message.

'What are you saying to him?' asked Bubblee.

'Oooh,' replied Mae, 'aren't we interested in what Malik has to say? Could the stony heart of our independent sister be melting?' she said, looking over at me as I raised my eyebrows.

'I'm wondering whether you'll always be this annoying, or if you might grow out of it,' replied Bubblee.

'Don't worry, Bubs,' she said, slouching on the sofa. 'We're all wondering the same about you.'

She made us all tea — Mae herbal, of course — and brought it over to the coffee table.

'I say we kick Jay out of the house and let him reap what he's sown,' said Bubblee.

'You know,' I replied, putting my feet on the coffee table, 'for once I don't actually disagree with you.'

The three of us sat in silence for a while. Mae

twirled the teabag around in her mug, Bubblee was looking into her mug as if she was reading her tea leaves and I just felt this emptiness around us. And this time it wasn't my husband.

'I wonder how she is,' said Bubblee, as if she'd read my mind.

'She'll be back soon, so we'll find out,' I replied. 'What does she say to you when she messages?' I asked Mae.

She shrugged. 'Just one-liners really, saying she's fine and Bangladesh is hot.'

Bubblee shook her head. 'Classic Fatti.'

'Do you think she'll come back and decide to pack her things, move to Bangladesh and never come back again?' asked Mae.

'No,' I replied. 'No; surely not.'

But the truth is, I wasn't sure.

'She may very well have found her spiritual home,' added Bubblee, which wasn't much comfort.

'But *we're* her family,' said Mae. '*This* is her home.'

Bubblee looked at her and nodded. 'I know.'

Mae took a few sips of her tea before she said: 'Don't think Jay likes Malik much.'

I had to laugh. 'Poor Malik, he's had a bit of a tough time with this family.'

'That's rich,' said Bubblee. 'Who the hell is Jay to have a say on anything? Sure, Malik's annoying but at least he's stuck it out with us. Especially, you know . . . considering.'

Bubblee raised her mug to her lips, but seemed to forget to take a sip. When you got past how irritating her constant pessimism was, it was quite amusing to watch her acknowledge she'd been difficult, without actually admitting it.

'School all right?' she asked Mae.

Mae lifted her legs to her knees, cupping her mug closer to her. 'It's fine.'

I looked at our little sister and realised that in all the chaos of our worlds we never think about what she's going through at school. Pooja told me that Sanjay said she was having a hard time and yet I hadn't once asked her if she was okay. This would be the time she could rail and rant about things and yet she just shrugs and says she's fine. It's funny, because to look at them you wouldn't think she and Fatti were alike, and yet they are so similar in so many ways.

'That's not what I heard,' I said.

'Who? Who's giving you a hard time?' said Bubblee, leaning forward.

'Oh, God, that Malik and his big mouth,' she said. 'You've got Bubs going,' said Mae to me.

'Malik?' I replied. 'What does he know? I heard it from Pooja.'

She shrugged. 'Oh. Whatevs. Doesn't matter.'

After we told her to give us the full story, she told us about the fight she got into and how Malik ended up dragging her away.

'Oh, Mae. You muppet,' I said. 'Why didn't you say?'

'Nothing I can't handle,' she replied.

'Why was he at your school?' asked Bubblee.

'God, don't act like you think he was perving on schoolgirls,' replied Mae. Then she explained that he'd come to see her because he'd been worried about her.

'He said he knew Fatti worried about me, and she was away so he wanted to make sure I was all right.'

I could see Mae's cheeks go a little red as she lowered her gaze. There was no accusation in her voice; if anything there was embarrassment that she was having to say these words out loud. I don't think it could've measured against the embarrassment I felt, or Bubblee seemed to have felt as she looked at me.

'Give me the name of this girl and I'll deal with her,' said Bubblee, her voice rising a decibel as it does when she's feeling a combination of embarrassment and anger.

Mae rolled her eyes and got up, putting her empty mug down. 'Calm down. It'll be fine and I don't need anyone fighting my battles for me.'

With that she said she was going to go to bed and went upstairs, leaving me and Bubblee on our own.

'Well,' I said, 'I feel like a failure of an older sister. Thank God for Malik.'

'Yeah,' said Bubblee thoughtfully. 'I guess so.'

She looked towards the door Mae had just walked through. 'Mae's always so happy, though. Well, not exactly happy, but *unbothered*.'

'Just goes to show, doesn't it?' I said, looking at her. 'You never can tell what a person's feeling.'

Bubblee locked eyes with me. 'No. I suppose you can't.'

17

Fatima

As the plane landed at Manchester airport I watched the rain drizzle in a way that looked as if it was unlikely to stop any time soon. My head was thudding and a bout of nausea rose inside me. I gulped it down. Now was not the time to get ill. Somehow I managed to leave the country and meet my birth parents only to return to the country I fled, unchanged. All my life I thought I'd been missing an epiphany and it turns out they don't exist. Not for me, anyway. It wouldn't have been so disappointing if it wasn't for the fact that I was so sure something would happen — that something would click into place like it does at the end of a film or book. But life is neither a film nor a book, and if it were, then mine wouldn't be a very fulfilling one. There was no more avoiding it; I'd have to see my mum and dad and family now, and who knows what they were feeling? Angry? Disappointed? Upset? Glad? Did this time away from me make them realise how unnecessary I was to them? It doesn't help to have feelings; to want to be liked or loved even though you're not sure what you've done to deserve it. That's the thing: your family have to love you when you're born into it — I'm not sure the same applies when you're adopted. Especially when you go off to try to find

281

something new, only to have failed. No-one wants to be second choice. But then maybe they'll know how it feels.

When I stepped out into arrivals, there were Bubblee and Malik, waiting for me. Ash said he'd collect me but Mae told me that Bubblee and Malik would be there instead. It didn't make sense to prolong the inevitable meeting. I wanted to turn around, get back on the plane and go wherever it decided to take me. Bubblee's arms were folded and Malik shifted on his feet as I walked towards them, my heart beating fast and my mouth going dry. It felt like I'd been away for years and as I drew nearer to them I wasn't sure what I'd say — it was as if they were both strangers.

'Hi,' I said.

'Fatti,' said Bubblee, who unfolded her arms and hugged me. 'Okay journey?' she asked, taking my suitcase from me.

I nodded, looking over at Malik. It was the first time I'd seen him since that day I found out about being adopted. I couldn't meet his gaze. I wanted to crawl under a rock. Perhaps my head wouldn't thud as badly there.

'Your parents send their love,' I murmured, looking at the ground as I walked with them.

He gave a tight smile and offered to take the suitcase from Bubblee, who said it was fine, before hesitating and handing it over to him.

'How's Mustafa?' I asked.

'The longer he's in the coma the worse it looks,' said Bubblee. I glanced at Malik whose flushed face was now looking pale.

'What does that mean?' I asked.

Bubblee sighed as we got to the car and Malik put the case into the boot. 'I don't know, Fatti. It means we have to pray for the best.'

I don't think I'd ever heard Bubblee saying to pray for anything. Especially when it came to Mustafa. I sat in the back of the car, staring out of the window, but would catch Bubblee looking at me from the rear-view mirror.

'Are you okay?' she asked. 'You look a bit peaky.'

'You do,' added Malik, turning around from the passenger seat. His eyes flicked towards the speedometer as Bubblee pressed on the accelerator.

'Headache. Plus, I'm not sure about some of the food I had on the plane.'

'Oh, God. Well, we'll be home soon, don't worry,' she replied.

I rested my head on the window and closed my eyes. Bubblee and Malik hadn't exchanged more than three words with each other; mostly just grunts or nods, and now there was silence. Truth is, despite wanting my bed, despite not being able to meet Malik's gaze, I wanted to be alone with him to ask him all kinds of questions about what'd happened here and his parents and brothers, but I couldn't bring myself to do that in front of Bubblee. He was the only person who might understand what my trip to Bangladesh really meant; who might help me make sense of it all.

'Mum and Dad have missed you,' she said, looking at me again through the mirror as I opened my eyes. 'We all have.'

Just then Malik's mobile rang. He replied to the caller with an urgency in his voice that made Bubblee turn to him.

'What's happened?' she asked, even though he was still on the phone.

'Okay,' he spoke into his phone, looking at Bubblee. 'We'll come straight there.'

He put the phone down. 'It's Mustafa. He's got worse. We have to go to the hospital.'

Oh, God. Please let Mustafa be okay. Please let me get to know the brother I never knew was mine. This time when Bubblee stepped on the accelerator, I don't think I or Malik minded.

★ ★ ★

Nothing prepared me for it. As soon as Farah saw me she stood up and fell into my arms, sobbing. *No, it can't be true.*

'I don't want to, Fatti. I don't want to lose him.'

I looked around at the others to try to figure out whether she *had* lost him. Mae wasn't in sight.

'Faru, be calm,' said Dad, stroking her head and looking at me.

She released herself from me and wiped her eyes as Dad pulled me into a hug.

'My beti,' he said, kissing me on the forehead.

'It's his heart,' said Farah to Bubblee and Malik, her panic rising again. 'It's getting weaker . . .'

I went to hug Mum, who pulled me into her

arms. At first I couldn't hug her back in the same way, but then I smelt her familiar flowery scent and tightened my grip around her.

'What's wrong with you?' she said, looking at my face.

'She ate some dodgy food on the plane,' explained Bubblee, her eyes flicking towards Farah.

'I'm fine. I'll be fine,' I said, even though I had to take quick breaths to try and settle the need to throw up. A few hours passed like this. I'd gone from feeling like I hadn't seen them all in years to feeling as if I'd never left — as if there never was a revelation that I was adopted. Dad brought me some paracetamol, which I took but which didn't seem to be making much difference. I wanted to curl up on the chair and sleep. When Mae came to the hospital from school she flew towards me and I think it might've been the first time I smiled since I came back. Maybe even since I'd been in Bangladesh. She looked so fine-limbed and easy with every part of her body that I knew it made sense I was adopted. I could never be sisters with someone like her; and yet I felt a pride that perhaps I'd never experienced before.

'Drama, huh?' she whispered to me, looking at everyone.

'Mae . . . ' Now wasn't the time to be flippant.

'Are you all right?' she asked, looking at my face, concerned.

I nodded, but I didn't feel fine. I felt like I was walking underwater or something and there was a sledgehammer going at my head, while my stomach seemed to want to burst out of my mouth.

'Were they . . . ?' She glanced over at Mum and Dad, I suppose to check they weren't listening in to our conversation. 'Were they nice to you? Your parents?'

'Yeah. They were fine.'

It wasn't a complete lie. They were fine. But then even the guy from the corner shop was fine.

'Fatti.' Dad had walked up to us. 'Look at you. You must go home and rest. We won't know any more for now. Bubblee, take her home.'

'No, no, I'll be fine.'

He was my brother. I had to stay because what if I left and something happened?

'Fatti, please go home,' said Farah. 'You probably shouldn't be around sick people anyway. Not good for anyone.'

There wasn't much I could say to that, but I told them to call me if anything changed and that I'd leave my mobile on loud. Just as we were about to leave Malik called out to me and walked towards me.

'We'll speak,' he said, pinching the bridge of his nose and moving his head as if to shake off the tiredness.

'Yeah,' I replied, looking at my hands and then giving him a brief nod.

I saw Bubblee glance at him and then look away before we walked out of the hospital and got back into the car.

'How've you been?' I asked her, grateful to have had some fresh air.

She let out a small laugh. 'Who cares how I've

been? I should be asking how *you've* been. But you don't look like you're in a state to have that conversation.' She paused. 'A lot's happened.'

'Hmm,' I replied, noticing that the rain had stopped.

'Listen, Fatti — '

' — Not now,' I said as she parked outside the house.

My home. I looked at it, thinking about all the years I'd lived in it, all the memories tangled up into a knot of something that was real, but not quite. I didn't think I'd be able to speak even if I wanted to. My mind and everything around me was a blur.

'You really are sick,' she said, looking at me in concern.

'Remember to call me if anything changes,' I said as I moved to get out of the car.

'Yes, of course. Will you be okay or do you want me to stay?' she asked.

I sat back. 'I'm just going to sleep for a while. I'll be fine in a bit.'

'The change in the climate doesn't help,' she said.

Just as I was about to leave, she held on to my arm and pulled me into a hug. 'You really need a shower.'

I laughed, for a moment forgetting about how nauseous I felt.

'Thanks.'

'Get rid of some of those ridiculous thoughts of yours while you're at it,' she added.

'What thoughts?'

'The ones that give you ideas about . . . God

knows what,' she said. 'That always keep you in your room.'

I looked at the dashboard. It was bad enough having these thoughts of not really belonging; it was even worse that someone might know about them.

When I got into the house I took some juice out of the fridge and drank it, sitting down for a while, waiting for the nausea to get better. I looked around the kitchen, taking in the familiar setting, made unfamiliar by how quiet the house was. Taking a deep breath, I got up and looked in the living room. The same brown sofa; the same pictures dotted around; picture-frames on the mantelpiece; embroidered rug. The juice seemed to have settled my stomach a bit and the paracetamol had finally softened the thudding head. I noticed the spot where Mae threw up her cereal once, when she was a toddler, and I'd cleaned it up; the corner where Jay used to hide from Bubblee when they played hide-and-seek; Mum and Dad's room and the bunk-bed they refuse to throw out; the chair I'd sit in and watch Farah potter around the house, picking up after Mum, clearing the clutter left behind by Jay. Another bout of nausea heaved inside me as I ran to the bathroom and threw up in the toilet. I sat there, looking at the bathroom walls and laughed at the idea that I was, quite literally, getting Bangladesh out of my system. My legs wobbled as I got up and I dragged myself to the sanctuary of my bedroom. My phone pinged. Ash. Normally I couldn't wait for his messages but not today. I didn't have the energy any more to think about my surroundings; what it meant that I was back here, once more, the familiarity of the place making me feel as if I'd gone back a step somehow in life. I rested my head on my pillow and managed to fall into a dreamless sleep.

When I awoke it was dark and for a moment I forgot where I was. I put my hand to my head that was thumping a little less. After recognising the familiar curtains and walls I checked my phone — it was eleven thirty p.m. and I'd received a few messages. Mustafa was the same. *Thank God he's still alive.* Ash wanted to know if I was okay. Getting out of bed, I realised that everyone seemed to be asleep as a wave of nausea came out of nowhere and had me reaching for the bin again. Someone had put a bottle of water by the bedside table and once again I fell into a stupor of sleep.

★   ★   ★

In the morning I'd been left a note:

Gone to the hospital. If you are better call and someone will come and pick you up. But you must rest if you are still ill. Your amma has left you food in the kitchen. Affa.

I'd sat up in bed, trying to get the energy to stand when my phone rang.

'Welcome home.'

It was Ash.

'Hi,' I said, smiling, my words coming out

croaky and uneven.

'You don't sound very well.'

I told him I'd been ill but that I was feeling better this morning, if a little weak.

'How was the reunion?'

I closed my eyes, wishing that my birth parents could've given me another story to tell.

'Fine.'

'That good?' he asked.

When I didn't respond he asked what I was doing today. I told him I'd rest and then get someone to collect me to take me to the hospital to see Mustafa.

'Well, why don't I do that?' he said.

'Oh, no, don't worry. I don't want to trouble you.'

Which I didn't, but at the same time it would've been nice to see someone I wasn't related to and could just act normal with.

'I know you don't.' He paused. 'But we're friends, aren't we?'

It felt slightly weird when he said that, though I don't know why. It made me sad and happy at the same time.

He said he'd pick me up before lunch but when he did, I didn't realise he meant that we were going for lunch.

'Or just a coffee,' he suggested as I looked at my watch.

I wanted to sit down and talk to him about Bangladesh but I also wanted to see Mustafa.

'Are you okay?' he asked. 'You look pale.'

'Still feeling a little sick.'

'Oh.'

He wiped his brow and cleared his throat. 'Just a half-hour?'

'Okay,' I said, nodding.

'So, the reunion was just fine then, was it?' he asked as we sat down at the table and ordered our drinks.

Now that he asked, the words wouldn't quite come out.

I shrugged. 'It must've been a bit of a shock for them.'

He'd had his hair cut and somehow or other he'd managed to get a tan. I think I perhaps looked at him a little too long, as he noticed me staring.

'They know they gave you away, don't they?' he said.

I stared at the table and the granules of sugar that hadn't been wiped off.

'Sorry,' he added. 'It's just that, if it's going to be a shock for anyone, it's you.'

I smiled at him.

'Your sister, Mae, she's quite a character, isn't she?'

I must've looked confused.

'She called me before you came back from Bangladesh,' he explained.

'Oh. Why?'

The afternoon sun came streaming through the window, and his eyes were more brown than black, I noticed.

'To tell me I wasn't allowed to pick you up. She sounded exactly like you'd described her,' he said.

I had to laugh. 'Oh, yeah, I'd forgotten about

that. She's not the type of person you forget in a hurry,' I said, smiling. 'And she has an opinion on everything.'

For a moment I wished she were a baby again and I could hold her in my arms like I used to.

'So, the parent meeting was a disappointment?' He sighed. 'Most things in life are,' he added, thanking the waitress for our coffees, not quite meeting my eye. 'As long as you know what you have *now*, that's the main thing.'

I twirled the cup in my hand, not really feeling like drinking its contents.

'Fatima, it might not be my place to say,' he said. 'But your family love you.'

I felt tears surface and the last thing I wanted was to cry in front of him. Again.

'Do you know that?' he asked. 'I mean, we all know our families love us — hopefully, anyway — but do you *know* that?'

I did know it, but something still felt amiss — as if I'd lost something I never really had, but felt its loss anyway.

'It just feels weird,' I said. 'I was ready to come home, but now being here, knowing that my birth parents don't actually . . .'

'What?' he asked.

The tears plopped on the table.

'Sorry,' I said, wiping my eyes. 'It's just that, my sisters — all of them — they seem to have it figured out. Their lives are so . . . well, *full*, and I was always waiting for mine to start. I thought this might've been it. The start of something new and meaningful. Not just hand-modelling and the inability to pass my driving test.' I shook my head and apologised again. He didn't need to hear all of that.

'Fatima,' he said, reaching over and putting his hand on my arm. 'It's time you realised that there are people who care about you. In the process of missing, or looking for something else, don't forget about them.'

Was it true? Had I spent so much time thinking about Farah and all she had, and Bubblee and Mae and what they were doing with their lives, that I'd missed something? When I looked up at him, his face was flushed. His hand was still on my arm when I glanced at it and he took it away.

'The truth is,' he said, staring at me. 'I wanted to . . .'

He looked agitated and every time he looked at me he'd look away again.

'What?' I asked. 'Are you okay?'

He shook his head. 'No. No, I'm not.'

'What's wrong?' I asked, leaning forward.

'Do you really want to know?' he said.

I nodded, because the least I could do was listen to whatever was on his mind, when he'd done nothing but listen to what was on mine.

'Your family's not the only one that cares about you,' he said.

It wasn't really clear what he meant — there wasn't much I could say to that. He leaned forward, his eyes looking into mine in a way that I felt I should look away from, and yet I couldn't.

'Listen,' he began. 'I've seen enough of people to know who's worth caring about and who's not.'

'Isn't everyone worth caring about?' I said, managing to look at my napkin instead.

He laughed and regarded me for a few moments.

'No, not everyone,' he replied. 'But . . . ' He paused. 'You are.'

I felt my face flush.

'Thanks,' I said, still not sure where to look, and so I looked at my phone, checking the time, and realised my battery had died. As much as I wanted to stay, it was time to go and see how Mustafa was doing.

Ash looked down at his lap and mumbled something. I'm not sure what it was but it sounded a bit like something not being easy, maybe.

'*I* care about you,' he said.

My cup was mid-air. The words he spoke wouldn't have felt so weird if he hadn't said them while he stared at me. I waited for him to say something else; something unrelated — maybe about the weather or something. I felt dizzy. What did he mean? When you tell someone you're not related to that you care about them, does it mean as a friend, sister . . . something else? The idea of something else got my heart beating a lot faster — so fast, it was having an effect on my stomach, which wasn't feeling at its best anyway. So much time had passed between what he'd said and my own thoughts that the only thing that came out of my mouth was, 'Perhaps we should go?'

For a moment his face dropped, still looking at me, and then he gave a smile. 'Of course. Yeah, let's go. You'll want to be with your family right now.' He got up as he added, 'Stupid of me wasting your time like this.'

'No,' I said, looking at him, wishing he'd see me smiling. 'You're the only person I can really talk to.'

'Really?' he asked, meeting my gaze.

I nodded. 'I mean, all the times I've failed my test and you've never once lost your patience with me — '

' — That's my job, Fatima.'

'No, yes — I know — but you're also . . . '

What was he? I tried to think of the words.

'A good friend,' I finished.

That didn't feel like enough, but then what else was he? He gave me a smile, but it seemed like a sad one. I don't know, though; I think everything is sad nowadays.

When we got in the car he was very quiet. Something had happened back there but I wasn't sure what. He drove into the main entrance of the hospital and I paused as I was unfastening my seatbelt.

'Thanks for the coffee and . . . everything,' I said.

'That's what friends are for,' he replied, not quite looking at me.

Something weighed down on my heart and as I got out of the car I paused and then turned around.

'Did I do something wrong?' I asked, looking into the car.

He took a deep breath, giving a short laugh as he shook his head. Leaning into the passenger's side, he said: 'No, Fatima. You didn't do anything wrong.'

He patted the seat, asking me to sit down, so I did. 'I should've said what I really meant.'

Taking another deep breath, he looked at me and said: 'I care about you. As *more* than a friend.'

For a second I thought: maybe this is a dream and I'll wake up any minute.

'Sorry,' he said. 'Maybe it's bad timing. Or maybe it's perfect timing. I just know that when you realise something like this you have to tell the person, because who knows what kind of obstacles life can put in your way?'

More than a friend? I noticed a couple come out of their car with their two children. Who were they visiting? A flock of birds flew overhead in a perfect V-shape and I wondered where they were going.

'You have a lot going on right now, though, and it's important that you focus on that. On your family.'

I noticed that his eyelashes curled upwards — it's the first time I'd realised that. And that he had a really kind face. Not the type that would stand out in a crowd, but the one you'd probably approach if you were in that crowd and had lost your way. I thought of Mustafa and Mum and Dad, and everything else that was such a tangle as I nodded.

'I don't expect anything,' he said.

Expect? What was happening? My headache was coming back. People cared about those around me, never *me*. The idea of anyone ever loving me like that was so ridiculous, I'd never even entertained the idea. Apart from when I first met Malik. The memory didn't help my nausea. There's a reason for being honest about who your birth parents are — accidentally falling for your brother being one of them. As Mae would say: *vom*.

'Oh,' I said, looking away.

What was I meant to say? Nothing had ever prepared me for a moment like this. I'd never expected it. If I spoke, I knew just a jumble of stupid words would come out.

'I should let you go,' he said.

Thank God he said that because I suddenly felt like I wanted to be as far from him as possible. Just him sitting there was confusing me. I couldn't stay any longer with all these thoughts and feelings that began tingling the surface of my skin. I gave a rushed goodbye as I got out of the car and the strap of my bag got caught in the door handle. I yanked it out, almost breaking the handle and my bag's strap in the process, slammed the door behind me and rushed into the hospital. My steps slowed down as I took in what had happened. *Ash* cares about *me*? My driving instructor *Ash*? *Why*? It didn't make sense. I turned around to see if he might be driving past, out of the car park. But he was no longer in view. So, I walked in the direction of Mustafa's ward, trying to calm the beating of my heart with each step that led me away from Ash.

★ ★ ★

'Where have you been?' exclaimed Mae, rushing towards me, still in her school uniform. 'We've been calling you.'

She looked so terrified, my heart sank. She grabbed my hand as we rushed down the corridor, outside Mustafa's hospital room. There was Farah, sobbing; Malik stood next to Bubblee, who looked pale and as if she was about to throw up; Jay looking at the floor with his hands in his pockets; Mum clutching her chest and Dad with his hand on her arm. I gripped Mae. And then I looked at Mustafa's bed.

'Oh my God,' I said, under my breath.

He looked at me and smiled.

'You're awake,' I said, almost in a whisper.

Farah turned to me and smiled through her sobs.

'Hi, Fatti,' said Mustafa, barely able to get the words out. Before I knew it I'd already rushed to his bedside and was hugging him.

I don't know whether it was because he was my brother, or that it meant that I hadn't given Farah the evil eye and she'd not be a widow because of me, or whether it was because, finally, the whole family was here, in a room together — and awake — for the first time.

'You're back,' I said, still hugging him.

'Ow,' he said. 'Just about.'

He looked at me as I drew away but he took my hand. Without saying anything, it was like he said he knew. I was his sister. As I sat up, taking in the fact that Mustafa was alive and awake, Jay rushed out of the room.

'He needs to learn that forgiveness doesn't come that easily,' said Bubblee.

Mustafa's eyes flickered towards the window. 'We both know that,' he replied, his eyes drowsy as if he were about to fall asleep again.

It was weird, because I'd never really had a relationship with Jay the way Farah did, or the love/hate bond he and Bubblee shared, and definitely not the little-sister, big-brother connection he and Mae had — but despite everything, I felt sorry for him. I could feel everyone's eyes on me as I left the room to find him. Typical Jay, he hadn't gone far — he was sitting in the waiting room.

'Hi,' I said, sitting next to him.

He regarded me for a while. 'Fatti. So. You're adopted.'

He never was careful with his actions or his words.

'You've dealt with it all a lot better than I would've if it was me,' he added.

'You've got enough to worry about,' I replied.

He laughed out loud before rubbing his face. 'Bangladesh's changed you.'

It hadn't occurred to me before — maybe it had. Maybe sometimes you're so busy waiting for change that you miss the fact that you yourself are changing.

'What about you? Has being away from all of us altered you?' I asked.

He gave a big sigh. He always had been a bit of a scrawny thing, and even though he'd filled out, was tall, there was still this gangliness to him. That's another thing he and Mae have in common.

'Not enough, according to some,' he said.

I leaned back in my chair.

'What?' he asked, looking at me.

'Jay — did you really think it'd be that easy? That you'd come home, say sorry, and now that Mustafa's woken up everything would be forgiven and forgotten? They're going to lose their house — their savings, everything they've worked for.'

I noticed the colour rise to his face, but he had to hear it. Why did he assume everything would just be so easy? Just because he's a man? I sounded like Bubblee — but then, I wasn't sure that was a bad thing, actually.

'Since when did you say what you thought?' he said.

'I'm a changed person, remember?' I leaned forward, thinking of just how much was happening in that moment: Mustafa was awake, I was talking to Jay and Ash cared about me. Was this it? Was this *life*? 'If you want to be a part of this family, then you have to do what it takes to be forgiven. By everyone.'

'Even Bubblee?' he said.

'Especially Bubblee,' I replied. 'But listen, and don't take this the wrong way. It's just that, if you can't do that, after everything you've put everyone through, then you might as well leave and not come back.'

The words felt so foreign coming out of my mouth and I could hear my voice tremble. These were all things I thought but never would've said if it were a month ago. Jay looked at me as if the words were as shocking to him as they were to me.

'Sorry,' I said. 'But I have to be honest. You can't just be here, but then *not* be here. It's not about you any more. It's about all of us, isn't it?'

As the words came out of my mouth, I couldn't help but think how they applied to me as well. Was I just as bad as Jay? I didn't think so because I hadn't ended up potentially getting Mustafa and Farah's house repossessed, but it still felt true in some ways.

'It's always the quiet ones,' he said.

'Listen,' I said. 'Things aren't exactly going to get better any time soon. Not with their financial situation. What are you going to do? Stay and help, or . . . run away?'

'That depends. Are *you* going to run away?'

I thought of Ash and the family, right now, in Mustafa's room. My family. Was that the moment; in Ash's car? Was that the moment perhaps I'd been waiting for — when life would actually change; *move* in some way? Or maybe it was right here, in the hospital corridor with my younger brother. Because even as I looked at him and thought of all the distance between us — the lack of any real bond — I couldn't help but feel, for better or for worse, that he *was* my brother.

'No,' I said. 'I'm here to stay.'

* * *

Pretty soon we were told to go home and let Mustafa rest. He was still weak and in and out of consciousness.

'Hasn't he had enough sleep?' said Mae to the

doctor. 'Shouldn't he be, like, ready to party now?'

Jay laughed and put his arm around her as I caught Malik frowning at him.

'This girl doesn't stop speaking,' said Mum as Dad laughed too, though he tried not to when Mum shot him a look.

We all left but Farah stayed behind in the hospital for a while. When we got home Jay said he was going for a nap and Bubblee said she and Mae would go to Farah's house to tidy it before she got home.

'Come with us?' said Bubblee to me.

I glanced over at Malik who'd gone into the garden to take a call. I shook my head because now was the time to pluck up my courage and speak to him. I could tell Mum and Dad were looking over at me as I walked past them, into the garden, just so I wouldn't have to be alone with them once Bubblee and Mae left. I wasn't ready to speak to them about Bangladesh yet.

Malik had got off his phone as I joined him in the garden.

'Hi,' I said, forcing myself to look at him, even though I could only manage it for about two seconds.

He looked tired and I wondered what it must be like to have had to deal with my family these past weeks.

'That was my parents,' he replied.

'Oh.'

Did they ask about me? Were they wondering whether I was safe or not? I couldn't bring myself to ask. When he said that they passed on

302

their salams and love, I had to wonder whether it was them speaking or Malik. He glanced over my shoulder and when I turned around I saw Mum was watching us from the kitchen window.

'Have they forgiven you then?' I said.

He glanced toward the window again and gave a wry smile. 'Yes. I have apologised. It was wrong of me, but . . . ' He shrugged. 'Still. I should've known better.'

'I don't suppose Mum was easy to please?' I asked.

'She was better than you would think, Fatima.' He looked down at the grass, putting his hands in his pockets. 'In fact, she said that in some ways she was relieved. The burden of carrying that secret and letting so much time pass must've been hard. It is not always how someone has acted — although, I'm not saying a person shouldn't think about their actions — but it is important to know what a person has felt too. If they have felt anything. At least your amma has felt it.'

I nodded, considering what he said. Some weeks ago, before Bangladesh, it would've probably made me angrier towards them, but today I could understand.

'Feelings are important,' I said.

We heard someone come out into the garden next door. I looked over at Paulo, putting out the laundry, just his naked shoulders visible from over the fence. It felt good to see him — the familiar — though obviously not *all* of him. He waved at me as I waved back. Malik looked over and then glanced at me.

'Your neighbours are . . . very interesting,' he said, lowering his voice.

I had to laugh at how disturbed Malik looked.

'So, I finally get to ask you properly: how was Bangladesh?' he said.

I noticed that the grass needed mowing. 'I got to meet everyone.'

'Ah, yes, my brothers, their wives and all my nieces and nephews too.'

'They seemed nice,' I replied.

'And my parents?' he asked. 'How did they seem?'

I paused, trying to search for the right kind of words.

'Nice as well,' I replied.

He gave a small laugh, bending his head to look at me as I still stared at the grass. 'You can be honest with me.'

I looked up at him. 'It's not that they weren't nice, it's just that . . . '

'They didn't seem to care like you thought they would?'

I nodded — in some ways it was a relief that he said it himself.

'This is why I wanted to go with you,' he replied, sighing.

'I am sorry,' he added.

'Don't be. It's not your fault. And really, like I said, they were fine, they just didn't . . . they just didn't seem to realise what they'd done.'

He furrowed his eyebrows as we meandered to the bottom of the garden. 'I can't make excuses for them, Fatima. I can only say that I know what poverty can do to a person, and what money can do when a poor person finally gets it.'

'Do you think they gave me away because they might not have been able to afford a dowry?'

He pondered this for a moment. 'Maybe,' he replied. 'Maybe not. They would have thought of it, though — at the time. It is no excuse,' he added, turning to me. 'I wished I could've grown up with a sister like you.'

I had to bite back the tears. 'Well, you're here now.'

He gave a sad smile. 'So much time has passed and you never can buy the kind of childhood memories you have with your siblings.'

Turning back towards the house, he looked at it, considering it.

'What?' I asked.

'A lot has happened these past weeks,' he replied. 'But your family felt very much like my family for a while.'

I looked at him for a moment and wondered: did he feel in Bangladesh the way I felt here? As if he didn't belong to the family he was born into? And did he find something here that I didn't manage to find in Bangladesh?

'Even Bubblee?' I said.

His smile disappeared.

'I know,' I said, when he didn't speak. 'She's not easy to warm to. But she has a good heart really. I mean, only if she loves you. It's just a bit hard to get her to.'

Malik put his hands behind his back as we strolled towards the house again. 'If it were easier, it might not be as worth it,' he replied. 'I suppose,' he added, as if as an afterthought.

I thought about Ash and something seemed to open in the pit of my stomach. When was the next time I'd see him? I still had a driving test to pass and yet how could I message him about another lesson, with everything that had happened? But it wasn't even as if the test really mattered any more. It didn't make a difference whether I saw him in the car, or in his home, or out in a coffee shop. It just mattered that I saw him.

'Have you never wanted to get married?' I asked him.

He looked a bit taken aback — it was slightly out of the blue. I'd even forgotten my initial awkwardness about speaking to him. He just wasn't that difficult to be around, I suppose. Plus, I really wanted to know: what *makes* you want to spend the rest of your life with someone? How do you know it's actually real or whether it's something you've made up in your head? How long can Ash care about someone like me? Just thinking about it made me anxious.

'I've never met anyone I wanted to spend the rest of my life with,' he replied. 'My parents would introduce me to a lot of girls, but I wasn't able to get to know them and their ideas and thoughts. We'd always be with family and how was I ever to have a proper conversation when everyone else was listening?'

I nodded, even though my thoughts began to wander.

'Why?' he asked.

'Just wondering.'

He gave me an inquisitive look and then just

smiled. 'Well, I'd better start looking into booking a ticket back home,' he said.

My heart sank. I was getting used to him being around. I wanted to spend more time with him, get to know him; *his* ideas, *his* thoughts. I loved Jay, but Malik was different — he seemed like someone I could go to if I needed advice. Plus, I knew Mae would miss him, even if Bubblee probably couldn't wait to be rid of him.

'Don't think about that yet,' I replied. 'Don't you want to spend some time with Mustafa now that he's awake? And the rest of us too?'

'Your parents are fine with me now, but still. I shouldn't overstay my welcome.'

'But everything is still so up in the air,' I said. 'We need to think of a way to help Mustafa and Farah not lose their house.'

What could we do? Whatever it was, it'd have to involve all of us chipping in somehow. Mum and Dad would be able to lend some money and I had a fair bit saved from living at home and hand-modelling.

'I will be able to lend some money too,' said Malik. 'Not a lot. You know how weak the taka is against the pound, but some.'

I smiled at him.

'Do you have any ideas?' he asked as we walked into the house.

'Not yet,' I replied.

I could tell Mum was looking at us as we walked in, watching out for what kind of conversation we might've been having.

'Are you both hungry?' she asked. 'Fatti, here's

your cheese and prawns. I've put them on crackers for you.'

I took it from her. 'Thanks, Amma.'

She put her hand on my face and I kissed her on the cheek.

'But maybe you should stop buying this for me,' I added.

Malik had walked over to the sink and started washing the dishes.

'Whatever you want, Babba,' said Mum.

'Maybe you should've stopped buying it for me a long time ago. Because, I know you meant well, but I don't think it's very good for me.'

She nodded. 'You are right. I made a mistake.'

I put the plate of prawns and cheese down, looking at her lined face, this one white hair that sprouts from her chin, and her big, kohl-smeared eyes that are kind whenever they look at me.

'No,' I said. 'You just did what you thought was best.'

'You are my beti,' she said, hugging me.

'I know, Amma.'

I held on to her until we heard the dishes clattering in the sink.

Mum turned around and wiped her eyes as she said to Malik: 'You go and sit down. Men don't help in the kitchen.'

'Kala, I'm trying new things.'

Just then the doorbell rang and it was Marnie with a tray of cupcakes.

'Oh, thank you,' said Mum, eyeing Mamie's clothes suspiciously.

'We thought you and the family could do with some treats now there's something to celebrate.'

Dad's footsteps came rushing down the stairs as he came to greet Marnie.

'Ah, so kind, Marnie. Isn't that kind, Jay's Amma?' he said, looking at Mum.

Mum pursed her lips, attempted a smile, and nodded.

'We love cupcakes,' added Dad, taking one from the tray and biting into it. 'Mm! Perfect.'

'My daughter made these ones,' replied Marnie.

'But she learns from her mother, no?' said Dad, nudging her and smiling.

Mum looked like she might shove the cheese-and-prawn crackers she'd made somewhere unsavoury if Marnie was naked.

'Well, I have been known for my baking, in the past,' she replied.

Something began to swirl around in my head as Mum led Dad into the kitchen by the arm and Marnie was left standing in the dining area.

'Really?' I said.

'Oh, yes,' she replied, recounting the various cakes she'd made for birthdays and anniversaries. 'People go mad for cake,' she added.

Of course they do. 'What if we made more cakes?' I said to everyone in the kitchen.

Malik turned around.

'I mean, lots and lots of cake.'

Mum looked at Dad, concerned. Maybe she thought I was going to make all this cake and eat it myself.

'Because people like it, don't they?' I said. 'You can't really go wrong with it if you make nice cakes. Like yours,' I added, looking at Marnie.

'Yes?' she replied, as if asking what the point of this was.

'What if . . . ?' No, it was a silly idea, surely. But then, what else did we have? 'Suppose if we did something like a bake-sale?'

Mum, Dad and Malik looked none the wiser with where I was going with this.

'A big one? I mean a *huge* one.'

'Yes, Babba, we can do whatever you want when things are calmer,' said Dad.

'Not for *me*, Abba.'

I could see Marnie nodding. 'Oh. Well, yes. I see.' She thought about it. 'But there's a lot to consider, and yet, I suppose . . . I mean, why *not*?' She seemed to be the only one who was understanding where I was going with this. 'But Fateema' — that's how she always pronounces my name — 'it would have to be a very *big* bake-sale.'

She seemed a little embarrassed as she cleared her throat.

'It's just that . . . ' Her eyes flicked towards everyone, as if apologising. 'We all know that Mustafa and Farah are having some financial troubles. And we gather that they're rather *big* ones.'

Of course they knew — everyone in the town did. But maybe that wasn't a bad thing now. Maybe it meant we could do something about it.

'What do you mean, bake-sale?' said Mum.

'I know,' I said, looking at Marnie. 'But isn't it worth a try? Something is better than nothing, isn't it? I just wonder — how willing would people be to help?'

Marnie gave me a smile. It was the smile of a person who loved a challenge. The kind of smile I think I had on my face too.

* * *

'Fats,' said Mae. 'Trust you to think the only way to keep someone's house from getting repossessed is baking cakes.' Mae was shaking her head as she ate her edamame. 'What are we going to do? Ice them with cheese from a tube?'

'Shh,' said Bubblee, who looked deep in concentration.

It was family meeting time. Farah was still at the hospital and I gathered everyone in the living room to tell them about my idea. Malik came in with two mugs of tea, and handed one to Bubblee.

'Oh,' she said, looking up. 'Thanks.'

Maybe it was a stupid idea. As if that would actually help get their house back. I checked my phone and wondered if there'd be a message waiting for me from Ash. Nothing. I tried to push the disappointment to the back of my mind and focus on what was happening now. *Why would he message anyway, after how I behaved? What must he think of me? I bet he's changed his mind already.* It wasn't the time to think about him though, or the way my heart dipped at the thought of him.

'It'd have to be a hell of a bake-sale,' said Bubblee, looking at me.

'Hmm? Oh yeah. It would,' I replied, just about catching what she said.

'Who would make all these cakes?' said Mum.

'Where would we have it?' asked Dad as he rocked in his rocking chair.

'Yeah, genius; and what about how much it'd actually cost to make all this stuff? Cakes don't grow on trees, you know.' Mae popped another edamame in her mouth.

I sat on the floor, because every seat was already occupied, and looked at the ground. My idea was a flop. Of course Mae was right. And so were Mum and Dad: who would make all these things and where would we even have it?

'Well,' said Marnie, who at Dad's insistence had stayed to 'give us her thoughts', 'Paulo's best friend works at the council. We'd just need to fill in the application form and . . . hang on.'

She got her phone out and called Paulo to explain what was happening.

'Yes. Mhmm. Okay.' She glanced at all of us as we all looked at each other. 'Right, fine. Good,' she added before hanging up the phone.

'Precisely,' she said. 'We fill in the application form under the pretext of a community fundraiser — which it is, of course — and use the park to put the sale on.'

'But it's not a community fundraiser,' said Bubblee.

'Oh yes it is, dear,' said Marnie, as if that was the final word on the matter. 'Paulo and I will fill in the application for you, get his friend to process it and we'll have permission within days. It pays to know people. We're going to turn this bake-sale into a fete.'

I had a new-found respect for Marnie.

'Right, well, that's one thing,' said Bubblee, looking impressed. 'Next problem.'

'I only have two hands,' said Mum. 'You will all help me but even then, to make money from it, we will need so many. Hundreds and hundreds and thousands.'

'Nonsense,' said Marnie. 'You have us.'

Bubblee picked up her mug of tea. 'To be fair, I'm sure plenty of Farah's neighbours and friends will help too.' She put the mug down and got her phone out, tapping on it before she looked up at us again. 'But still, I mean, even if you sold cakes at an average *maximum* of two pounds per cupcake or slice, or whatever it might be, you'd have to sell at least fifty thousand of them for it to be worth it. There are only around five thousand people in Wyvernage. And they're not all going to buy cake. It doesn't even include the cost of making all of them.'

It was looking grim. Every time I got excited at the idea and thought it might work, there was another hurdle to consider. For all of Bubblee's cynicism, there was no denying that she was right.

'Hang on, hang on,' said Jay. 'I have a lot of people who owe me favours.'

Apart from Marnie, there wasn't one person in the room who didn't look at Jay with doubt. Even Mum and Dad looked sceptical.

'All right. Do these people happen to be in prison?' said Mae as Mum shot her a look.

Marnie cleared her throat.

'No, Squirt. They happen to be people who own bulk-buying stores.'

313

'Jay,' said Bubblee. 'If people owed you money, then why would you be broke and have none yourself?' She glanced over at Marnie who really was finding out a little too much about the Amir family.

'You might find it hard to believe, but I have helped people with things in the past. And some favours,' said Jay, getting up with his phone in his hand, 'aren't the money kind.'

He left the room to apparently make a phone call.

'I'll believe it when I see it,' said Bubblee.

'Listen,' said Malik, leaning forward and clasping his hands. 'If we can somehow get bulk ingredients from Jay's . . . ' he cleared his throat, '. . . *friends*, then we could make boxes of cakes to sell so people will spend, I don't know, eight or ten pounds for a box.'

'Oh my God,' said Mae, putting out her hands as if she'd had an epiphany. 'We could call them *Rescue* Boxes.' She smiled eagerly. 'Get it? Because they'll rescue Mustafa, Farah *and* people who are addicted to sugar. Well, actually, they'll just feed their addiction rather than rescue them from it, but you get my drift.'

Malik smiled at her, showing his teeth. 'Such a clever one.'

Mae took a very low bow.

Dad sighed and stroked his chin. 'This is good, but we still have the problem of making *enough* money. Bubblee is right. This town is small.'

'Oh!' exclaimed Mae, who dashed out of the room.

She appeared again, a minute later, this time with her laptop in her arms.

'But, my dear Abba, the Internet is *not* small,' she said, tapping on the laptop, frowning in concentration.

'These youngsters and their gadgets,' said Marnie.

'What are you doing?' I asked.

'Taking advantage of the wonder of the online world, my dear sister,' she replied. 'Creating a Facebook page.' She laughed to herself as she typed.

'What?' I said.

Bubblee shook her head. 'What's this going to do?'

Mae looked at Bubblee as you'd look at a child. '*Create awareness*, Bubble, bubble, toil and trouble. *And* . . . ' she said, 'get people to donate.'

Mae explained that she could set up a Funding Page explaining the aim behind the fete.

'Why would people just give their money to someone they don't know?' said Mum.

'Because, my cynical mother . . . ' Mae looked around the room. 'At least we know where Bubs gets it from — they'll get a Rescue Box for every ten-pound donation. It might only have three cupcakes in it, but them's the breaks. People love the idea of 'helping' while getting something in return. And obvs, they pay for their own postage and packaging.'

I looked at her in amazement. 'Is this all possible?'

Jay walked back into the room, puffing out his chest and smiling at us all.

'Done. Marnie, I'll need a list of the main things we'll need, apart from eggs and flour and sugar, and then anything beside that we'll just have to pay for out of our own pockets — but that we can manage, right?'

Mum and Dad both looked at him, not beaming, but relieved that at least he'd managed to help in *some* way. Though Bubblee still looked sceptical.

'Wait a minute,' I said. 'Are we saying this might actually work, then?'

Bubblee leaned back and played with a short strand of her hair. I looked around at Mum and Dad, Malik, Mae, Jay and Marnie.

'You know,' said Bubblee, 'I think it just might.'

Mae was tapping furiously at her laptop still, her brows knitted in concentration. 'Especially,' she said, her eyes skimming across her screen, 'when I contact our lovely local paper for a news story.'

★ ★ ★

The first thing I thought about when I woke up was Ash. *Maybe I should message him? But then what if he didn't actually mean what he said? Perhaps I should ask Bubblee? But it's not as if she thinks very clearly when it comes to that kind of thing, considering what she thought of Mustafa. And Mae would just laugh and make a joke of it. Farah has other things on her mind. I*

316

could ask Malik but the very thought of it makes me so embarrassed, I want to crawl under my duvet.

Just then Mae came charging into my room and said Farah was on her way. We told her to come to Mum and Dad's house before going to the hospital because we needed to speak to her. I dragged myself out of bed and tried to forget about Ash. There were other important things to be done.

'Oh my God,' sang Mae, as she hopped about like a rabbit when Farah entered the house. 'Have we got news for you!'

'What?' snapped Farah.

'Oh yeah, sorry. First of all I meant, how was Mustafa yesterday?' asked Mae.

Farah came into the living room and looked at all of us as she took a seat on the single sofa.

'Weak; sorry about what's happened; alive,' she replied.

Farah played with her wedding ring and I noticed Bubblee pursing her lips as if she was stopping herself from saying anything. Mum and Dad were still in their room.

'As if sorry's going to bring our home back,' Farah added.

She put her face in her hands and sat there for a while, the three of us looking at each other, unsure about what to do. That's when I explained the fete idea to her. At first I wasn't sure whether she was listening, because it was a while before she looked up at me.

'A fete? To save my home?' She didn't sound very convinced.

'Yeah,' I said, glancing at Bubblee and Mae. 'We sat here yesterday and figured out how it could work.'

'It was Fatti's idea,' said Bubblee.

'But we all came up with a plan together.'

Mae came forward with her laptop and clicked on the mouse. She'd prepared a vignette of clips from her video and uploaded it to the Facebook page: shots of Farah and Mustafa together; in their home, in our home, laughing and bickering. Farah took the laptop from Mae. The following shots were of all of us in the hospital; the doctor coming to tell us Mustafa's in an induced coma; a shot of Mrs Lemington's poodle; Dad staring at the vending machine; Bubblee and Mum sitting side by side; a close-up of Farah's face. Every step of the past few weeks, recorded by our little sister and collated into three minutes and fourteen seconds of images and conversation that made tears fall from Farah's eyes.

'Mae . . . ' whispered Farah, looking at her. 'This is . . . *beautiful*.'

'Oh, you know. Whatever,' she replied. 'Anyway, see that.' Mae pointed at a figure at the bottom of the page. 'That shows how much money people have donated so far.'

'Oh my God,' said Bubblee, staring at the four-figure sum.

'It's not much,' said Mae. 'Yet. But wait until the news story runs.'

Farah began to read comments and messages from friends, neighbours, but also strangers. 'But these people don't even know us,' she said.

'But they know someone you might've known.

Or Mustafa might've known.' I looked at her. 'People like him a lot.'

'The whole thing is incredible, to be quite honest,' said Bubblee. 'But with the bad rep that banks have for repossessing homes of families, maybe it's struck a chord with people. Plus, they've all been invited to come to the fete.'

Farah came up with all the objections we'd already gone through. When I told her what Jay was doing she became very still.

'Where is he?'

'Gone to meet with the person who owes him the favour,' I said.

'Oh,' she replied. 'Well, we'll see if they're just like his other promises. Empty.'

'Far,' said Bubblee. 'I've decided that pessimism doesn't suit you. Leave that to me, please.'

Farah looked at her and nodded. 'It's catching.'

'Ugh,' said Mae. 'Keep away from Fats, then. Or we'll all be doomed.'

I checked my phone again. He wouldn't message this early anyway. He wouldn't message at *all*. But I wasn't going to despair, or compare how one of my sisters would've dealt with it, or how it would've turned out for them, because this was *my* life; I had to live it. I got up.

'There's a lot to do,' I said as they all looked up at me. 'Don't you think we better get started?'

18

Mae

'Sorry — Mae, is it? Yes, could we have you with your phone in a natural pose? Yes, just by the sign with your road name.'

'Natural?' I said to the reporter. 'There's no such thing as natural when it comes to phones and photos.'

'Mae . . . ' warned Fatti, rushing past and into the house with a three-tiered cake. 'Bubs,' she called out. 'We need more icing.'

Bubblee, who was already getting into her car with Malik, shouted out: 'On it.'

'Like a car bonnet,' I added to journo lady, who obvs didn't have an appreciation for rhyme.

'How do you feel about your role in the way this small town has come together to save two of its treasured inhabitants?'

Treasured was taking it a bit far. Since when were Mustafa and Farah *treasured*? But this lady meant well and I was on a verbal ban — as in, I wasn't allowed to say anything that might be taken the wrong way and used in the media against us.

'Well, it's great, isn't it? I mean, are baked goods really the best way to raise money when you think about how it's going to raise everyone's cholesterol? I think not, Miss Reporter. But you have to give everyone credit,

320

don't you? Plus, no-one wants to spend three quid on a kale smoothie.'

She laughed. 'Yes, wise words.'

So wise, she was taking notes, even though the camera was rolling.

'And do you believe it's going to work? Will this save your sister and brother-in-law from losing their home?'

I mean, if someone had told me about it I'd be, like, are you kidding? How can cupcakes save a house from being repossessed? But then, this was more than that — this had become a bigger team effort than anyone could've thought possible. Before I could answer Paulo and Marnie came bursting through their front door — fully clothed — with more trays, rushed past us smiling and into the house.

'See those people, right there?' I said. 'Those, Miss Reporter, are a few of our saviours. Nudists,' I whispered to her, leaning forward. 'Not that I care, but I don't know how Health and Safety would feel about them baking starkers.'

'Terry,' said the reporter to the cameraman, 'make sure we get an interview with them.'

You couldn't make it up, really. When we went into the house it was buzzing with people — I saw Mum watching Dad as he spoke to Marnie and took the trays she was carrying. Jay and Fatti were stacking up bunting, ready for the fete tomorrow. They always had a functional sort of relationship so I don't know what happened over the past week or so, but something changed. Maybe they discovered they had more in common than they realised. What's even funnier is that Bubblee and Malik were actually speaking to each other without Bubblee giving him evil looks. I swear, baking makes people go soft.

'Mae,' Fatti called out.

'Yes m'lady,' I said, leaving the reporter to speak to Paulo and Marnie.

'Do you have the video vignette prepared to show on the big screen?'

I sighed. 'Oh ye of little faith.'

My school had allowed us to borrow their big-screen television so that we could show the video I'd put together at the fete. Fatti looked at her phone and put it down again.

'Who are you waiting to hear from?' I asked. 'Everyone you know is within about three metres of here.'

She shook her head as Jay raised his eyebrows at me. 'Everyone says you ask too many questions, Squirt. I think maybe you don't ask enough.' Then he gave me a wry smile, picked up a box and went to put it in the boot of the van that Farah's neighbour had lent us.

'Something you're not telling me, Fatti Batty?' I said.

'Go and do something useful, Mae.'

I jumped up on the kitchen counter. 'My uses are indefinable.'

She carried on taping up boxes and stacking them.

'Have you told your driving instructor friend about tomorrow?' I asked.

The good thing about having experience in videoing people and watching them while editing is that you can read every kind of movement they make.

'Can you make sure we have enough napkins?' she said.

I had to smile at her, working away, pretending as if nothing was up, when *everything* was up.

'Yes, ma'am,' I replied and hopped off the table, swiping her phone while I was at it.

People say they're not proud when they interfere with other people's personal stuff, but I'm not that type, because sometimes you need a mediator to get things going. So, I messaged Ash, told him about the fete tomorrow and asked him to come, pretending the message was from Fatti. The only problem, of course, was if he messaged back and Fatti saw, but as with most important things in life, it was a risk I was willing to take. After all, I couldn't be told off any more than I had been this past month.

★ ★ ★

Paulo and Marnie really did come through for us about being able to use the park — I mean, we were contributing to the community, if you think about it — but it wouldn't have happened if it weren't for them, and obvs Paulo's mate at the council. The place was teeming with people: couples, children, dogs. Jay even got some Union Jack bunting that we put on all of the stalls. It also turned out that the old town-folk could be quite inventive when needed, with tables full of home-made cakes and biscuits, trifles and pastries. There were some camera crews and reporters interviewing people; I swear it was the event of a lifetime for Wyvernage. And miracle of all miracles, it was sunny. Mum said that's because God was on our side. It's good that she didn't hear Bubblee say that the coma and repossession of the house must've been someone else's plan, then. Just when I think she can't get any more cynical.

'All right, Abbauuu?' I asked Dad, smacking him on the back.

He was looking at all the stalls manned by neighbours and friends, I guess keeping an eye out for any potential disasters.

'Where's your wife?' I said.

'Helping Marnie,' he replied.

I laughed out loud.

'Careful, or your wife might start sharing Marnie's — let's say, life philosophy.'

'Mae . . .' he said in warning.

I sighed, and looked around the park with him as he patted my hand.

'Oh no,' he said. 'Who's that person parking in the children's play area?' with which he rushed off.

It gave me the chance to get my camera out and record. There were Bubblee and Jay with Sasha who'd driven up from London, being haggled by Nora the Borer; Fatti and Malik seemed to be talking about something important. I zoomed into their faces as he smiled at her and gave her a hug. I know he's a Bangladeshi boatie, but I kind of hope he'll stay for longer. I looked around to see if there was any sign of the driving instructor. I wondered if it was him Fatti was looking for every time she glanced around the place, even when in deep conversation with someone. There was Mum, eyeing Bubblee and then looking over at Malik. I mean, the woman never gives up, even after all that's happened. Good luck getting those two to tie the knot. She came over to me and told me to stop recording and get the two of them to man a stall together.

'Mum, it's not going to happen. I mean, she doesn't hate him as much as she used to, but she sure isn't going to marry him,' I said.

'You don't know,' she replied. 'When you're older then you will realise things.'

I wanted to go into detail about what these mysterious 'things' might be, but Mum had rushed off as quickly as she'd rushed towards me because she'd caught sight of Dad chatting to Marnie. There came a round of applause and I turned around to see Farah get out of her car, with Mustafa. He looked embarrassed. I'd have been too: *Congratulations! You lost all your money, and now have a cake!* But it was the thought that counted, I guess. Plus, it was good to see Farah actually smiling, especially when Bubblee and Malik walked up to them.

'*Oh em geeee!*' cried someone in my ear.

I turned around and it was Anne, Sarah and Sanjay.

'Don't ask,' said Sanjay. 'My mum made me come.'

He pointed over at Pooja who had a stall of traditional Indian sweetmeats.

'Whatever, liar,' replied Sarah, hitting him.

325

'You were counting down the days.'

He laughed as he rubbed the back of his head.

'This is, like, *phenomenal*,' said Anne, looking around her. 'So many cakes and so many people.'

'Yeah, well,' I said. 'I just hope it works.'

Sarah put her arm around me and squeezed my shoulder. 'Of course it'll work.'

But who knew? It was so much money.

'Everyone handed in their coursework?' I asked.

They all nodded.

'And now for the exams,' I added. 'That's going to be fun.'

'Yeah, but then think of the summer holiday,' said Sanjay.

I thought of the long stretch of time ahead of us and what we'd do. Because let's face it, one thing Mustafa's coma's taught me is you have to make the most of your time.

'Oh my God,' exclaimed Anne. 'I know! We should make a film.'

'A *film*?' I said.

'Yes! You could write a script and film it and we could act in it,' she replied, indicating to herself, Sanjay and Sarah. Sanjay was nodding as if he wasn't completely bored by the idea and Sarah looked at Anne, eyes widening.

'*That* is the best idea I've *ever* heard.'

Anne squealed and jumped up and down.

'Really? You think we should give that a go?' I said, looking at the three of them.

'What else are we going to do?' said Sanjay. 'Something better get me out of the house or my mum will start giving me cooking lessons.'

Pooja waved at all of us as we looked at her. She is what Farah likes to call a progressive. I reckon we need more of those. I put my arm around Anne and walked up to a stall that Mum and Dad were guarding for Marnie, to buy Anne a cupcake. Why didn't I think of it? Anne was right — it was a genius idea! And already I was thinking of what I could write about — what the story could be. That Anne, she's really not so bad at all.

'Are you keeping out of trouble?' asked Dad as we approached.

I sighed. 'Yes, Dad.'

He bent under the table and handed me a bottle that had some kind of green liquid in it.

'Apple, mint and cucumber,' he said to me, looking rather proud.

I eyed it with suspicion. 'Are you sure that's not code for *our hedge*?'

'You're just like your amma. Never forget a mistake.'

Mum looked at me and the bottle, making a face as if she'd smelt a fart as she asked Anne to help her with some biscuits. Well, I guess I knew where this bottle would end up going, but you had to give Dad points for trying. Speaking of trying, I watched Jay as he was on his own at a stall, counting cash.

'Thief!' I cried out from behind him as the notes in his hands went flying in the air.

'You little squirt,' he said, whacking me on the leg and bending down to pick up the notes that had fallen.

'Hope you're not planning on taking all the profits,' I said, going to help him. 'Doesn't matter, anyway. We've got police at all the borders, just in case.'

'Thanks for the vote of confidence,' he replied.

'Oh, I kid, I kid, big bro,' I said. 'Anyway, where would you go? Messed everything up royally, didn't you? So now you're stuck here.'

He sighed and looked around at the masses of people, the gingham tables and colourful banners as people laughed and chatted.

'So, this is my life then,' he said, gripping the notes. I did wonder whether there was any chance of him running off with as much money as he could get his hands on.

'Yep, and you might as well get used to it. I snatched the money from him and put it in the cash box.

He looked over at Farah. 'Well, I guess I should be happy she's at least saying hello to me.'

Jay's not exactly easy to like. Obviously I like him because I can't be bothered to waste energy not liking people. Plus, he's my brother, and that means something. But it was kind of a relief to know that it mattered to him whether Farah did or didn't say hello to him. Maybe he wasn't a complete lost cause like Bubblee said he was. He locked eyes with Mustafa from across the crowd. Mustafa gave him a nod, then looked away.

'Maybe she'd have forgiven you quicker if you'd gone into a coma too,' I said.

It hardly seemed fair that Farah still wasn't saying more than five words at a time to Jay when she was walking around, hand in hand, with Mustafa as if nothing had happened. He gave a wry laugh.

'That's love for you,' he replied.

'What's that got to do with anything?' I asked.

He laughed as he got me into a headlock.

'Get off me!' I exclaimed.

He eventually gave up messing up my hair and we both stood, observing the expanse of the park, his arm still around me.

'Everything, Squirt. It's got everything to do with it.' He took a deep breath and said: 'Man the stall for me, will you?'

I watched him walk towards Farah and Mustafa. He stood in front of both of them and extended his hand to Mustafa. Mustafa looked at it, then at Farah, whose face was unreadable. Then he took it, put his hand over Jay's and pulled him into a hug. Jay didn't see Farah breathe a sigh of relief — but it's okay, because I caught it on camera.

* * *

As the day wore on and the crowds began to thin I wondered how much money we could've made. The figure on the fund-raising page had hit five figures a few days ago and it was still growing.

'Listen, Mae, I know you created that Facebook page and made that video, but have you actually lifted a box today?' said Bubblee, putting some cake in her mouth as she walked up to me with Fatti.

'Leave her alone,' said Fatti.

'Yeah, Bubs, I focus my talents for optimum outcome,' I said.

'Exactly,' said Fatti. 'That page might just mean we'll actually succeed.'

She might feel less gracious towards me if Ash appeared — though it didn't seem likely since it was nearing the end of the evening. I hoped for her sake that he would. Not that I could really see Fatima in a grown-up relationship — seemed completely weird — but anything to stop her from becoming the Fatti who spends most of her time in her room.

'Yeah,' I said to Bubblee. 'Careful what you say or I'll go and make Mum force you to marry Malik.'

Fatti glanced at Bubblee who went red in the face and started blabbering about how inappropriate that comment was, and that Mum should respect the choices she had made and . . . the usual, really.

'Still,' she added. 'He's not awful. I mean, as a human being. Or man.'

I was making kissing noises at Bubblee when we saw Farah. She began walking towards us, leaving Mustafa to talk to some of their neighbours.

'Looks like you've forgiven your husband then,' I said as she approached. 'You crazy lovebirds, you.'

She glanced at him. 'Yes. I mean, it's not as simple as it looks.'

'You seem happy,' said Fatti.

Farah considered this. 'I'm happy he's back

and getting healthy again. But it makes you think, doesn't it?'

'What?' asked Fatti.

'That you can't take anything for granted. And I don't mean accidents and comas. I mean, the life you live, or think you have.'

'Talk about killjoy,' I said.

Bubblee nudged me.

'I just get it,' Farah said, looking at Bubblee. 'I don't mean I agree with you — I'd marry Mustafa again if I had to do it all over, but I became complacent and it wasn't good for me. Especially when I couldn't have a . . . '

'I know,' replied Bubblee.

'He needs to earn my trust again,' said Farah. 'And I need to figure out what I'll do with my life. What'll happen to our home — because even if we save it, he's still lost so much money, I don't even know if we'll be able to afford to keep it.'

I guess we'd all forgotten that it was a long road ahead. I told her to have some cake. I mean, she actually deserved it.

'We don't have to worry about you flying off to Bangladesh though, do we?' Farah asked, looking at Fatti.

I switched my camera off and put my phone away. 'Not if I hide her passport, she won't.'

'It's not that we can *make* you do anything,' said Bubblee. 'But, you know, *this* is where you belong. With us.'

Fatti's eyes filled with tears, which was hardly a surprise — but even my own eyes filled. She nodded and looked around the park again, her eyes darting from corner to corner.

'I know,' she said.

'Because, Fatti, all this,' began Farah, opening out her arms around the green, 'it wouldn't have been possible without you.' She looked at Bubblee and Me. 'All of you. You know that, right?'

'Oh yeah. Without us you'd have topped yourself, for sure,' I said.

Bubblee elbowed me again and laughed. 'You'd have coped without us too, Far.'

Farah shook her head. 'No, I really don't think I would have.'

Just then another car turned into the parking area and parked up — it was one I recognised. I grabbed Fatti's wrist and squeezed it, hardly able to contain the excitement I felt.

'What?' she said.

'Just remember not to kill me, okay?' I said as I pointed towards the man who'd just got out of the car.

'Isn't that your driving instructor?' said Farah.

Fatti froze. '*Mae . . . what* did you do?' she whispered, but more as if she was going to turn around and run away rather than kill me.

'Call me cupid,' I said, doing a little curtsey to show my cupid prowess.

Farah and Bubblee both looked at me, then at Fatti, and then at Ash.

'Go on, then,' I said. 'Go to him.'

'Mae? What's going on?' asked Farah.

'You guys need to open your eyes.'

'My God,' said Bubblee. '*That's* the friend? Of course it is!'

'*Duh*,' I said.

Fatti was taking deep breaths as she watched him walk over to Jay — they shook hands, and just as Jay pointed towards us Fatti turned around so her back was to him.

Farah was smiling so widely, all her teeth were showing and even Bubblee cracked a smile, saying, 'In all the chaos I forgot to ask.'

'Well?' said Farah, grabbing Fatti's arm. 'What are you waiting for?'

'Nothing,' replied Fatti, looking at all of us. She took another deep breath and turned around to face towards Ash. 'I'm not waiting for anything any more.'

Acknowledgements

Writing is a passion I have had for such a long time but learning how to put together a whole entire book was something I had to learn quickly. This is the perfect opportunity to thank all the people who have helped me put this book together. So I will reel off a list of ludicrous amounts of thank yous like an intoxicated, overzealous surprised award winner. If I may . . .

A massive thank you to firstly my agent, Anne, for holding my hand all the time. Not a word of lie when I say she holds my hand metaphorically and literally. Thank you for taking me deeper and deeper into the realisation that I can do it even when I am afraid.

Thank you to the team. Thank you Lisa Milton, for being the first person, the first set of eyes and ears to believe that this was even a possibility.

Thank you Ayisha for helping me through my writing process. For honing in the story, the ideas and the madness that ensued. For helping me create a story that I am so very proud of.

Thanks to Anna Baggaley and Rhea Kurien. If I go back to the amount of food and white board markers we went through all I can think about is our waistlines and the squeak of the ink running out.

Thank you to Alison Lindsay, Louise McGrory, Sophie Calder, Nick Bates, Darren Shoffren, Taryn Sachs and all at Team HQ.

Thanks to my family giving me some valuable material. They are comedy gold and if they keep going as they are I can write till the end of time. The weirdest, most dysfunctional and funniest people I know. We like a bit of topsy turvy, that's what makes everyone look at us sideways!

Thanks to my husband Abdal, my kids Musa, Dawud and Maryam, for quite simply putting up with me. For covering me when I fall asleep on the couch, for not waking me up at 4am and asking me if I'm asleep, for arguing with the door shut. Thanks for being considerate but still entirely my extraordinary family. Don't change.

We do hope that you have enjoyed reading this large print book.

Did you know that all of our titles are available for purchase?

We publish a wide range of high quality large print books including:
Romances, Mysteries, Classics
General Fiction
Non Fiction and Westerns

Special interest titles available in large print are:
The Little Oxford Dictionary
Music Book
Song Book
Hymn Book
Service Book

Also available from us courtesy of Oxford University Press:
Young Readers' Dictionary
(large print edition)
Young Readers' Thesaurus
(large print edition)

For further information or a free brochure, please contact us at:
Ulverscroft Large Print Books Ltd.,
The Green, Bradgate Road, Anstey,
Leicester, LE7 7FU, England.
Tel: (00 44) 0116 236 4325
Fax: (00 44) 0116 234 0205